DRONISH

A WALKER SAGA BOOK SIX

JAYMIN EVE

For all of us in the #AddictedtoWalkers club. I love that our numbers grow every day.

Dronish

Copyright © Jaymin Eve 2015

All rights reserved
First published in 2015

Eve, Jaymin
Dronish

No part of this book may be reproduced, stored in a retrieval system or transmitted in any form or by any means, without the prior permission in writing of the publisher, nor be otherwise circulated in any form of binding or cover other than that in which it is published and without a similar condition, including this condition, being imposed on the subsequent purchaser. All characters in this publication other than those clearly in the public domain are fictitious, and any resemblance to real persons, living or dead, is purely coincidental.

1

SAPHA

Home to all of the fifty thousand Drones that remained after the last collapse, Arotia was the last city left standing on the world of Dronish. The long-lived race were energy consumers, vampires in a manner, needing constant renewal of their life-force by taking that of others. Through their own greed and need, they had razed the once strong, thriving world to the ground. Only the dregs of a society remained.

Sapha lived her life in constant fear that she would be consumed by the desperate people ... fear that her secret would be discovered ... fear that she would always be alone. She had two weapons in her arsenal, and without them she'd be dead ten times over. Her mother had protected her as a babe, but, in the end, she'd succumbed to the urge and tried to kill her. Luckily, the attack had come in Sapha's ninth year and she'd been strong enough to fight back and escape. She hadn't seen her mother since.

Until today.

Sapha had snuck into the market square, cloaking herself in shadows, and in the half-darkness of Dronish, lit only by the sliver of moon that remained. Standing in the long lines of those waiting for their daily replenishment from the sacred mineraline crystals was the tall, slender form of Cletia, her mother.

Her primary gift: Sapha had no need of the crystals. Her energy was replenished with simple nourishment from the fungi that grew around her cave outside Arotia.

She'd only ventured into the square to keep a close eye on her one friend. Marl was a youngling, ten and one year. He shared the caves with her, and made the journey once a week into the city for his nourishment.

Sapha was invisible to all at the moment, although seeing her mother had caused her to almost lose control of her cloaking energy, her second ability. She could use the shadows and camouflage herself. Sapha was grateful that her large source of internal power was somehow hidden from the Drones. They would hunt her down and drain her. She had enough power to nourish the city of Arotia for many half-moons.

She did not remember Dronish when it was filled with the sun's warmth and five moons. It was long ago that the gluttonous nature of her people had consumed the sun and all but a sliver of one moon's energy. Those dead rocks still littered their sky, but could not be seen in the darkness. She wouldn't even start on the cold. Luckily, between their layers of skin and muscle, they had a thin coating of fat dense enough to keep them from freezing to death.

Marl was at the start of the line now. Seven guards surrounded the mineraline stone before him. It was black, glittering in the dim light. Sapha lurked closer as he opened his mouth and his throttle emerged. Unraveling from where it rested inside his throat, the snakelike extension's end attached to the crystal.

As he absorbed the energy, Sapha was still amazed to see the changes in her friend. His skeletal frame filled out slightly, flesh instead of just skin actually encasing bone. His scaled and cracked hide filled back in, and even glistened with some protective oils again. All drones had lithe frames, but now Marl stopped swaying and stood strong and tall. His large, single eye – which was one of the many differences between Sapha and the rest of the Drones – cleared of yellow and turned back to blood-red. He looked so much healthier. If only they could take this nourishment more than once a week.

According to the market gossip, they were about to extend the waiting period between feedings again. Many wouldn't survive that. In the end, once a week was only just allowing some to endure. One more day would be their death. Marl would be fine, though; she secretly fed him energy during his trance state – not enough that it was noticeable, but enough that he would always survive.

Suddenly shouts could be heard, more than one voice and more than one language. Sapha drifted away from the crowds, hugging the side of a building where she could observe without anyone accidentally bumping into her. She was cloaked but still corporeal. Marl was off to the side as well, so he should be safe enough from whatever disturbance was coming.

A male burst into view, tall and thin like the rest, but plumped out a bit more. He was one of the high priest's men. Kan, the priest, was the leader of Arotia, and his contingent always seemed to be a little more nourished than the average inhabitant.

"Sound the alarm, a group approaches our city. Guard the walls and hide the mineralines."

Just like that, the guards snatched up the precious life-giving crystals and were gone, their dark forms disappearing back into the palatial structure where the priest, his harem, and the guards were holed up praying for redemption, or whatever they were calling it.

Those who had still been in line waiting for their small slice of energy cried out. Their shrieks and wails were testament to the pain and hunger plaguing the world.

Sapha lost sight of her mother in the chaos, which left her with an uneasy churning in her stomach. It was sad that this was what their world had been reduced to.

It was over a thousand years ago that the Dronish civilization realized their growth as a people, and their need for energy, was overtaking their world's ability to survive. The leaders of the time – for there had been many cities – had tried to reverse that which had been wrought, but it was too late. Millions perished in the fighting and wars which ensued. Everyone wanted to capture for themselves whatever free energy remained, and more importantly one of the mineralines which were able to provide renewable food. They had drained the crystals so many times that the sun and moons eventually succumbed to the loss of energy.

When the dust finally cleared, all that remained were the dregs of a once-thriving, cosmopolitan world. Those who had ventured out to explore told tales of a dusty land filled with the skeletons of cities and civilizations. Arotia had the last stores of crystals, and eventually all of the Dronish survivors had made their way here. But the energy continued to ebb away. The stones required the light of the sun or moons to recharge, and there was only a sliver of moon left.

Sapha knew it was just a matter of time before there was nothing left of Dronish. The world was on a path to destruction and they were all waiting for the final flicker of moon to die out.

The priests had tried their best. They had made it a death sentence if anyone took energy from anything or anyone now, except for their allocation of crystal, and had declared the same fate for anyone who procreated without permission. They allowed for some new life, otherwise the Drones would have died out a long time ago.

Her mother, of course, had not received their permission. She had always said that a foreign male, one who had much power, had seduced her with energy. She had woken after the overload and she was with young. Knowing Sapha would be different and easily detected, she had left Arotia and settled in an abandoned farmhouse outside of the city.

As a child, Sapha had been left alone while her mother went into town to replenish her energy, but otherwise they had lived a quiet, hidden life – until the day her mother had tried to drain Sapha dry. It was just after they'd extended the feeding period to three days. This time period proved to be too long for Cletia. She'd been overcome by her need for sustenance.

Sapha rubbed at her chest. She could still feel the attached sucker, the panic that had flooded her veins as the well of energy inside her started to drain away. There should be no greater love than that of a mother for her child, but in the end the hunger had proved greater. No wonder the Drones couldn't stop themselves before they destroyed the world.

Sapha followed the crowds as they moved toward the large barriers that had been erected near the entrance to the city. She kept the shadows wrapped tightly around her. She would be invisible to everyone unless they looked really closely. No one had ever appeared to notice her before.

Except for Marl.

After his mother had died from lack of energy, he'd been abandoned in the market square. Tiny little thing, only four cycles old, he'd noticed Sapha as she skirted the area, having come in for a slice of companionship, even if no one knew they were providing it. She went a little crazy stuck in her cave all the time. He'd had no fear coming straight up to her and asking her what she was. They'd been together ever since.

Marl moved gracefully to her side. The small Drone trailing along beside her, they walked with the crowd.

"Sapha, you need to be careful. I saw your entire body a moment ago."

His words would have been hard to understand if Sapha hadn't had so much practice with the Drone's strange way of phrasing words. The sucker made it difficult for them to pronounce certain sounds.

"You only saw because you were looking for me," she said, keeping her voice low.

He snorted, his single eye flashing red in the mild light.

"What do you think is coming?" He was worried. Sapha could always tell by the jitter in his voice.

"I have no idea, but surely nothing would have survived outside the city." Sapha left the rest unspoken.

If something had survived, who knew what type of monster it might be?

When they reached the barriers, everyone paused. The gates were high, but there were handholds all the way up. Then those that had received their weekly energy began to climb. The others would not risk any more of their strength.

Sapha stayed close to Marl, off to the side. Together they scaled the fifteen-foot wall. Sapha got her hand on the top of the hold and paused before she pulled her head up to see over. It was dark outside the gates, just a speckle of moonlight to break the endless night. She squinted, and then as the scene came into focus she almost lost her grip on the fence and plunged to the ground. It was only by sheer will that her fingertips stayed gripped to the fence.

There was a massive group of Drones just outside the city barrier. Those standing in the front held large poles with black mineralines tied to them. This cast enough light to illuminate their fierce expressions.

The Arotia Drones started to mumble amongst themselves. Sapha could hear the fear, the worry, and maybe even the slightest hint of hope.

There were other survivors.

The male who was next to Marl started to chatter. He was wondering if they had stores of energy hidden away somewhere. Were they saviors?

Sapha bit into her lip. She had a bad feeling about

this. If these foreign Drones had lots of energy stores, why would they have journeyed to Arotia? They were here for a reason and, judging by their massive numbers and hard features, it wasn't to form a community and celebrate life. A glance along the fence showed that there were no priests or guards along the perimeter, no one to defend the city. Where were Kan and his guards?

"This is bad," she muttered.

A commotion had her spinning to the left. Finally Kan had emerged from his home. Surrounded by guards, he was making his way to the watchtower over the main gate. Despite her previous thoughts about his absence, his presence didn't exactly reassure Sapha. So far the high priest had proved to be more than useless.

"We should go, Marl," she said. That nudging sensation to flee was not one she ignored; it had saved her life on more than one occasion.

Without hesitation, she scaled back down the fence, and Marl, who trusted her implicitly, followed.

"I want to know what's going to happen." He continued, craning his head as they started to backtrack away from the front gate and through the town.

They didn't speak again until they'd arrived at the piece of metal which hid the hole in the fence they used to leave the city. Luckily, it seemed as if the foreign Drones were only at the front entrance, so they did not have to sneak to their cave.

It took a bit of time to cross the darkened plains. Sapha had marked the route many years before; she could have walked it with her eyes closed. Their faces reflected relief as the thorny bush that hid their cave came into view. It was always a good outing when they made it home without being detected. Scooting around the outer area, they made it inside the large rock cavern. It was a huge single room, with an arterial that exited out the other side. It was perfect because they had two ways to run if it ever came to that.

The moment Sapha was safe inside, she dropped the shadows that cloaked her, revealing her tall, thin frame. She was not as shapeless as the average Drone, but still did not have much extra weight on her bones. Her long, dark purple hair was secured to the nape of her neck with many twines of string. Unlike the Drones, she had two eyes, but they were still red around the pupil, the iris darkening out to gold. Her skin was chameleon-like, changing color according to her surroundings. But generally it was somewhere in a rich brown tone.

Marl strode around the sparse room. There was not much in the dark interior besides a few padded surfaces for his meditation, some bones they used for games, and tomes of information that Sapha had hoarded away. The moss creatures which clung high up on the wall cast shadowy light. Luckily the town didn't know about these light-givers; otherwise they would have drained their energy long ago. Sapha had never seen them in the city. They seemed to only exist far away from civilization. In fact, she was starting to wonder now how many other organisms might be out there, surviving, learning how to function in the dying world.

The army out the front of Arotia suggested there were quite a lot.

Marl finally expressed his unease. "Where did they come from? What do you think they want?"

"I've no idea," Sapha had to admit. "But something

tells me that Arotia is not going to like the reason, they either want our city or our crystals, and either way it will be the end of the people here."

Marl was already deathly pale, his skin white, translucent – like all of the Drones – muscle and bone visible beneath, but he seemed to shrink even further into himself. "What will happen to me?" He knew Sapha needed nothing to survive.

"I'll keep you alive," she whispered to her only friend, the little boy she thought of as a brother and would die to protect. "Don't ever fear death from lack of energy; I have enough to keep you alive."

Marl hugged her, his cold thin body melding into her own for a brief second. The Drones did not hug or touch much. It was not in their nature – too easy to want to suck the life-energy from another. But Sapha craved touch, so these brief moments meant everything to her.

"I'd give you energy now, but I know that if anyone sensed it on you, they'd want to know where you got it from and they'd kill you."

They would think Marl was stealing energy and they would not hesitate to end his life. Their laws were brutal now. Martial law ruled Arotia.

"You give me more than enough." Marl patted her arm once before withdrawing back into himself.

He really didn't understand the power Sapha wielded.

THERE WAS no day or night on Dronish to mark the passing of time, only the almost-dead-moon which drifted across the sky. From this they knew when to rest in their meditative state and when a weekly cycle had passed so they wouldn't miss Marl's next chance with the crystals.

Sapha wished they didn't have to go into Arotia at all, but Marl wore tracking bracelets, as did all the other Drones. If someone did not show up for feeding time, the authorities searched for them. The priest said it was for the protection of the masses, but it was really about control. Now the trackers were deactivated, the lights along the edge of the ankle bracelet dull and lifeless. They would light up if activated. But they only did that on rare occasions. The priest wouldn't waste power unless he needed to find someone. Sapha dreaded the day that Marl's lit up. She didn't have one, of course; she'd been hidden since birth.

IT WAS the next moon when she approached Marl. She'd been working on a plan all night. It felt like now was the time to break all ties with Arotia, especially if a battle was coming.

"I think I've figured out how to remove your ankle tracker. I just have to be sure that my power won't be detected."

Marl shook his head, his eye blinking as he stared. "Why bother? They won't call it in. No need to risk exposure."

Sapha clenched her hands together. "What if those other Drones have infiltrated the city? They might have the energy to activate every tracker. They could find us out here. We risk detection either way now."

"Can you sneak back in under your shadows and see what's happening?" He crouched down on his pillow. It wasn't time for meditation, but he often sat and absorbed the fine particles of energy in his surroundings. "That way we know the true risk either way."

"I already planned on going," Sapha said.

She had not rested for the entire meditation period. She had to know what was happening and she had to know now.

She left Marl, after making him promise many times he would not leave the cave, and made her way back to Arotia. She called her shadows to her the moment she was in the clear plains. It was nice when the shadows wrapped around her, warm and comforting, giving her the touch she desperately craved. Yes, they were not solid, but had been there her entire life; she would have gone crazy without them. She slowed outside the fence hole, pausing for a moment to make sure there was nothing or no one to worry her on the other side. It seemed to be clear.

She slipped through. There wasn't anyone close by; she could detect life-force pretty easily, except on those who were close to death. Wandering toward the town center, her eyes flicked left and right, waiting to sense the presence of the town's people. Arotia was not a spread-out city. To conserve energy, all the inhabitants lived together in large buildings. Each dwelling had layers, one on top of the other; literally thousands inhabited each of the stacked-on structures.

Staying close to the edges of the buildings, hidden by the shadows under the overhanging eaves, Sapha crept toward the front gate. She ground to a halt about a hundred yards out. She couldn't move any closer. It looked as if the entire population of Arotia was surrounding the gates. Kan and his men still sat in the watchtower. No one moved or spoke.

What the hell is going on here?

It was hard to get closer without running into anyone, but sticking with her darkness Sapha managed to get right into a small corner of a dwelling. From there she could climb some latticework and make her way to higher ground. The first level she reached wasn't high enough, so she continued to climb, working hard to keep her movements silent and hidden. Finally the second story allowed an uninterrupted view.

Holy mother of all energy, Sapha cursed under her breath as she blinked out into the darkness.

The crowd of foreigners outside the barriers had grown to massive proportions. They were at least as numerous as those inside Arotia, and they had moved closer to the city. Sapha couldn't tell what was happening, but it looked as if they were preparing to enter.

Shouting broke the silence. The words of the ancient Drones' language. Not the tongue Sapha preferred, but one she understood.

A young foreigner stepped forward. He wore a long, dark cloak like the rest of their society, his pale skin lit with red carvings which accentuated his very red eye.

"We warned you. Surrender your city and mineralines to us, or we will end you all." He wore his energy like a cloak, and he was filled to the brim.

In fact, all the people outside the gates looked flush with strength.

"You have one more cycle of the moon." This was his last warning before he turned and gestured to his people.

They all backed away, and then moved to their camp.

The Arotia priest turned, facing out to the thousands who waited on his words.

"Everyone into the town square now. We are bringing out the emergency crystals. Energy for everyone, so we have a chance to fight."

Sapha gasped a few times before scurrying down the side of the building. She fumbled near the bottom, missing the last few rungs and landing on her hands and knees. The hard rock that formed the dry ground bit into her delicate skin, tearing it and spraying free the liquid which lived under her skin. She was the only Drone she knew who had this red flowing in her body. It was a real pain. Thankfully she wasn't too hurt and managed to make it to her feet and take off for the cave. She had to stay ahead of the others and she had to either remove Marl's tracker or get him back to the town. They were sure to turn on the trackers for this. It was definitely an emergency.

The Drones were going to war again.

2

ABIGAIL

The group that gathered on the grassy area before the beach was large. We were at the wedding slash mating of my best friend, Lucy, and her mate, the wolf-Walker Colton. We watched as Cerberus, a two-headed hellhound, and Lina, a massive, shiny black unicorn – her long sparkling ivory horn tipped with a deadly-looking spike – galloped along the sand toward us.

Yes, you heard me correctly: hellhound and unicorn.

As Lina stepped closer, I was stunned to see a pair of shiny black wings tucked in at her side. I hadn't noticed them before. Unbelievable. She wasn't just a unicorn, but some sort of hybrid. Like a Pegasus and unicorn combined.

"I'm almost afraid to ask what the other five sacred Walker animals are going to be," I heard Lucy murmur.

She was next to me, still decked out in her stunning white gown, and tucked under the arm of her equally stunning mate. Colton's white-blond hair was tousled. He watched the creatures approach us.

"If Cerberus is bonded to me," I said, "does that mean each of these sacred guides will choose one of the half-Walkers?"

I tilted my head upwards and was captured by the velvety brown of my mate's eyes.

"Yes," Brace said. "That's what the legends tell us."

As the creatures approached, I felt a draw to step toward them, the same pull that had been there when I found Cerberus in pixie land. I clearly wasn't the only one. Fury, Talina, Ria, and Delane followed me off the grassy area and onto the sand. The half-Walker girls.

My heels sunk in, but it took no effort to kick the uncomfortable death-traps free. I reached out and linked hands with Fury on the right and Talina on the left. In turn, Ria attached to Talina, and then Delane – our most recent friend from the world of Nephilius – hesitated just briefly before she took Ria's other hand.

The five of us were linked physically, but as we stood waiting for the animals to reach us, unity, strength, and something a little more connected us at a cellular level.

"What's her name?" I heard Delane whisper. There was a sense of reverence coating her tone. "And what sort of animal is that?" I wasn't sure I'd ever heard such emotion from the warrior-Walker.

"On Earth we called them unicorns, but they don't usually have wings," I said. "So I guess she's a pegacorn."

"Or a unisus," Lucy chimed in.

I laughed. "Probably just easier to stick with unicorn. And her name is Lina."

Cerberus reached me first, and his two heads bobbed

as happiness exuded from him. My hellhound had been alone for so long, and now he was reveling in the Walker love around him. Not to mention his fellow animal guides were returning.

Lina paused six feet from us. She had large eyes, a shimmery silver color. With an inclination of her head she acknowledged each of us half-Walkers. I found my own head lowering slightly in return. She was majestic; there was no other way to describe her. The energy that swirled around her was so strong I kept expecting to see visible strands.

Lina, who stood heads taller than all of us girls, trotted forward and stopped in front of Delane. The Nephilius half-Walker's eyebrows drew together and her lips parted slightly. She pulled her hand free from Ria's, and then with little pause lifted both hands to gently rest them against Lina's long, horse-like nose.

Suddenly Delane's short, silky black hair lifted in whirls around her face and the caramel of her skin darkened as energy flowed between them. Both Delane and Lina's wings shot out from their bodies, standing many feet above their heads. We all had to jump back or we'd have been clobbered by the massive, razor-sharp appendages.

"She's mine?" Delane choked out. "I can't ... I don't know what to say." She turned her head to face me. She hadn't removed her hands from Lina. I could see the shock in her wide, dark eyes.

"They're our guides, helping us through this war, protecting us when they can," I said as I also freed my hands and reached forward to hug Cerberus. "We've been blessed, but I'm thinking we need to do some research. I've no idea what the sacred animals' abilities are."

"We can help you with that, baby girl." I spun my head to the side and found Josian standing there.

My lips lifted in a broad smile as a flood of joy washed through me. I was so glad he had made it back before the ceremony was over. He'd had to leave in the middle of Lucy's wedding, but I always felt better when he was close by. Something was going on with my father. I had sensed it for a while now, but still his presence was so essential in my life that I felt a little lost when his massive personality wasn't around.

"Who's we?" Ria asked.

Which was a good question, since he was standing there alone.

He grinned, showcasing his perfect white teeth. "The princeps of all seven clans are due to meet later. We should have enough knowledge between us." His red hair shifted around him in the breeze off the ocean.

I had so many things to be doing in the next twenty-four hours. I needed to go to the laluna and see if I could reform my melding bond with Brace. I had to meet with the princeps and find out about our animal guides. And I needed to get moving to the next world, Dronish, and gather the sixth half-Walker.

We were in a race against the clock. Four of the Seventine were out there and they were gathering energy and working to free the last three of their brothers.

And speaking of gathering energy, I also needed to find out what Fury had discovered on Crais. I had a terrible feeling there was something big about to go down on one of the planets. I just didn't know which one or how to prevent it from happening.

"But I think now it's time for a dance," Josian said, spreading his arms wide. "Can I have the honor, baby girl?"

His words had the crowds dispersing again. They moved back to the positions they'd been in before the arrival of our second sacred animal, mingling on the dance floor and seated around the tables eating and drinking. I caught Lucy's eye and she gave me a wink before turning to Colton. He took her into his strong arms. Brace was standing where I'd left him; his features softened as I blew him a kiss. I strode across to Josian, still barefoot, while the other girls remained gathered around the sacred animals.

A quick glance behind me confirmed that Delane still had a shell-shocked look.

I turned away to meet the bronze-eyed gaze of my father. "I'd love a dance." I linked my arm through his. "We missed you earlier. Where did you go?"

I wasn't good with secrets. Hated them. And he was keeping a big one from me.

He didn't hesitate with his answer. "I had to leave to see my laluna." The sadness on his features tugged at my heart. "They want me to bring you and Brace to them before you reform the melding bond. They have some information to release."

I reached up and smoothed the frown lines framing his stunning eyes. "What's wrong, Dad?"

He hesitated a moment, as if he were about to say something, but changed his mind. His eyes dulled even further. "I wish I could tell you, baby girl, but there're some things that are outside my control."

After Brace, Josian was the most powerful Walker I knew, and it scared me a little that my dad was so stressed out. That he was keeping secrets from me.

As we moved around the dance floor I wracked my brain trying to figure out what could be bothering him. Clearly it was something he either couldn't tell me, or didn't want to. Was it about the Seventine? If it was, he most surely should be clueing me in. I needed every piece of information to try to best them in this final battle.

Josian's eyes never left my face as he gracefully swirled me around – I was as uncoordinated as always. If I wasn't mistaken there was pleading in his bronze depths. He wanted me to figure it out. But I just couldn't think. Maybe his laluna was a hint. He'd mentioned them without much pressure from me, but that made me think that it wasn't about them. Except, what if it was to do with the stones and he could only tell me so much?

Were they threatening or controlling him? But that would mean they had to be in his head. I needed to talk to Brace about this. I'd avoided mentioning it to anyone besides Lucy, because I didn't want to create any suspicion around my dad. But Brace was smart with these things, and he knew how the Walker world worked. His ideas would probably be a hell of a lot closer to the truth than mine.

Speaking of, I smiled as my mate danced past with his mom, Lasandra. She was laughing and grinning up into her son's handsome features. The moment he turned to rest tender eyes on me, her smile dried up. Yes, she was still not a fan, and I was hoping that we didn't need to deal with that anytime soon.

I was distracted then. A hum of foreign energy suddenly infiltrated the wedding party. It seeped across and then slammed against me with a recognizable force. I turned my head to try to pinpoint it, and I wasn't the only one – every Walker in the vicinity was locked in on this new power.

Josian straightened, his hands falling as he let go of me. "Well, I wouldn't have believed they'd leave their home. Your little Lucy is an important lady." He grinned. "And this is the answer to a question you asked me long ago. You're about to meet Lucy's father. The moment I first saw her I sensed his energy, but considering she was from Earth, I thought it nothing more than a weird coincidence. Until Malisna explained what had happened."

Josian was chattier than usual, probably overcompensating for all those things he couldn't tell me. And I guessed his words meant the faeries were coming.

The large cloud of power continued moving from the gates of Angelisian toward us. The energy was strong, humming through the air and clashing with the Walker energy inside. Brace moved to stand next to me, which wasn't a surprise; he was extra protective of me now.

"What is it, Abbs?" Lucy fluttered to my other side, her exquisite, translucent wings moving so rapidly I almost couldn't see them. "Colt's gone all growly, and his mind has shifted into this weird black-and-white landscape."

I widened my eyes, a broad grin spreading across my face. "Are you telling me he thinks like a dog?"

"Wolf," he growled at me. "I'm a bloody wolf."

I waved him aside. Growly-wolf-Colton was such a common occurrence there was no need for worry. Although I noticed the way Brace was watching his best friend. If I'd still been able to hear his thoughts, no doubt I'd be seeing my mate's mental images of punching Colton in the face.

Malisna, the stunning and petite pixie queen, flew over to us. "Lucy!" Her face was pale, the green more prominent than usual and her blue-and-gold eyes were wide and glassy. "Lucy, it's your father. Promise me that you'll go nowhere with him. He's not to be trusted."

Behind her was Refis, Lucy's brother. He had his little dagger drawn; it seemed to be a knee-jerk reaction for him in stressful situations.

"Father," Lucy repeated in a stutter. "As in faeries ... freaking faeries are coming toward us."

A warm voice washed over us. "Well, I'm not so sure about the freaking part, but faerie we are."

Then from the shadows dozens of faeries emerged. Malisna snarled and moved to stand in front of her daughter. Colton also pulled Lucy back behind him.

I felt Brace's hand on my arm, stopping me from moving forward. I hadn't even realized I'd been trying to get a better look.

I stared with more than a little fascination. They were like the tall versions of pixies, with pointed ears, multi-colored eyes and delicate feline features. But despite these similarities there were many differences also.

The faeries stood over six feet, every single one. They had long sweeping hair that reached their ankles. Even on the men. And while the pixies' skin seemed to exist in shades of green and ivory, this fey group had a plethora of colors going on. Some sported skin as black as night, as black as the Crais inhabitants, contrasting so strongly with others whose skin was so white it almost hurt to stare too closely. There were also red, yellow, purple, and many shades in between.

Their tri-colored eyes stared back at us from their alien features. They had that ancient, carved-from-stone look that was a trademark of Walkers. Unlike the pixies with their leafy covers, they were dressed in regular clothes, like that of First Worlders.

A male stepped forward. He wore an understated but heavily adorned crown of jewels. It held back his long waves of blond hair. His clothing was all black, a silky open-collared shirt and slacks. And yes, his power had that distinct feel of Lucy's. Ten to one this was her father.

The pixie queen confirmed my thoughts. "What are you doing here, Latinti?" Her words were low and bitingly cruel.

I almost winced as she lashed out with her power-laced question.

"I'm here for my daughter's mating ceremony. I'm her father, after all." His voice was low, rich, and with just a hint of laughter behind each word.

"You lost all rights to Lucy the moment you stole her from me." Malisna's bi-colored hair was starting to lift as her power increased. "That you dare show your face here tells me that you have learned nothing from these very long years. You have suffered nothing that I have. You must suffer. You must be punished."

Lucy escaped her guard-wolf and dived to Malisna's side.

"Mother, please, don't do this here." I heard her

urgent words as they fell into the pixie queen's ear. "He can't take me from you again; I'm no longer helpless. He'll soon see that a reunion between us is a rocky and difficult road for him to walk."

While she was talking down her pissed-off mother, I continued to watch Latinti. From the moment his blue-, gold- and black-flecked eyes had found Lucy, everything in his demeanor changed. Gone was the cocky arrogance and half-smartass expression. He lowered his face, but I still saw the sorrow and fear that stretched his features.

My head snapped to the side at the sound of a low growl. It was Colton.

He stepped closer to the faerie. "You watched Lucy from the window the other day. Your scent is different, but I recognize it ... you've only masked the top layer."

Shit. Well, if anyone would know it was the wolf-Walker; he had senses like no other.

Latinti nodded his head once. "Yes, it was me. I heard the pixies were free. I knew that ... Lucy had returned."

He hesitated over her name. Something told me that he had known her as something else. Maybe the name Malisna had called her, or maybe something different.

"Why are you really here?" Lucy finally faced the man who had stolen her and dumped her on Earth. She didn't seem upset. Her doll-like features were relaxed, eyes calm.

He didn't pretend not to understand her question. "I do want to meet you. And ..." he hesitated just briefly, before his cool eyes shifted to Josian. "We are joining the war. This is a big one, we can feel it, and the land whispers with the prophecy words. Pixies are gathering and faerie will also stand with Walkers."

Brace stared him down a little. "You've never involved yourself in Walker battles before."

Latinti's expression hardened, the benign smile falling from his lips. "This war is different. Should this one be lost, then it will end our existence as we know it. This is not silly Walker politics in which faerie have no interest. This is a battle to live."

I lifted my chin to meet Brace's gaze.

"The faerie is right," I said with conviction, projecting my voice loud enough for all to hear. "I've been thinking for a while that we need to gather these different powers. Maybe we should ... I don't know, set up a war camp."

Josian stepped to my side. Lallielle, as always, was right beside him.

"Already ahead of you, baby girl. At the last princeps' meeting we decided to start gathering our clans. We planned to meet in the large field again. We were taking the first steps in setting up a war council."

I'd been so busy lately I knew that I'd missed lots of what was going on with the Walker leaders.

Josian continued. "I'll contact the others. We need to move the time-frame forward." He waved a hand toward Malisna and Latinti. "We welcome the involvement of pixie, faerie, and any others who arrive on our doorstep. But be aware, this is a Walker battle. In the end you must heed our commands."

"We'll see," Latinti said. "I've never denied that Walkers are the supreme power, but in your arrogance, you often miss things which might aid your plight. Don't discount us yet."

Malisna let out a long breath. "I will retrieve the rest of pixie, and the forest sprites and we will meet you at the war camp." She kissed her daughter on the cheek, still fixing narrowed eyes on Latinti. "See you soon, daughter, I am honored to have been here today at the mating to your beloved." She fluttered up and kissed Colton on the cheek too.

As she dropped down, Lucy reached across and hugged her mother, arms a little awkward over the wings.

Latinti watched these exchanges with fascination, before he chimed in. "We'll also take our leave for this camp," he said. "It's probably best ..." His eyes flicked to the right. "If you set up separate territories for all fey involved."

Judging by the scowl from Malisna, the pixie and faerie camps should be on opposite sides.

"It will be done." Josian didn't smile. Instead he saluted the faerie prince.

Then just like that the different fey factions disappeared off into the air. Or wherever they went.

"Guess that's the wedding over." Lucy sighed. "We were lucky to have as much time as we did."

She hugged Lallielle and then moved over to hug me also. "Colt and I can't thank you enough. This was the best day ever."

"Yes, we owe you for organizing such an amazing celebration." Colton's gruff tones spoke of more than his words.

I punched his arm. "Aw, you big old softie."

He growled deeper. "Stop saying that. I'm tough. I'm a freaking Walker, a warrior and a wolf."

Lucy and I snorted out our laughter.

"Sure, sure," I said between splutters. "The three Ws of Colt."

Colton turned to Brace. "Control your woman."

Brace held up both hands. "Are you kidding? No one controls Red. She's got it all over me. We're just going to have to live with the fact that, with these two around, we'll never again have out of control egos."

My heart started galloping in my chest at the thought of the rest of my life with Brace. I was more than lucky to have him. He was my perfect other half, and the fact that he still didn't have all of his memories of our brief life together rankled with me. We needed to get back to the lalunas soon, before I moved on to Dronish.

"I love you." I leaned in close and let the soft words trickle toward him. I hadn't said that since before the bond was broken.

His features froze. I had taken him by surprise: for him, that was the first time he'd heard those words from me. The sudden shimmery reflection of his eyes and the emotions on his face almost broke my heart. With a sort of rumbly growl he pulled me toward him. I went willingly. I had to bury my face in his chest to hide the tears that had formed in my eyes.

Everything of Brace washed over me: his scent, strength and energy. It was like being cocooned in my favorite blanket. For a brief moment I was safe and protected, like nothing could touch me.

Soft words added to my happy-place. "There should be a word stronger than love," he whispered in my ear. "Something so unbreakable that nothing in any of the worlds or even gods above could tear it apart. If there was a word that defined this, then I would use it every day for you. But for now, I love you, Red."

Oh. My. God. He was killing me, but in the best

freaking way.

I had never doubted his feelings for me. Despite the fact he was relearning about our life, the emotions between us had never gone anywhere. His love for me ... well, the lalunas had never had the power to sever that.

"And there's that sappy romance we've been missing." Lucy broke the moment, but I was okay with it. This wasn't exactly the place for anything more.

Lallielle made a distressed noise. "I still can't believe you allowed this, Josian." She had not been happy about us keeping her in the dark about the broken melding bond. "You tampered with something so sacred ... a blessing which has been lost to Walkers for many lifetimes."

I reached across and took her hand. "I'm sorry, Mom, we thought it was the only way." My next few breaths were ragged as I fought my emotions.

Josian didn't say anything, but his face suddenly had that carved-from-stone look that Walkers pulled out when they were mega pissed off.

Fury distracted us. "While I totally get your reasoning, you should have let the half-Walkers know. We're a team ... you can trust us with anything."

Cerberus came closer and licked up the side of my face. The hound had an innate sense of when I needed comforting.

I sucked in a few more labored breaths. The air filled my lungs, but I was still lightheaded. "I do trust you all. It wasn't about lack of trust; it was ... I don't even know. Fear, thinking I had no other choice, thinking I was the one who had to shoulder the responsibility to save these worlds." I hung my head. "I'm really sorry. It was stupid.

Keeping secrets has done nothing but cause problems, even if I had the best of intentions. So, from now on, full disclosure. No more secrets."

As I spoke, Josian's gaze fell. My worries flooded back. I hoped that this meeting we were going to with the laluna would clue me as to what sort of problem Josian was having.

Ria's arms went around me then, and I hugged her back tightly. I knew she had accepted my lack of disclosure of the melding bond. She could be so kind when she wanted to.

"Alright, so what do we do now?" the Regali queen asked, her demeanor calm.

It was never difficult to see the methodical intelligence that Ria used to rule her people on Regali.

"We go to this war camp." This was from Delane, of course. Warrior-Walker.

The Angelica had her massive wings tucked in behind her. She spoke with confidence but her expression was filled with unease. Life on Nephilius was solely about training and battle. Lucy's wedding was a big – uneasy – first for her.

"We must gather together, figure out the strengths of each group and plan our strategy. Not to mention that we half-Walker females need to tether our powers. We must strengthen ourselves and learn to work as a team."

"I agree," I said. "I've been thinking for a while that the half-Walker females need to spend more time together. When we're close our energy bounces off each other. We have complementary powers, and they need time to blend." I exhaled loudly, my breathing finally coming easier. "But equally as important is me finding the last two of our group. I'll make sure I continually pop in and out."

Talina laid her cool hand on my arm. "Finding the girls is really important, Abbs. While you're gone the rest of us can still research and train. Then hopefully once you're finished finding the last two, we'll be ready to take the step as a complete power."

Josian interrupted us. "Jedi contacted me last night; he has some information from the pixie library. He'll meet us at the war camp. He has a few scrolls to go through." He glanced at our faces. "No one will be sitting around waiting for Aribella to return. We all have to do our part."

That was good. I couldn't be everywhere at once. I had to trust that others could handle some aspects of this entire Seventine battle.

Lallielle started to move. "I'll send off all the First Worlders, and then we can focus on this impending war."

She scurried off to farewell those guests still lingering around the beach area. Brace and Colton left our group for a moment, stepping across to where Lasandra, Caty, Magenta, Petal and her dad were gathered in a group. I could see the men's lips move as they updated the Walkers ... eventually Magenta opened a doorway. Caty was the only one to turn back and give me a friendly wave as they all left via that doorway. Lasandra never glanced back.

Magenta's white-blond hair disappeared, along with the scowl that was pretty much permanently on her face. She'd made it perfectly clear to Colton that he was mated into this Seventine mess, and it had nothing to do with her. Magenta wasn't a fan of mine because she'd wanted

Brace – or mostly to be the princeps' mate. And Lucy she hated and detested on a cellular level – to her my pixie friend had stolen her twin brother's love and loyalty away. If the bickering and snotty comments continued between those two, sooner or later it was going to come to blows.

After a few minutes of goodbyes it was just our core group left: the five half-Walkers and our mates, as well as Lucy, Colton, Josian, Lallielle and Quarn – who had made it in time for the ceremony. At the back of the group, sort of in a guard-like position, were our two sacred animal guides.

Since we finally had a spare moment, I took three steps and threw myself at my guardian. Quarn caught me easily, anticipating my hug.

"Ah, it's been too long, miquerina," he said.

I knew now those words meant *my little one*. It still made me smile when he said it.

"How's the castle security going?" I asked as we pulled apart. I wished we had more time to catch up.

"Great, except for Lucas having his moody crown on lately," Quarn said. "It's been quite the strained environment."

I glanced across at Ria, and noticed the subtle tightening of her features, especially the feathering around the delicate skin of her eyes. She had heard his words. It wasn't a huge reach to guess the emperor's recent asshat mood was because of the stunning Regali half-Walker. I didn't believe these two could ignore their connection for too long. In the end these types of cosmic links, whether they were true mates or not, always came to a head. You had to deal with it, or it would force you to.

Lallielle crossed her arms, all businesslike. "So, to

reiterate, everyone is off to the war camp in the same field the Walker gathering was held. Except for Abby, who has to go to Dronish and find the half-Walker." She rested her soft gaze on me. "While you're gone, we'll be making plans and gathering information; if all the Seventine are released, we'll be ready for them."

Fury also crossed her arms. "Sounds about right, but I need to go back to Crais ... well, Dune and I do. We have to check out this energy-gathering spot."

They'd been in the middle of investigating something on Crais when I'd called her to attend Lucy's wedding.

Ladre distracted us by stepping forward. In his right hand he held a device that pumped a fine mist of water toward his face. All Spurns – except Talina – needed to keep their hair moist or they could dehydrate and die. Ladre used the machine whenever he was away from the water.

He spoke slowly so we could understand his lispy words. "At some point Talli and I should also return to Spurn. I have a few more locations to check for Seventine activity, and it's time for the council to elect a new Baroon leader. I must assist in this transitioning."

Wow, it sounded like Ladre had most definitely chosen a life with Talina over his life on Spurn. I caught her small grin and I was so happy for my friend.

I waved my hands a few times. "Okay, since we can't ignore other responsibilities, you all should go do what you have to. But keep in mind that at any point I might have to call the half-Walker girls to me." I narrowed my eyes on Fury. "And if you do find anything to do with energy-gathering or the Seventine, you have to let me or Dad know. This is not something you can deal with on your own, and the half-Walker girls are too important to risk." I smiled to soften my words. "And I personally couldn't stand it if any of you were hurt."

Fury met my unblinking stare, one side of her lips rising in a grin. "Fine, Supes, you win. I'll let you know." She persisted with the nickname, but it was still better than Super Abby.

At least she had finally given me the promise I'd been trying to get out of her for days.

"As will I." Talina, as always, was agreeable.

Great, one thing dealt with. Time for the next.

I stepped closer to Delane before reaching out and gripping her hand. The Angelica's features froze. She was not used to personal contact, which was part of the reason I did it. She needed to bond with us, and to do that she had to loosen up. Also, she needed a purpose and I was about to give her one.

I spoke to the rest of the group. "While I'm gone I want you all to spend some time training with Delane. She's an amazing warrior, with a battle-ready mind. Something we're in desperate need of."

Delane's expression didn't change, but her black eyes flashed something in their reflective depths.

I focused my attention on the four half-Walkers. "All of us have different strengths, but together we make a complete package. It's time for us to cement these bonds between us." I pushed back a few curls that had fallen forward. "I know that I'm not going to be here much for the next little bit, but that doesn't mean that we can't bond. I'll connect as much as I can; we'll strengthen our combined power."

"Hear hear, Supes." Fury clapped a few times. "But I'll

reserve judgment on whether I follow warrior here. She needs to prove this battle mind to me."

Delane did not hesitate. "Challenge accepted."

"Oh, my god. Let me be there when Fury gets her ass kicked." Lucy raised her head as if she were really praying.

Laughter rang out. A smile even crossed Delane's face. Fury was the only one with her signature scowl.

I let go of the Angelica's hand. "Well, that seems like a good plan for the next few days, and with that in mind I'm changing out of this dress and going to find me a laluna."

A thrill went through me as I shot my head around and clashed eyes with my mate. I let myself have a moment to eye-devour the heck out of him. He had been silent, letting us have our discussion, but my awareness of him was as strong as ever. As we stared, tension built between us. There was this slight curve to his lips as he caressed my features. That look filled me with heat.

I had no doubt that he was excited to be reforming our bond. Actually, judging by that expression, excited was an understatement.

Quarn distracted me. "Why do you need to go to the lalunas?"

I refrained from fanning my face as I turned to my guardian.

He stepped closer, his expression shuttered. "Everything I've heard of the stones is that they're trouble."

On this I wholeheartedly agreed with him, but I would deal with creepier McCreeps than them for Brace. I quickly explained about the broken melding bond, knowing he had probably already heard most of the story, since he talked to Lallielle all the time. His concerned expression never abated. In fact, as the story went on, he looked graver. Which was giving me that bad-feeling cramp low in my gut.

I was just finishing the story when a flash of light and energy flickered over the group. I glanced down. My blue laluna had just appeared in my hand.

"Well, hello there," I said. "Haven't seen you for a while."

The blue flashed in a series of strikes and different colors ricocheted through the stone.

I choked on my next breath because all of a sudden the stone was burning hot.

"What's happening?" I gasped out.

Brace was at my side in a second, but no matter how much he tried he couldn't touch me.

I couldn't stop the choked screams that were spluttering from me. "The laluna's doing something."

Josian stumbled a little closer. "This is the first stage of the transformation," he said, looking stricken.

Just like Brace, he couldn't move any closer to me. His bronzed, autumn-leaf eyes drooped at the corners, and it almost looked as if he were going to cry.

The heat crisping through me increased, my whimpering screams amplifying in pitch. By my estimate, in about five seconds my hand was going to char right off my arm. Just when I thought I couldn't take the pain any longer, the stone started to change shape. I watched as it kind of ... melted. It was reforming into something else.

My face began to ache from my alternate screaming and clenching of my jaw. Closing my eyes, I dropped to my knees, my sole focus on the simple act of continuing to breathe. The pain was almost beyond my ability to process. I wondered what would happen when my capacity to withstand this agony reached its pinnacle. I guessed I would pass out, a welcome relief.

Although my eyes were closed I could feel the melting stone. It started to twirl around my hand, smoothing out, flattening, and curling around my wrist. The same wrist which had the purple, tear-shaped birthmark of my mother's line.

Finally, as I puffed in and out, the burning started to cease, before dying off altogether. I sucked in a few more ragged breaths, the air drifting over my raw throat. It hurt. I'd screamed myself hoarse.

The pain continued to ease, until finally it was completely gone. My eyelids flew up, and I dropped my chin to see my hand.

What the hell?

The stone had turned itself into a piece of jewelry. A shiny, blue bracelet curved in thin lines around my wrist and up my arm a little way. Okay, it was beautiful, but definitely not worth the pain.

I flexed my hand. Despite the stiff, unbreakable feel to the cuff, it shifted easily. It didn't limit my movements, which was a relief.

Brace's arms closed around me as the energy disappeared altogether. I sank into his familiar comfort, just for a brief moment. No matter how strong I was or would become, he would always be my rock. My true strength. His body was steady, although his arms shook a little as they held me tight. He wasn't speaking, but something told me he was too stressed or pissed off to open his mouth.

Eventually I pulled away ... well, as far away as Brace would let me. Which meant I was pressed firmly against his hard chest. I turned my head to the right and found Josian hovering close to my side. I held up the bracelet.

"Is this what generally happens during a transformation?"

He stared down at the sparkle of blue flashing up from my wrist. He shook his head slowly, once and then again.

"No." His voice was barely above a whisper. "I don't know what this is, but it appears your laluna doesn't want to be separated from you."

The familiar, comforting warmth I'd always felt around the laluna was flowing through me. Along with power. My Walker side started to hum with contentment. If there was something my energy well inside loved it was power, and the laluna was pure undiluted energy.

Lucy broke the tension. "Okay, well let's add that to this week's weird."

I snorted out my laughter. "Truthfully, besides the pain, which I could definitely have done without, the rest doesn't even feel that weird. I'm starting to just expect these kinds of things."

"Word!" Lucy, Talina, Fury and Ria all exclaimed.

Delane was the only one not quite up to our Earth slang yet.

I couldn't help the full-bellied laughter that followed. In some moments, like right then, when my arm was no longer charring off my body and I could look at the faces of my loved ones, I knew how lucky I was.

Even if we only had these brief moments, I wouldn't change one thing.

3
———

During the next hour everyone dispersed to their destinations. Some entered a doorway to the First World war zone, and others traced to their youngling planets. After seeing them all off I had just ducked inside to change out of my beautiful emerald dress. Brace and Josian were waiting for me downstairs. We were heading for the laluna.

Lucy was with me, standing in my dressing room. "So you're sure that you can handle these wacko faeries without me?"

The pixie's stunning white-green dress had already been replaced by jeans and a black tank with custom-made cuts in the back for her wings. White and green flowers still threaded her long curls.

"Yes, Luce, you go and finish the final Walker mating step. You don't want Colt to get heat mange from stress."

"Damn smart-ass Walker," I heard her mate mutter from where he stood at the entrance to my room.

Lucy grinned at me before leaping forward and

wrapping her arms tightly around me. "I'm going to miss you. I promise we won't be long, but I know the urgency to get to Dronish, so I'm afraid we might not be back in time. You better take Brace with you – and be careful."

I returned her hug tightly. "If I end up leaving before you return, I'll make sure to come back often and see that you've made it home safely." I raised my voice then. "You better look after her, Colton, or I'll find you."

And I would. Although, I did trust her mate. He would die for Lucy and you couldn't ask for more than that from anyone.

With one last kiss on the cheek I watched my oldest friend in any of the worlds, my sister and soul mate, fly out the door. Yeah, Brace was also my soul mate; he owned the vast majority of my heart and soul. But there was plenty there for Lucy too. There are some people who walk into your lives and change you. Never again will you be the same person. If I lost Lucy I wasn't sure what sort of person I would be after, and right then I hoped like hell that wasn't something I ever had to experience.

Stepping further into my closet, I shimmied out of the beautiful gown, placing it on the end of the rack to be cleaned. I was dressed within moments. Jeans and a shirt didn't take much time to choose.

Just as I was stepping out to wash my hands in the bathroom, I paused as a light wash of energy entered my room. Weird. I had not expected to see him today. Or any day really.

I stared at the man who stood awkwardly near the end of my bed.

"I'd have knocked," he said, "but I wasn't sure you would open the door for me."

"What do you want, Samuel?" I focused on the dark eyes of my brother and felt the familiar tendrils of emotions course through me. A mix of anger and guilt.

He'd been the person to take Brace from me, which in turn facilitated the release of the third Seventine. But in other ways I knew I was being a little unfair, judging Samuel without the full story. I'd done some pretty questionable things myself lately, thinking I was doing the right thing, but still ending up causing trouble. Who was I to throw stones in glass houses?

He pushed back his dark hair. "I don't know why I'm here. I feel as if the entire world has been out of control since I was taken by Que. I've been tortured and mind-wiped and caused so much pain and trouble. But ... there's something inside me that needs to make things right with you."

He bled sincerity, and pain. I recognized agony quite intimately now, and it blazed from every facet of Samuel.

"I swear to you, Abby, that I never intentionally did anything to hurt you or Lucy." He ran a shaking hand through his hair again. "I might have been weak, allowing myself to be manipulated, but I'm not a bad person ... deep down. I know I'm not."

I was feeling all sorts of extra emotions now. Guilt, anger, worry and pain. Because I hated to see anyone suffering the way I could see Samuel was.

"You weren't at Lucy's mating."

His features fell even further. "No," he said, shaking his head. "Despite everything, I just couldn't watch her belong to ... another."

In his own way, Samuel had loved Lucy, but his problem was that he was just too broken. He'd been so busy trying to make sense of all the missing pieces of himself that he'd never truly appreciated Lucy.

Colton was broken too, but he was old and had had a long time to come to terms with the new individual he was. And it didn't hurt that Lucy and Colton were true mates. You can overcome a lot in those circumstances.

Colton also knew something which Samuel had not figured out yet; being broken doesn't mean there's no hope for you. You just have to find the new person you are, learn how to exist with a few less pieces. And maybe Samuel was finally starting to do that.

He stopped fidgeting and stared straight at me. "You're my family, my sister. I might not have appreciated that in the first few months of discovering you were alive, but I don't want to lose you."

In so many ways this man was a stranger to me. But it didn't have to be like that. Both of us had made mistakes. My heart was telling me that it was time for both of us to work harder.

"I'm willing to try and build a relationship with you." I reached out, briefly hesitating before finally grasping his hand. "But no more lies and secrets. Full disclosure."

He met my gaze. He had to look down a little to do so. "I can agree to that."

I pulled away. "I'm sorry I don't have time now, but soon I'd like to have dinner with you. Catch up on your life. I want to know who Samuel was before the kidnapping, but more importantly, who you are now."

He moved swiftly and hugged me. My breath

whooshed out in a loud exhalation. I hadn't expected that move, but I returned the gesture.

"Thank you, Abby, thank you so much for ... not dismissing me."

My heart ached a little at his sad words.

"I'll let you go now. Be safe and I'll see you when you return."

He pulled away and started to leave before turning back at the doorway.

"In the spirit of full disclosure ... I might be imagining things here, but be careful of Josian. When I was influenced by Que and the Seventine, I had a few weird dreams ... your dad had two faces. He was being controlled with these strings on his arms and legs." He shrugged his broad shoulders. "I know that it's just a dream, but I've learned to not completely discount these weird occurrences."

With one last half-smile, he left the room.

I clenched my hands into tight fists. Samuel's dreams sounded an awful lot like the dream Lucy had had of Josian. My throat seized. I tried to breathe around the thought that my father might be in trouble. I knew in my soul he was a good man – he would move mountains for his loved ones – but was he involved in something that was outside his control?

If this meeting with the laluna didn't reveal anything I was going to have to spend a lot of time with my dad. I couldn't help, unless I knew what was happening to him. I was definitely going to talk with Brace about my worries; he'd have great insights. He always knew more than I did.

As I stepped out onto the front grassed area I saw that

only three figures out of those who had taken part in the previous wedding celebrations remained: Lallielle, Josian, and Brace.

And Cerberus, of course. He was stretched out enjoying the twilight.

My family was in the middle of a conversation. Their relaxed expressions indicated that the discussion was not about anything serious.

Lallielle pulled me into a hug when I reached her side. "I wish you didn't have to leave so soon, Aribella." Her grip was tight and her words low. She was generally so calm, especially amongst all of us volatile and emotional beings, but she was overflowing a little today. "I just want one normal day with my daughter. We never have enough time together."

"I know, Mom, I wish for that too." I buried my face into her familiar scent. "It's for this very reason that we fight the Seventine so hard, so that one day we'll have so much time together we'll be bored."

As he'd done many times before, Josian enclosed us both in his long arms, his strength adding an extra dimension to our dynamics. In that moment I prayed for a million more hugs like this. Despite my shaky faith in the gods, I needed hope that there was something bigger than me out there giving us a helping hand.

As we untangled ourselves I decided to provide my mother with a little bit of happy. "I talked to Sammy," I said.

Lallielle's pale-green eyes met mine, and I saw the hope light them.

"We aren't suddenly besties or anything, but there

was some healing and I think ... well, one day soon, I hope we have a normal sibling relationship."

With a shriek, Lallielle cupped my face in her hands. "Oh, that makes me so happy to hear, baby girl."

In my peripheral vision I could see Josian and Brace. My father's expression was a little wistful, and a little resigned. He wasn't Samuel's biggest fan, and while most of us had pretty much accepted Samuel hadn't willingly betrayed us – he'd been influenced – Josian still retained some suspicion.

Brace, on the other hand, was smiling. He'd been friends with my brother for a long time and had always encouraged me to look deeper into what had happened, to dig for the whole story. Too-clever-for-his-own-good Walker. His advice was always geared toward making me a better version of who I already was and, really, that was a pretty amazing quality to have in one's mate. Instead of tearing you down, they built you up.

Lallielle and I pulled away as Josian spoke.

"We need to go now. Get this *laluna* meeting over with so that Aribella can move on to Dronish."

His voice had an unusual inflection when he'd mentioned the laluna. They were his little world, so why did he seem less than excited to take us there? My suspicions grew further.

I glanced down at the sudden burst of power and heat from my new bracelet.

Were they warning me too? I already knew to tread carefully with Tenni, and I hadn't forgotten I owed her a favor. Which I wasn't looking forward to fulfilling. Damn, I really hoped Josian's issue wasn't to do with the favor I owed.

With one last kiss on the cheek we left Lallielle and Cerberus on the beach and took a Walker doorway to Josian's cave planet. I knew it was hard for Mom to always be left behind, but she was our trusted delegate on First World; she kept everything functioning. Her plan was to go across to this war camp. Quarn would take her in his little buggy. Knowing Lallielle, she would move between home and the camp as needed. Lallielle often played a behind-the-scenes role in this battle, but that didn't make her any less important. For the time being my hellhound was to stay by her side and keep her safe.

Brace held my hand as we traversed the vacuum-worm-hole. Josian strode beside us, quiet, expressionless. It took us no time to cross through the cave and into the garden that hid the laluna world. The weird little faeries were waiting for us, Tenni front and center, as always the spokes-crazy for the rest of them.

Unlike the last time when I was devastated by the decision to break my melding bond, now I could really pay attention to what was going on in this little cave alcove. Tenni moved closer to Josian, and as she moved so did the others. It was slight, but it seemed as if there were invisible strings connecting the laluna creatures. They moved as one unit.

"Hello, our precious bonded one," she said to Josian, and even I felt the wash of power directed toward him.

The fine skin around his eyes tightened. It was ever so subtle, but I was paying attention.

"Hello, Tenni." He exhaled loudly. "As requested, I've brought Aribella and her mate."

His greeting was a hell of a lot colder than it had been the last time we were here. If I had to guess, he'd had a fight with his laluna ... why the hell would he fight with them? I exchanged a glance with Brace, but now wasn't the time for more questions.

"Why have you come here, our bonded one's daughter?" Tenni asked me, even though she already knew the reason.

"I'm going to reform the melding bond with Brace, but Josian though it prudent that I check in with you first, just in case you wanted to tell me something."

I carefully phrased my sentence. I didn't need or want their permission, and I sure as heck wasn't owing them anything more.

Tenni looked from me to Brace, her eyes lingering on the way our hands were tightly connected. "Why have you changed your mind so quickly? Do you no longer care about the fate of the worlds?"

Brace spoke this time. "I wasn't involved in the decision to break the bond. Had I been, I would have told you all that a melded couple is the strongest force in the star system. In no way could our melding weaken Abby. I have no doubt that she will need my strength in the final battle, should it come to that."

I nodded a few times. "Yeah, what Brace said."

Tenni didn't pull any punches. "You owe us a favor ... we order you not to reform the melding bond. We believe the initial visions were correct. We work to protect the worlds."

Ahhh, eff me. What the hell was I going to do now?

"So your favor is that I never reform my melding bond?" My voice held all the horror of my thoughts.

"No," she shook her head, "just until after the final battle."

My swallowing sounded loud in the cavernous room. The walls were spinning a little, and I thought I was going to pass out. I wasn't sure I could survive that long without Brace. It felt as if my skin were paper thin now, and I was moments from turning to dust and dispersing into the air.

Brace's stance was confident as he spoke. "Just one small problem there." His eyes were not black, so he wasn't too pissed off. What did he have up his sleeve? "Abby's an original power, as are you."

Tenni smiled, as if that acknowledgement of her status pleased her. But that expression disappeared with the next words from Brace's mouth.

"Original powers cannot owe or ask favors from each other. You know that. It throws off the natural order of the worlds."

What? I mean, what the eff?

I spun to stare at my silent father. Josian had his eyes lifted, as if he were observing the ceiling. What was he looking at? There was nothing above us but stone. Was he even paying attention to this conversation?

Surely he knew original powers couldn't owe each other favors, so why hadn't he mentioned this when I initially broke the bond? And why was he not looking at me now? My heart clenched tightly. Whatever Josian was involved in was bigger than I'd imagined, and right then my brain was churning out some very unappealing options.

Tenni was solemn as she stepped closer to the edge of her area. "You know your history, young Walker. Due to Aribella's dual nature, we did not initially know she held original power." Her tone indicated that she still had her doubts about my abilities. "We do not want to anger the gods, so ... in regards to this we concede that there is no favor."

My body tensed and my heart jumped for joy. For a brief moment I imagined I could reform the bond without repercussions. But then she spoke again, shattering that brief moment of joy.

"We still cannot allow you to reform your melding bond." As Tenni hesitated, all of the faeries swayed forward. "We control Josian, and in turn we can make him do anything we want."

The words fell from her lips and shattered across me in jagged spikes. My instincts had been correct. My brain had been slowly lining all the dominos up and now they were falling around me in a splash of pain and light. I really hadn't been prepared for her to confirm my suspicions.

The world continued flashing at me. Bright, loud, quiet, dark. I'd stumbled a little. Brace must have reached out to help me. It took me a few moments to notice his warm hands cupping my elbows.

"I don't understand," I whispered. But I did understand. I couldn't lie to myself any longer about what the truth was here.

Brace pulled me closer. "Tenni is behind the Seventine." He was quick to put the clues together. "I would say they've been aided by Josian and Que. They needed puppets. Original powers can't directly influence the end of the worlds."

Tenni was listening closely. "We've never hidden our intentions from those that we required to know; the worlds are corrupted, evil, greedy, and warring. A cleanse

Dronish

is needed, a renewal. The Seventine were simply the easiest tool for us to utilize."

"Aren't the Seventine original powers?" I asked in breathless tones. Not to mention so were the half-Walkers.

Tenni nodded. "Yes, but the Seventine are simply doing what they were created for. Severing tethers, dispersing energy. This shouldn't directly end the worlds, but the timing of the convergence was our perfect opportunity."

So as long as we were doing what was natural, it was okay to save or destroy the worlds. Even with original powers. Sounded like a gray area to me.

I touched my father's arm. He didn't move or acknowledge me, but I sensed the swirls of energy inside him.

"Everyone answers to someone more powerful," Tenni said simply, her crazy logic rearing its head. "Josian has no choice."

"And we all know that you answer to someone powerful also," Brace all but snarled. "You won't get away with this."

Tenni's small glittering eyes looked from one of us to the other. "We already have. All the pieces are in place and the countdown is on. You have no hope to stop this. The Seventine are powerful, a well-oiled machine. They will never rest until their task is complete. In the end, we will remake the worlds, which was always the lalunas' role."

In that moment I gathered together the fragments of myself. Put on my big-girl panties and accepted the truth about what had happened.

Josian was our betrayer.

But it was not as simple as that. He had not known of his actions; it was no different to someone being drugged and raped. They had no control over the actions of others, and neither had Josian. Right then I forgave my father for anything he'd been involved in. I didn't even need to know all the details. In reality, I didn't *want* to know them.

The blue bracelet on my wrist started to heat and suddenly, for the first time, I wanted to be away from my stone. I clenched my fist around the cuff. Damn the lalunas. They'd rolled Josian, controlled him because he was bonded to them. I did not want the same fate from my own stone. Although, as an original power ... would I have a chance to fight them?

The crazy faerie stepped closer. "You can leave now. We are done with this."

Keeping the hand with my laluna hidden behind me, I dropped down to reach the same level as Tenni. "Just so I understand your barely veiled threat, if Brace and I reform our melding bond, then you'll do what to Josian? Kill him?"

She sucked in sharply, her flowing gown shifting as she swayed. "We love Josian. We would never hurt him."

Hell to the no. As if they knew what love was.

"But, we can make life very difficult for him, trap him here with us for all of eternity and bar this world to any. Removing him from your life, his mate's life, and the Walker clan that he governs."

Which was pretty much the same as killing him. If we could never see him again, then he was still gone.

"And if we don't reform the bond?"

Tenni pursed her lips. I could see the mind calculating behind her tiny face. "Then we will do nothing, and as an added incentive we'll free Josian from all obligations in this war now, allow him to regain full control of his mind and powers. We will step back from our battle and allow it to play out as it would in the natural order."

"You have no choice but to do that," Brace said. He was standing right above me now, and I could tell he wanted to yank me back from the crazy faeries. "My guess is that you're treading awfully close to too much involvement, and you're about to get your ass stomped by the mother of all."

Tenni didn't say anything, although I could sense a tension that filtered through the laluna.

"We will give you a moment to make your decision." She dismissed Brace's words by turning her back on us.

Brace hauled me up and dragged me away. Josian still didn't move. They weren't letting him leave until we agreed.

The moment we were out of the garden, words burst from me. "What do we do?" I was shaking as adrenalin and fear warred inside me. "We can't fight lalunas as well. Josian always said they were so strong, they have the power of creation."

In that instant Brace's arms were around me. As he held me close I used his calm and even heartbeat to ground myself and slow my own racing pulse. He didn't pull back until I was composed, moving just far enough away to see my face.

"They're powerful, but they also have rules and order to follow like the rest of us." His hands were gently running over my back, offering comfort. "I won't lie to you, Red, it's not an ideal situation, but at least now we know who's been controlling these events. We can adjust our plan."

My face flicked back to my motionless father and tears filled my eyes. "What do we do about Josian?" He was so strong and to see him reduced to nothing but a puppet. I was devastated, and resisting the urge to sob my heart out. "We have to help him."

"You know that Josian is probably the one who has facilitated much of the lalunas' plans. Que was a pawn, but Josian is bonded to them. He would have been there since day one." Brace's quiet words cut through my heart.

"I don't care," I said strongly. "This is not his fault, and I refuse to place one ounce of blame on him."

My father was my rock, my pillar of strength, and knowing the cause of his strange behavior, well, I was almost relieved. Plus I was steadfast in my belief that none of this was his doing. The blame lay squarely with the laluna. It was kind of nice to have a place to lay blame now, even if it freaked me out that it was something so powerful.

Brace kissed my cheek. "That's my girl. I was just checking on your true feelings."

I blinked up a few times, my eyes caressing his masculine features. The urge to throw myself at him was as strong as ever. Our bond, as always, was pushing us to be together. The next words were painful as they ripped from my throat.

"We can't reform our melding, not right now. We have to figure out how to save Josian first."

Brace nodded; in his thinned lips and crinkled brow I saw the lines of his pain. "I understand, and while I want to protest, I won't do that to Josian. But ..." He sighed. "Maybe for the next little bit we'll have to spend some time apart. Otherwise, the bond will be forced on us."

My heart tightened, that heart-attack-stabbed-in-the-chest thing happening again.

"We need your answer." Tenni's high voice cut across the space to us.

I clenched my fists until my nails cut into my skin, but when I turned to face her I knew my expression was calm. Without pausing I strode back into the garden, Brace right behind me.

My eyes were cold when I rested them on her. "These are my terms: we will not reform the melding, and you will free Josian of all obligations in this battle ... and you will return all the memories you stole when the melding was broken." I narrowed my eyebrows. "Every single memory to every single person who lost them."

"Agreed." Tenni didn't even hesitate. Which told me how concerned she was about our bond. "But if you meld, either by accident or choice, you will lose Josian forever."

I wanted to scream. Like at the top of my lungs, until all breath fled my body and I collapsed from exhaustion. This was so unfair. I needed Brace, I couldn't handle the pain any longer. But I also needed my dad.

"You're strong, Red, you can do this." Brace's whispered words brought me back from whatever dark place I'd gone to.

Tenni raised her hands and the same bursts of light which had stolen our bond and memories blasted out into the atmosphere, spreading to return a fraction of what was lost. Brace didn't fall, but he stumbled as he was hit, his hands rising to clutch at his head. It was over in seconds, and I froze waiting for the reaction. How would Brace feel now that all of our memories together had been returned?

Arms encased me and lips crashed into my own. I groaned as his taste flooded me and the passion washed over us. I opened my mouth, inviting him in, and his tongue boldly stroked my own. And then it was over, as fast as it had begun. My head swum as I stumbled against him.

"I've missed you, Red," he said.

My heart buckled as I stared into his eyes. It was all there again. Our love, our history, all of it. The new and the old feelings combined. In some ways I was the luckiest person in the world. I had a man who had fallen in love with me twice now, seen all my flaws and mistakes, and still wasn't walking away. On the other hand I couldn't bond with him, my father was a puppet, and the fate of the worlds rested heavily on my shoulders.

I burst into full-on ugly sob-my-heart-out tears. I must have cried for a long time because when I finally pulled myself together, Brace's shirt was wet and we were out of the garden and in the living room area of Josian's cave. I hadn't even felt him carry me. He was simply holding me, his large body cradled protectively around me as I shook and cried.

"I'm sorry," I stuttered out. "The more I try to do the right thing, the worse everything seems to go."

"I disagree." Brace's voice was smooth, but I could hear the huskiness beneath. "So far I think you've done the very best you could and far better than most. You've found four of the six girls, prevented the Seventine from destroying Nephilius. Freed many First Worlders who were marked for death." He gently captured my chin, before laying the lightest of kisses on my lips. "My calculations have your good deeds far outweighing the few ... rash choices you've made. And, Abigail, you're eighteen years old. The fact that you've managed to achieve anything speaks of your old soul and strength of character."

My eyes were locked on his face.

"We'll beat them, baby; we'll save Josian and the worlds. I refuse to consider any other option, because I want a life with you bad enough that ... well, there's no other way."

Hot damn. I'd be proposing marriage right then if I didn't already have him locked up for eternity.

"Baby girl?"

I lifted my head and looked back over my shoulder. Josian stood there, strong, tall and glowing softly as he always had. I had been a little worried how I might feel the first time he was back with us. But I knew immediately: I still trusted and loved him. The same emotions he'd invoked in me from the first moment he'd burst into my life. I accepted that he had made a colossal eff-up in trusting his laluna, but it was time to rebuild and move on from this.

I untangled myself from Brace, stumbling forward until I was before my father. "I think you have some explaining to do, Dad."

He blinked a few times, before running his right hand through his hair and leaving the smooth red waves in disarray.

"You must hate me."

His first words were rushed, and I could see the anguish in his shiny bronze eyes.

I let the slightest smile cross my lips and took another step toward him. "No, had you betrayed us willingly, then I would hate you. But as far as I'm concerned, this is the same as Samuel: you were used by something much more powerful, and I'm sure ..." I hesitated here just briefly, "that feels a lot like torture or rape; when you have no control over your mind and actions. Forced to do something that you hate."

A single tear fled the corner of his left eye. I followed its slow trail as it drifted down the sculptured lines of his face.

"I think maybe you should tell us everything though, Josian." Brace's voice was a little harder than mine, but still sympathetic. "Your laluna wasn't that forthcoming with information, but they seemed to think they'd stacked events in the right direction, the damage had been done. They weren't that concerned about concealing their involvement any longer."

Josian laughed a few times. It was harsh and in no way did he sound amused. "No, trust me they didn't want to tell you. They just believe it's of utmost importance to keep you and Aribella unmelded." He turned to me. "And I'm here right now asking you to meld with Brace. Don't worry about me. I might be stuck in these caves for an eternity, but you need to beat the Seventine."

I sucked in a loud, ragged breath. "I would accept their offer, Dad, except I know that they have another plan, and another. In the end, I won't forsake you, only to lose to the Seventine anyway. Not to mention we're going to need your help to eliminate the lalunas."

"Don't say anything more, Red," Brace bit out. "Can they hear your thoughts?" he asked Josian.

My father shook his head. "No, they've never been able to do that. They contact me, and can force themselves into my head to control me. But I know when they're there; their presence isn't hidden. They don't hear thoughts the way a mate would."

That was a relief.

OVER THE NEXT hour Josian told us everything that he could remember about his laluna. Even though I hadn't wanted to know the details, it was actually good to feel there were no more secrets.

I was thankful to know that he hadn't been aware of his actions for a lot of the nasty shit. Every one of his reactions when he first met me had been genuine, and that was important to me. His love and unwavering support was a precious memory I held on to.

I had to bite my lip when he spoke of kidnapping Lucy, which had allowed her to be goddamned tortured on Earth by Olden. I might have had a few nasty thoughts about Josian then. But in the end I accepted what he said. It could have been any of us; it could have been me. Brace had it right: the laluna needed a puppet. My poor father was just the easiest one to manipulate. Samuel and Lucy's dreams of the strings on Josian's arms and legs made perfect sense now.

Brace had tightened his grip on me a few times during the story. But he refrained from expressing too many thoughts. Right until the end when he chimed in.

"You need to tell everyone of this, Josian. All of the

princeps and the Walker clans. I'm guessing they'll ask you to abdicate as princeps."

Josian nodded. "I've tried many times to reveal this information, basically from the moment I started to be aware of my actions. Tenni wouldn't let me. They tied up pretty much any avenue I had to confess."

"No!" I said, Brace's words running through my head. I didn't want another princeps for Doreen; Josian was the best. "I don't want Dad to lose everything because of this. We have to fix it."

Josian reached out and captured my hand in his huge one. "Thank you, baby girl, but as long as I have you and your mother, I've lost nothing. Besides, no one is going to trust me anymore. You can't hold the mantle of leader without trust. It's fundamentally important."

Brace's gaze softened as he met my angry stare. "Josian speaks the truth. I'll throw my support a hundred percent behind him, but he'll have a battle to regain trust."

"I'm ready now." My father stepped a few feet back and in the same instant opened a doorway. "Let's go to the war council. The princeps should all be there. It's time to figure out how to break these lalunas down."

As he spoke the cuff on my wrist started to heat.

"Is my laluna going to do the same thing to me?" I spilled my current worry. "Why has it attached itself to my wrist?

Josian's eye flicked down to my arm. He stared at it for a few tense heartbeats before exhaling loudly. "Lalunas aren't bad. In fact, they don't even understand the concept of good or bad, right or wrong. They're original powers and have one real job to do: keep the balance in the universe. But something happened to Tenni. Once they burst from their stone, they started to develop a consciousness. Feelings. Emotions. And with this allowed the seeds of crazy to bleed in."

He looked from Brace to me. "They're certain that they're doing this for the greater good, that the worlds are corruptible and need cleansing. There's no malice or greed in their actions. They still don't have the capacity for that."

That was the scariest part. Those who believe very strongly in their cause will do anything to make sure it comes to fruition.

"So you're saying that Tenni is a once-off and there's very little chance that my laluna will be going bonkers anytime soon?" I double-checked.

Josian gave me a real smile then, the first I'd seen from him in a while. "Yes, baby girl." His strong arms wrapped around me and I didn't tense; I truly was not mad at him. "I don't deserve you."

I patted his arm. "If it hadn't been you they used as a pawn it would have been someone else." I knew that. Powerful beings don't stop in achieving their end game. "And now they can no longer use you. I promise that we'll do everything to make sure you remain free."

He was more serious as he pulled away. "You and Brace have to be careful. A bond as strong as yours ... it's going to try and force you to meld. If you're serious about remaining unmelded for the period of time it will take us to dig through a million years of ancient scrolls to find if there's any way to contain a laluna, I think you two will have to stay apart."

Brace growled low then, shaking his broad chest. "I

can't let Abby go off to planets by herself. It's too dangerous."

Josian sucked in deeply. "I understand. Maybe you two will be strong enough, but try not to be alone too much. Take others as a buffer between you, and try not to touch too often. Touch increases the need."

Not touch. Holy shit. I'd have better luck not breathing. I tried to slow the rapid exhalations I was emitting from my mouth.

Brace was sort of resembling the stone walls behind us, his features rigid. "Maybe Josian is right," he finally said. He spoke slowly, as if it were hard work getting these words out. "I can just stay in mental connection with you and see you on occasion so I don't completely lose my shit by being permanently away from you. But you're still not going to Dronish alone."

That plan was so not cool with me, but we had no other choice.

I sighed. It had been a long day, and for the fiftieth time I wanted to scream and stamp my feet. But again it was time for Abigail to put on her grown-up hat and acknowledge that I was going to be suffering a little longer.

"Alright, let's head to the war council. It's time for me to face the music," Josian said. His expression was grim, and something told me it wasn't about to get happy any time soon.

4

We'd spent so long on the cave world that it was early morning when we returned to First World.

It took a long time to deal with the fallout of Josian spilling his massive secret to not only the Walker community but also to the faeries, pixies, sprites and random other feys who had joined our movement.

Let's just say there was quite a lot of screaming, power balls and tears. The Doreen contingent were particularly devastated. They loved Josian and his actions cut them deep.

Eventually Brace blasted out a few shock waves, which worked to startle the masses out of their hysteria. He told them to pull their heads in and act like the incredibly complex and ancient beings they were. This was not a black or white situation; it was solidly gray. When you lived hundreds to millions of years, there was no way to have perfectly clean hands. All of them should be able to understand what Josian had been through. I was happy that a sense of calm descended after a few of these home truths were voiced.

I knew eventually everyone would come to terms with what had happened with the lalunas and, to be fair, most seemed to have accepted Josian's role and forgiven him. The real emotion behind their initial anger had been fear. They feared the power of a corrupted laluna, something which had never happened in billions of years.

In the end it was a mixed vote from the princeps about whether Josian should abdicate. My father had been the one to decide to step aside. His second, a red by the name of Gerry, had been elected as the interim leader. There wouldn't be time for anything official until after the final battle.

The one who took all these revelations the hardest was Lallielle. She had been shocked – to put it mildly.

"I knew something was off with him, but I never guessed in a million years that the lalunas were controlling him, that he was the facilitator for so many of the woes in our lives."

My mother and I were in the Doreen area. I'd pulled her aside after the vote to see how she was taking the news.

"I'm not sure what to think about this, Aribella ..." A few sobs escaped her. "I can't believe it."

Josian was on the other side of the territory, stuck in endless debates and discussions about the lalunas with the seven princeps. They were grilling him for any tiny snippet of information. There was no Walker with as much laluna knowledge as Josian.

"It wasn't his fault, Mom." I softened my voice. My hand reached out to stroke Cerberus. Since I'd returned, my faithful hound had barely left my side. "He was mind-controlled, and for most of those events wasn't even aware of his actions."

"Logically I understand that, but emotionally I still feel betrayed." She clasped my biceps in her hands. "Why aren't you taking this harder? Have you fully considered everything his actions have caused?" Her voice rose.

Uh-oh, Lallielle was pissed. And I could understand that. She'd lost both her children for many years, and the thought that Josian had anything to do with that, even second-hand, was riling her momma bear.

I started to speak, my words slow. "I'm not happy about it, that's for sure. But in my mind it wasn't Josian; it was just a shell used for the lalunas' bidding. If it hadn't been Dad's shell, it would have been someone else's. Josian's innocent, and he's beating himself up worse than I ever could."

She huffed a few times, before crossing her arms. "I think I need a few minutes," she muttered, before walking off.

I watched her as she strode away, head held high, tension riding her entire frame. I was thinking the next part of the journey was going to be a bumpy road for Lallielle and Josian. But I had every faith that they would make it. I knew from my melding that mate-bonds were hard to break; the connection was soul deep. Cerberus nudged me gently and I started scratching his ears again.

"Hey, Supes."

I smiled as Fury and Delane wandered across to me. Lina was close behind her Angelica. The massive unicorn cut a path through the milling Walkers with ease. In a way it was lucky that the sacred animals had started reappearing. It had helped ease some of the fear caused by Josian's revelations. A positive light in the very dark days we were living.

"Where's Dune?" I asked Fury.

Her face got all dreamy. "He's on Crais, looking into the energy thing." She recovered quickly, her gray eyes pinning me to the spot. "We hadn't discovered anything yet, since you called me back like eight seconds after I left."

It had been more like five hours, but I understood her point. I'd had no choice. We needed to regroup and the half-Walkers needed to know about these new developments. Delane was silent as she reached out and rubbed Lina's smooth, shiny black forehead.

I picked at an edge of my nail. "I know my timing sucks, but I said no more secrets, and I knew you'd all want to know who the big, bad Seventine-releasing asshats were."

Fury shook back her mane of white hair. "Honestly, I'm a little shocked. Firstly, poor Josian. I know everyone's jumping all over him right now, but I'm kind of feeling sorry for him."

I'd found it unexpected and slightly amusing the way Fury's big heart took over, forcing her to do things that were out of character. Most would think she'd have been the first to judge and berate Josian, but instead she'd been one of his biggest defenders.

"And secondly," she continued. "I did *not* suspect the lalunas, those evil little suckers."

My bracelet warmed as she spoke. It had been doing that a lot. Especially during the explanation to the clans about Tenni and how the laluna was the superpower behind the whole release-the-Seventine-in-time-for-convergence plan. It almost felt like it was apologizing for its brethren's involvement in the entire thing.

"Where's Brace?" Fury asked.

Everyone had their memories back now and seemed constantly surprised that we weren't attached at the hip.

"In some sort of serious Princeps' meeting." I sighed. "Josian is still getting the third degree and they're trying to formulate a plan for the lalunas."

"Shouldn't we be in that meeting?" Delane said, just as Talina and Ria joined our group.

"They offered, but I declined," I said.

Delane opened her mouth. I cut her off before she could start arguing.

"There's no point. They don't have any new information at the moment. We need to wait for Jedi to finish his research, especially now he knows about the lalunas." I looked at the four girls and realized how much I missed Lucy. It wasn't the same without her. "I think we should spend this time right now connecting our powers? I can't leave for Dronish yet."

I didn't have enough information about this world. I needed to talk with Brace and Josian before I left. I had never gone to a planet on my own, and I doubted I was about to start then. They'd have some type of plan, and at least I could trust everything about Josian now. The lalunas had to keep their word. They could do nothing unless I reformed the melding bond.

So right now I didn't want to waste this time waiting for the meeting to be over. We needed to be building power.

Ria tucked her chestnut hair behind one ear. "Yes, I

think that's a great idea." With the same hand she reached out and squeezed my fingertips. "I'm so proud of you, Abby. I see your strength increase every day ... and I mean more than physically, or even power. Your mental strength and character are to be commended."

I stilled, her words hitting me right in the heart. "Thank you." My voice was just above a whisper. "I feel as if I'm barely hanging on. We scrape ourselves over one hurdle, only to find ten more have risen."

"Yep, and these ones have poisonous spikes on the top," Talina said.

"Word," I said. I was reminded of Lucy again. She'd better be okay. "Come on, let's go somewhere with more space."

As the five of us started to move out of Doreen I decided not to waste another moment. I threw out my tethers and connected us together. With a whooshing flood I could now feel them, their energy, distinct powers, not to mention multiple voices in my head.

I spoke first. *We need to learn how to be in each other's heads and still focus on our surroundings. And something has been bothering me about how one-sided the control is like this. I'm not sure I'm supposed to have so much of the control. We need to figure out how to spread the power.*

It was getting easier to mental-talk and also focus on the outside world, dodging around the multitude of different species milling around the center field.

Delane spoke next. *So Jedi said that each of us will hold one of the elements of the ancients, right? Who has what power?*

I answered her. *Walkers' powers in general are built on seven elements. Fire ...*"

Which is me, Fury piped up.

Yes, fire is Fury, I said. *Water is Talina. Earth is Ria.*

I was interrupted by the Regali half. *I'd think I was more nature. Are you sure?*

I nodded, which was stupid. No one could see me. *Yes, earth and nature are the same. One can't exist without the other. You seem to have power over the living earth components, in comparison to Grantham, who controls the inanimate earth components, such as rock and stone.*

We were all quiet for a minute, absorbing this information, then I continued. *Delane, you're ... wind, I'm guessing.* I'd never seen her powers directly. Just, from the fights on Nephilius, she'd often seemed to use the winds to push away her opponents. But I could be wrong.

I wasn't.

Yes, I can control the elements of the air. I can take away breath or force so much oxygen in that you black out. I can use the minute particles of air to see things no one else would, and they whisper information to me. I can spy. I can send out gusts and buffets to stop any in their tracks. I'm wind.

As always, the warrior-Walker was all facts and succinct information.

Wicked, Fury said. *I love my fire, but sometimes I wish I could have all these powers.*

I laughed. *I guess that's what my role is. As the conduit, I bring all the other elements together and form one big superpower.*

We were drawing a few stares as we sauntered casually through the crowds. Half-Walkers were still mythical creatures to most Walkers and we weren't often in a large, visible group like this. Not to mention when we were connected there were glowing tethers flowing around us.

I'd seen it through Brace's eyes before, and we looked scary and powerful. Not to mention we had a unicorn and hellhound following us around.

So we still need shadow and spirit? Talina asked as we came to a halt in the center.

We'd discussed all the elements in the early days, so she knew the seven.

Yes.

Connected as we were, I could feel the muted powers of the two unknown half-Walkers. Their tethers were there, but sort of invisible, not tangible.

Delane had told me that she'd never felt any connection with me until I'd arrived on Nephilius. With that in mind, I was hoping once I made it to Dronish I could throw out my tether and pinpoint the half-Walker female that way. The closer I was to the half-Walkers the stronger the connections were.

We now stood in the middle of a large space, our two sacred animals waiting patiently off to the side. The five of us were silent. There was no movement of our energy, powers were muted and we were simply connected to each other on a mental level.

I was comforted to have Cerberus and Lina close by. Not only were they beautiful, powerful and loyal, they were also very useful for crowd control.

From the corner of my eye I could see a Doreen Walker striding right near my back, and suddenly there was a massive two-headed hellhound standing between him and me, growling and showing his lethal fangs. I refrained from laughing as the male literally cried and ran away.

Go, Cerberus.

Dronish

Call your power, I said, focusing back on the girls.

One by one, I felt the surge of energy. Talina, who could literally pull water from the very air, was surrounded by her turret of liquid. It didn't happen much now, but her clear lens flicked down to cover her eyes. It was little things like this that reminded me how diverse our group was. We were all half-Walker, but for some the other half was quite alien.

Next was Fury. She was encased in blue flames.

Ria had vines, grass and flowers bursting up from the ground and lovingly embracing her.

And lastly was Delane; a whirly bird started to form beneath her feet, and the short strands of her very black hair began to fly around her as she was surrounded by an air whirl, but she somehow remained safe in the center.

In fact, none of us seemed to be harmed by the powers of the others when we were connected.

What happens now? Delane asked. *Because I'm struggling to do anything else with my power.*

I was trying my best not to pull all that delicious energy into myself. My greedy little well inside loved itself some half-Walker power.

Generally Abby controls us when we're like this, Fury said. *She can move the energy around, allowing it to go where needed.*

To demonstrate, I sucked energy from Fury, Ria and Talina, and sent it into Delane. All of a sudden we had a massive hundred-foot-high twister on our hands. Walkers, pixies, faeries and sprites flew through the air around us.

Whoops; I quickly dialed it back. The five of us worked together, each lending control so we could safely set all our victims back on the ground. I was surprised and impressed by the finesse we demonstrated; it was a group effort, all the girls helping to anchor me. We got more than a few glares as those near us scurried away. Surprisingly enough, our sacred animals had not been affected. They were unmoving at our side.

Okay, so our power seems to have increased just a little. Ria grinned, showing all of her perfect white teeth. *I'm liking this.*

I could feel the surge of emotions in Delane. Connected like this, it was hard to keep them private, but I also knew she was struggling after so many years of subjugation and training to individualize herself.

We're a weapon. She finally voiced her emotion. *Unbelievable. And you say we'll only become more powerful with each half-Walker we add?*

Yes, I said. *The strength seems to increase ten-fold with each female. I just hope we can control this in the end, because although the power is ours, it's damn strong and, as we've seen with Josian, even the strongest of us can be dominated by those more powerful.*

Josian had been a sobering but important lesson for us to learn.

WE SPENT the next few hours testing ourselves and our elemental powers. We learned that if we focused together, the girls could help me control the energy, including directing and targeting it. In fact, I relied on them quite a lot, because no one knew the inner facets of their individual powers better than they did.

Despite the very real possibility of being blown into

the air by a whirlwind, we had drawn quite the crowd around us by the time we were finished. Brace was standing to the side. I'd known he was there the moment he strode up. We were attuned to each other, our bodies craving the togetherness. I'd had to stop myself from breaking our power chain so I could run to him.

The golden bond that lived inside me, the one which I used for tethering, was also the force trying to push me into melding again. I wasn't sure how much longer we could be around each other before it was taken from our control. I was afraid that Josian was right, we'd have to stay separated for a while. This very thought made me want to take the masses of power I was wielding and blow shit up. Like maybe a laluna.

Talina distracted me. *The more we're joined together and use our power like this,* she said, *the stronger my energy feels. I can't even believe how afraid I used to be of my abilities. I did my best to keep them locked down, and then they'd overwhelm me and take control. Now it feels as if there's a bond; we exist together, not in battle.*

It was a long speech from the normally quiet Spurn half, and it was clear that she was excited and happy. Which was nice. After losing Raror, I'd worried that she was broken, that her gentle soul was damaged beyond repair. I think it was Ladre's love and acceptance, plus the bond with us half-Walkers, which had given her a reason to live.

I was afraid of my abilities too, Fury confessed, with what sounded like a little reluctance. She didn't like others to know of her weaknesses. *Afraid I'd hurt someone because I couldn't control them.*

Ria spoke formally. *It sounds like we've all gone through*

something like this. But I'm forever grateful for my abilities now. My energy and the meditation of the packs are allowing us to slow the death of Artwon. Of course, we still have to return the sacred tree or the jungle will eventually fall, but we're giving it time that we wouldn't have had.

I'd been meaning to ask Ria how Artwon was managing after the Seventine destroyed the most important tether in their jungle: the sacred tree which had housed their gods.

Have you heard from your mother or any of the nature spirits? I asked her. *Since the loss of the sacred tree.*

No. She sounded sad. *I can feel that they're there, but there's no way now to communicate between the mortal realm and theirs.*

Effing Seventine, I growled. *Those effers are getting on my last nerve.*

There were a few chuckles as I started cursing my head off.

You sound like Lucy now, Fury snorted. *And I'd never thought I'd say this, but I miss her annoying pixie butt.*

I was missing her so much and she'd only been gone for like half a day. I wondered who the seven witnesses to their mating would be. Apparently they were called by the great mother and Walkers had no idea who it would be until they arrived.

The entire time we'd been chatting, we were still exercising our abilities. We started with one girl and one element at a time. We'd run through the range of abilities and together we'd form the power into weapons. Our control was still not the best. Sometimes we missed our target completely; other times the energy fizzled out before it could become anything dangerous. But sometimes, when the stars aligned and we all worked together, we created something so crazy powerful that it was a little scary.

A perfect example occurred in the five minutes before the end of our training. We were just about to pull apart, when Fury and Delane got into an argument. I won't go into details, but suffice to say the Crais half did not like to take orders from the Nephilius half, despite the fact that Delane was full to the brim of useful little battle tactics. Fury fired up, and we all knew what happened when she did that. She sent her blue flames into massive spiraling turrets into the sky. The only problem was, she was still connected to the rest of us and suddenly every single half-Walker's power was shooting up into the air around us.

Water, fire, wind, and earth.

For the first time the elements were not individual. The powers started to swirl around each other in a massive storm above our heads. I parted my lips to let out an extra exhalation of breath. As the conduit I could feel that the five of us were connecting further than we ever had before, the elements blending into each other, fire merging into the air, which swirled to the water and earth.

In the last minute, just before the storm grew large enough to descend and surround us, I pulled the energy into myself and severed the connections. I wasn't sure, but it felt like we were about to lose control of what we had formed. It was going to take off from us and gods only knew what damage it might have wrought.

"Why did you cut that off, Abigail?" Fury got right

into my face, hands on her hips. "We were just starting to create something powerful enough to be useful."

I stared at her for a few moments. My eyebrows rose of their own accord as I fought against my instincts to smack some sense into her.

My tone was short when I finally answered her. I seemed to be lacking in patience without my melding bond. "You're always so caught up in the power. The fire drives you, Fury, which is the main reason you didn't even notice that that was too much energy for us to control. We were going to lose it, and then what would have happened?" I waved my hands to indicate the masses surrounding us. "People would have died."

She slammed her mouth shut then, and the dark gray of her eyes glistened as she breathed deeply. I could see her trying to gain control of herself, of the fire that rode her emotions.

She threw her hands into the air. "Shit. Sorry. I know better than to let the energy control me." She lowered her eyes and shook her head a few times.

I reached out and gripped her forearm, my hand gentle. "That's why my conduit abilities are important. You all control elemental powers. They're strong and link to your base instincts. I'm here to make sure we keep control of such immense energy. That we're responsible with what we wield."

Fury surprised me by reaching forward and yanking me into a strong hug. "I never say things like this, but I need you to know, I'm so happy to have met you and all the other girls." She pulled back and looked at everyone. "I ... care about you all." Her hesitation spoke volumes. She'd wanted to use another word there.

"I love you all too!" Talina was always the sweetest, and most loving.

And then suddenly it was group-hug time.

Delane seemed a little uncomfortable with the affection, but I could see the softening of her eyes. She'd only been with us a short time, but the bond between us was strong, unbreakable. We half-Walkers were formed of past lives and old power.

"I've never had many friends, besides Klea," Ria said. "But you're all my best friends, and even though the Seventine are trying to destroy everything, I'm so glad we found each other."

It was such a perfect friend moment, where you're surrounded by so much love and strength that you kind of feel you might burst from it. If only Lucy were here.

"Please don't tell me you biatches are having a bonding moment without me?" We all spun around to find a fluttering pixie-doll about ten feet from us. "Cause I'm totally owed some love now."

Lucy held her arms open and we ended up in a huge girl pile. I had arms and knees digging into me, but I didn't care. By this time, we'd lost most of our curious onlookers. They wanted to see power, not girls crying, hugging and bonding with each other.

Colton and Brace both braved our pile, their long arms reaching in to fish us out. The wolf-Walker hauled his mate free. She was the smallest by a fair amount and had been on the bottom of the pile. I felt muscled bands surround me, and before I could blink again I was in Brace's arms. He set me on my feet. We were trying to keep our distance from each other, but he hadn't been able to stop himself from 'saving me'. Protective as always.

Lucy and Colton drifted to our side. "So I'm guessing your mating was accepted?" I asked the happy, glowing, way-too-beautiful-for-their-own-good couple.

"Yes!" Lucy exclaimed. "It was incredible, floating in space, no gravity, and then all of this stuff happened at once." Her blue-and-gold eyes softened as they rested on my face and then looked from Brace to me. "You'll see for yourself soon enough."

I closed my eyes briefly, her words reminding me that she didn't know about Josian and everything to do with his laluna.

"Actually –" I started to say, but she interrupted me.

"I already know about Jos. We ran into Grantham over the other side of the field." She waved a hand dismissively. "That's not what I'm talking about. I see that you and Brace will bond soon."

"You don't seem worried or surprised about Dad and the lalunas." I furrowed my brow.

"Josian is a good man, and he'll become a great man now," she said cryptically. "The secrets were holding him back; now he can be free."

Fury snorted as she crossed her arms tightly over her body. "I might have missed some aspects of Lucy, but her weird 'I'm a pretend soothsayer' babble was not one of them."

"Hey, fiery Fury," Lucy said, smiling or kind of baring her teeth, "I have a surprise for you."

Fury stilled, her animated face shutting down as she regarded Lucy. "Why do I have a feeling you're about to drop a bombshell on me?"

Lucy shifted her head to the right, her chin lifting as she searched for something. I followed her line of sight and was surprised to notice a man standing across the field. Walker, most definitely.

His energy felt a little like Fury's, which meant he was from Grantham's clan, Relli. The man started to move in long strides, eating up the distance toward us. As he closed in I registered the broad planes of his features. They were harsh, weather-beaten.

Which was very strange on a Walker.

He looked like a man who had seen too much and had been systematically washed over like the side of a rock face. No longer smooth, his experiences had shaped an entirely new face. When he drew closer, my lips parted as recognition shocked me.

Without any doubt in all the worlds, he had Fury's very expressive gray eyes. Same shape. Same sardonic slant to the eyebrows.

Lucy's voice was low. "He was one of the seven witnesses called for my bonding." The Walker was almost upon us. "I knew as soon as I saw him. I had Colt mentally contact him and explain about Fury. Your father decided to come and find you." She directed the last part to the stunned-looking Crais half.

Fury lifted a hand to cover her mouth, before taking a staggering step toward him. She seemed to halt herself, shaking her head a few times when she realized what she'd been doing.

"I've waited a long time to meet my father," she whispered, "and now I feel that this is a big mistake."

She turned to run, but at the last moment Lucy stepped in front of her. "Put your big-girl pants on,

Fury. You're tough; you can manage five minutes of small-talk to see if there's anything there for you to build upon. All of us have had to come to terms with our messed up families. Now it's your turn to suck it up."

Lucy could be beyond blunt; right then, though, Fury kind of needed it. She'd wanted to meet her father since we first found her on Crais, and the big moment was here now. She would regret running from him.

I heard Fury's breathing increase. She sounded awfully close to hyperventilating. The weathered Relli was now five feet from our group. He had stopped and seemed to be patiently waiting. Fury spent the next few moments examining his features. She must have found something there. She walked straight up to him, halting mere inches from the man who had gotten her mother pregnant and then abandoned her all in the name of protecting Fury.

"What's your name?"

They both asked the question at the same time, and straight away it was clear that Fury had inherited more than his eyes. The blunt, borderline arrogant tone of speaking that she had down pat. Well, this Walker mirrored that.

"I am Lukalien." He spoke slowly, as if he were unaccustomed to using English. "Your mother was the only being who called me Luke, and you can also use this name."

The look on Fury's face was comical. "I'm Fury," she finally spluttered out.

The Crais half looked so astonished that I couldn't help the burst of laughter that escaped me. And that was all it took to set everyone off. Lucy howled louder than anyone. Even Delane cracked a smile.

Lukalien blinked rapidly as he glanced from one to the other. I could see he had no idea what was so funny.

Lucy was speaking in between gasps of laughter. "Damn ... no DNA test required there. He's the man version of Fury. Now I know where she gets all her mean snarkiness."

"Ignore them." Fury waved her hands. "Where have you been? Why are you here now?"

And the unasked question. Why did you leave my pregnant mother to die alone on Crais?

I'd been there when Dune had told Fury that Gena, her mother, had died of a broken heart. And having lost Brace on more than one occasion, I could completely sympathize with the agony her mother must have felt.

Lukalien's voice was rusty. "I have been mourning for many years. I knew when my mate perished, and I returned to Crais to check on you, but could not find any trace of our young. I thought you had died too." The rustiness cracked then. He sounded defeated. "I still can't sense your energy?" It was a question-statement.

Brace moved closer to the group. "Half-Walkers have an inbuilt protection. They can't be traced or sensed in the normal Walker manner." I could feel him at my back, his heat reaching out and tempting me.

Lukalien lifted his eyes slightly, just barely acknowledging the rest of us. Damn, there was no doubt. This was what a broken man looked like, even worse than Samuel.

Fury stepped closer to him. "We have a lot to talk about. Let's go for a walk." Her big heart was getting the better of her again. She'd be mothering this poor man within minutes. "I need to get back to my mate soon. How long do we have?" She started ushering him toward the Relli area.

"I'll stay as long as you need. But I don't like people ..." His voice trailed off as they moved away.

My mouth was for sure hanging open. "Did that just happen?"

Lucy cracked up again. "I was thinking the same thing the entire time he was witnessing our ceremony. That Walker has zero people skills. He makes Fury look darn-right hospitable."

"I wish Dune were here," I mused.

"Why?" Delane asked.

I stared into her obsidian eyes. "Just to confirm he's who he says he is. We can't be too safe, and I don't want Fury hurt."

I knew how much she'd wanted to meet her father – even if it was just to yell at him – I didn't want her hopes dashed.

The Angelica stared at me for a few moments, before giving me a succinct nod. "You are worthy."

I felt strangely honored. I knew her well enough now to know she was tough to please. The approval in her tone and gaze touched me.

I was distracted from these thoughts as Brace stepped in and swept me off my feet. The movement was unexpected and my heart rate sped up. Even more than it usually pitter-pattered around my mate.

"You and I need a moment." He was all growly.

That voice should most definitely be outlawed in public. It was as sexy as hell.

"Be right back," I said to the girls, without even

turning my face away from my gorgeous mate.

"Heard that before," Lucy muttered. "The next thing I knew there were huge dangly bits and bare asses parading down the hall."

I stifled my laughter as Brace strode away. He had the slightest smile on his face too. He finally remembered our moments, which was the best thing in the world.

"I don't even want to know what you're talking about." Ria's voice could be heard behind us, along with the low rumbles from Lucy's pissed-off mate. Colton was going to be on his toes for all of eternity.

"What's happening with Dad?" I asked Brace. "Is he okay? Has he talked with Mom yet?"

She would be raring to rip him a new one, but I felt that they needed to have their fight, get it out in the open and move on.

"Everything is sorted with the clans. They seemed to feel that his stepping down as princeps was more than enough punishment. We're all in agreement that he wasn't at fault, and in reality has given us a slight advantage by bringing it to everyone's attention."

I wasn't actually that surprised by this.

Walkers – while hotheaded and arrogant – were also ancient beings with very logical brains. In most situations they saw the bigger picture. Except when it came to their mates. Then they were cavemen with pea-sized brains and zero logic.

I needed to see Josian. I wanted to reassure him again that I was not mad with him. I knew the guilt would be eating him alive. He was an emotional man and felt things very deeply. I just hoped that Lallielle wasn't too hard on him, although I understood that her sense of betrayal ran even deeper than the rest of ours. She just needed time to remember the unwavering faith she had always shown in her mate.

But before I could search out my father, I knew Brace needed a moment of my time.

5
———

We were crossing the green fields. Off to the side were masses of forest. Brace's arms were tightly wound around me as he strode without effort. I'd protest all the carrying – but I didn't want to.

"So, not that I'm complaining, but is there a reason for this current show of manliness?" I kissed his cheek, my entire body straining to be closer to him.

"I have to go back to Abernath for a while. Mother needs to see me," he said. "Then I'll be in war meetings with the other princeps for the rest of the day."

My heart sank a little. Even though this is what we had planned on, I was still effing annoyed that Brace and I were going to be apart. It wouldn't have been as bad if we were melded; I'd have him in my head. But this way ... was damn lonely.

"Open your mind to me, baby." His whispered words caressed my senses like the lightest touch.

I didn't hesitate, dropping the barrier, and then he was everywhere: in my thoughts, body, soul, and heart.

Not that he was ever far from those places. As his heat and distinct power burned through me, it was the closest I'd felt to complete since the bond was broken.

An image crossed my mind. It was a very strange, dark city with barriers around the outside and a few black crystals glittering on the edges.

That's the city of Arotia. The last living civilization of Dronish. You should find your female there.

Brace's words echoed across my senses, and then with a sigh of regret he withdrew his presence from me. I wanted to cry at the loss. I was cold and alone again. I understood why we couldn't stay merged. We were practically taunting our bond into taking over and forcing our meld. But still ... it effing sucked the big one.

With a sigh I shielded my mind again. Brace drew me into his arms, his hands running up and down my back in a soothing manner. After a long time we pulled apart. He stared down. His dark eyes reflected my image in their depths.

He brushed back strands of my hair from where they had fallen across my face. "We didn't discuss who you were going to Dronish with, but you should take the half-Walker girls."

I blinked at him a few times.

He grinned at my confusion. "Dronish is a world of energy-craving inhabitants. They've razed their world's resources to the ground, existing now on just a few shards of power. Enough to keep them alive, but weak." He locked me in his gaze. "The half-Walker's protection will ensure that your energy isn't felt. The moment any Walker has explored there in the past they were swarmed by those trying to steal their power." His voice lowered into that I'm-dead-serious register. "They're dangerous, Red. Don't underestimate this race. They're desperate, and it's about survival for them."

I filed away that information. It was sure to be important later. "You're deliberately separating us, aren't you?" I tried to keep the sadness from my voice, but I wasn't too successful.

"No, sweetheart, I'm tempted to tie you to my side. Forever." He was all fierce now. "But I have to acknowledge that we have jobs to do, and right now we can't reform the melding bond. My current focus is to make sure I destroy the lalunas. I won't rest until I find a way." He dropped a brief and sweet kiss on my lips. "There're no other options. I will remeld with you," he whispered against my mouth.

"Soon," I practically begged.

He groaned. It was low but I heard it. "For the love of my sanity, please stop begging."

I couldn't help the snort of laughter that escaped me. I may, just a little, adore my power over him.

With great reluctance he set me on my feet. "Okay, Red. I'm going to walk away now, while I still possess the ability to."

He turned away, but was back in a blink of an eye and I was in his arms again. Our lips met in a scorching kiss. He broke away first, since I was never willingly going to remove my lips from his.

"I love you," he said.

He left me there dazed and confused as he walked a few steps away and opened a doorway behind some trees. His serious eyes caressed my features briefly before he touched his fingertips to his lips and blew me a kiss goodbye.

And then he was gone.

Ah, eff. That was painful.

I must have stood there for a long time. Thankfully, as a Walker, I could have probably stood there forever without too much discomfort. Turning to make my way back to the girls, I stopped when I almost bumped into Lucas. He looked as if he'd been standing about six feet from me, just watching my back.

"Uh, hello, Emperor creepy. What are you doing?"

The side of his mouth lifted slightly, but he was minus his usual mirth. "You looked like you needed a few minutes, and I –" He broke off, before running his hand through his blond hair and sighing. "Well, I understand that quite strongly at the moment."

I ran my eyes over the handsome First World Emperor. He looked disheveled, which was not his usual suave façade. Something was going on with him. I hoped it wasn't to do with the running of First World, because I wasn't even close to having time to pick up my side of that responsibility.

"Are you okay, Lucas?"

He shook his head a few times. The repeated motion was odd. "Actually, no, I'm not."

I opened my mouth, but he cut me off before I could ask.

"It's not First World. Things are as smooth as can be expected. Since you dispelled all of that negative energy in the dark mountains, we've had a resurgence of the balance. Less darkness has resulted in less unease. Of course I'm still having my issues with the mayoral heads, but nothing I can't handle." He laughed. It was harsh and derisive. "My father prepared me well for this mantle, even if others think I wasn't ready for the challenge."

"So what's wrong then?" I asked as a light breeze blew through the field, lifting my curls off the back of my neck. There was the slightest hint of cool in an otherwise balmy day.

His icy blue eyes locked onto my face. "These damn dreams are keeping me up at night. I'm being haunted by all the choices I've made. Mostly what the hell to do about Ria and whether I'm failing at running First World." His words were jumbled, as if he were trying to figure it out himself. "But I do feel better knowing what your place is in my life. I hated the disloyalty I felt toward you when I still couldn't forget the woman from my dreams." His eyes narrowed playfully. "Despite the fact you were constantly lip-locked with that giant, pain-in-the-ass Walker."

I took a step closer to Lucas. It was easier to be around him now. We both understood the connection we shared, and knew it was nothing to do with romance and everything to do with a ruling partnership. I didn't have to worry my actions could be mistakenly construed as a romantic advance.

"I'm really sorry that I'm not around to help with some of the stresses," I said, and I meant it. "I just seem to have more hard choices than easy ones nowadays and time is not my friend."

Lucas reached out and took my hand. It was unexpected, and I fought the instinct to rip myself free of him.

"The worlds are lucky to have you, Abby. I see the sacrifice, the struggle. I've been there before and it's a tough life to be a leader, a savior." His soft tone washed over me. "And you do it so seamlessly that most people wouldn't even notice the personal cost. I notice," he finished fiercely.

I hugged him then. Yeah, I'd wanted to pull my hand away a minute ago, but then I'd changed my mind. What? I'm a complicated woman and right then I'd needed his encouraging words.

"Thank you," I said, stepping back again. "And I think you should talk to Ria. She deserves an explanation. She deserves the same considerate words you managed to find for me."

Lucas was a different man to the cocky individual I'd met when I first came to this world. Every obstacle he'd faced, his father's death, taking on the role as Emperor in a time of war and crisis, finding and hurting his dreammate. Well, he'd grown a little more with every hardship.

"I'm proud of you," I said to him. "You seem to finally be a worthy leader for our people."

A lazy grin crossed his features. "What a lovely, backward compliment."

I shrugged. "You're welcome. Why are you here anyways?"

"It looks as if this battle is going to go down on First World. I've been called in as part of the war council." His brows drew together. "I know it's just a formality. The Walkers definitely don't need or want advice from a young, newly appointed Emperor. But still, Quarn is assembling our army and we're having our own area set up in the camp."

Wow, I was impressed. They'd started to pull together a wide variety of soldiers in a short period of time.

Dronish

"I have to go now. Make sure that everyone isn't killing themselves in our zone." He touched my arm briefly. "I'll think on what you've said about Ria. Maybe it wouldn't hurt to talk to her, try and mend some of the hurt between us. I might actually get a decent night's sleep," he finished on a mutter.

"We have to go to Dronish now, but when we return you'll have plenty of time." I straightened, shoving my hands into the pockets on my jeans.

"Ria's going with you?" His voice lowered.

I nodded, my eyes examining his features.

He didn't say anything for a few heartbeats. It looked as if he were counting to ten. Finally he all but growled. "Look after her for me. And yourself." He swallowed loudly. "I would be loath to lose either of you." He marched away, his broad shoulders rigid and arms stiff at his side.

I watched him for a while before turning to make my way back to the girls.

HOURS later the five of us were ready to head to Dronish. Fury had returned. Her father had had enough of the crowds and was off hiding, but she seemed to think they'd made a small inroad to building a relationship. Although she still wasn't sure if she liked him or not yet; he was 'damn weird' had been the main observation she'd made.

Lucy was by my side absolutely fuming mad that she wasn't allowed to go with us to the vampire planet. She was starting to look like a green glitter sprinkler. I could barely see her through the mist. She wasn't really talking to me as we stood near the war council area.

The entire camp was a little messy at that moment, filled with fighting, confusion and unease. Everyone striving to be the leader, but there were too many different groups, all of whom wanted to be heard. I hoped when we returned they were a little more organized. I felt uneasy leaving before having a chance to speak with Josian, but I hadn't been able to find him. Despite the fact I'd searched for a few hours.

Just as I had that thought, my head whipped to the side as his energy drifted toward me. Five seconds later he stepped out from behind the Doreen tent, an area which had been set up for our new princeps and his council to confer.

"Give me a minute," I said to the others, before marching across to Josian.

He was not looking in my direction as he strode in slow deliberate motions across the space. His expression was that of a shattered man and that hurt my heart all over again.

"Hey, Dad," I said, coming to a halt a few feet from him.

His head flew up and bronze eyes locked in on me.

"Baby girl," he croaked out, his voice low and rough. "What are you doing here?"

"I'm about to head to Dronish with the other half-Walkers."

He reached out and grasped my hand.

I squeezed it tightly in return.

"I tried to talk with your mother. She's still fairly upset. But ..." He cleared his throat. "Do you have any time for me to explain a few more things before you leave?"

I nodded. "I always have time for you, Dad."

Under the watchful eyes of my friends, their mates and a few other onlookers, Josian and I made our way out of the main area. We stopped near the waterfall and lake.

He started slowly. "I'm going to say it again, because you deserve to hear this more than once. I am so sorry, baby girl. I know it'll take me a lifetime to make this up to you, for you to trust me again –"

"No!" I said, my voice fierce. I was on my feet, hands on my hips. "No, you have to stop saying crap like this." My hands went from my hips to waving wildly in the air. "Are the lalunas still gone from your head?"

He nodded twice. "Yes, I haven't felt their presence since we left the stone world."

I reached out and grabbed onto his forearms. "I don't forgive you, Dad."

His face fell so I hurried to finish.

"Because there's nothing to forgive. In my mind you did nothing wrong. This is all on the lalunas, and they're going down. Now tell me what we need to do to beat them?"

His bronze eyes hardened, the gold threading through. "I've been thinking about this for a long time and ... the only way to limit their power is to lock them away, in the same prison as the Seventine."

"What?" I said. He'd taken me by surprise. "Is it a wise idea to place two sets of the most powerful entities in our star systems close to each other?"

Josian shook out his very dark red hair. "Once they're imprisoned, they'll have no power. We'll use the lalunas to strengthen the protections on the prison. If the stones are part of the wall, then I don't think the Seventine will ever be able to escape again."

I mulled his words over. "And if they're locked away they'll no longer have power over you? Or anyone?"

"They'll have no power unless they escape."

My bracelet warmed then. I gasped, holding it up in front of me, but thankfully there was no pain. Just a sudden burst of warmth. Then it started to melt again, dripping off my hand and reforming into a blue stone nestled on the forest floor.

Josian and I both stared at it.

"What does that mean?" I widened my eyes.

A broad grin crossed my father's face. I blinked a few times. It was odd to see him so joyous. I hadn't seen that expression in a long time. Then he threw back his head and laughed.

Great, the stress had gotten to him and he'd lost the plot.

"They like my plan, baby girl," he spluttered through his laughter.

How the hell did he know that? Shaking my head, I knelt down and curved my fingers under the stone, prepared to pick it up again.

The moment my palm wrapped around the blue surface, I flinched as whispers of energy crossed my mind, and then there were voices in my head. It says a lot about my recent life that my shock lasted all of a second before I was okay with what was happening.

Lock away all of the lalunas. We are too powerful; we will contain the Seventine and right the wrong of our brethren. We must right the wrong.

A symphony of voices continued to echo through my mind, and I was reminded of Francesca's prophecy from a long time ago. That the end of days was written in mineral. Maybe that was to do with the stones, and the bindings on the prison. I had a brief thought of my aunt. She had been lying low in the beach house, depression claiming her ever since her gift of prophecy had fled. I knew Lallielle checked on her all the time. I hoped it was enough.

Pushing these thoughts aside, I stood up and faced Josian. "My laluna does like your idea. We need to gather all fourteen lalunas and lock every single one away."

He straightened. "Did they tell you that?"

I nodded. "Yes, they want to repair the damage from their brethren and contain the Seventine."

Josian stood taller than I'd seen for a long time. A light descended over him and he started to glow, in that same way he had when I first ever saw him. I hadn't realized but over time his light had faded out, and that probably had something to do with his laluna manipulating him. Especially once he started to remember it. Now, though, he looked like the gods that Walkers were worshipped as. Furious, fierce and utterly spectacular.

"I'm going to find the stones, baby girl, and we're going to lock them away."

I bit my lip. I was thrilled at his enthusiasm, but – "How are you going to find them on the worlds?"

He reached across and took the stone from me. "We already have the First World pair. Tenni will have to be last. The others I can find using this." He held the stone aloft. "They're beacons for each other."

My lips parted as a grin forced itself across my face.

The fact that my laluna didn't disappear from his hands meant it was definitely agreeing to this plan. I moved closer and, standing on my toes, waited until he leaned down so I could kiss his cheek.

"This is going to work, Dad. We'll lock them away forever and imprison the Seventine and live happily ever after."

Fairytales were awesome for a reason.

He chuckled uneasily before it was cut off abruptly and sadness descended again. "All of that sounds simpler than easing the hurt I've caused Lallielle."

I knew Mom had not been far from his mind. He would have no respite from his own hurt and guilt until his mate forgave him.

"Mom is an incredibly strong and forgiving woman." I offered the comfort I could. "Just give her some time; it's a remarkable healer."

"Time, hey?" He ran his hand through his red mane. "I'm not very patient, but I'll do my best."

We walked back to the Doreen area and I left Josian at the main war tent again. He was going in to explain his plan to the princeps, and then, with my laluna in hand, was going to be jetting off to the worlds to find the other stones. We'd probably cross paths with him on Dronish.

Lucy was in my face as soon as I found the girls again. "So you're absolutely sure you don't want me on this trip?" she demanded. "Who's going to watch your back without me there?"

She was being mean now because she was pissed off. She knew the half-Walkers had each other's backs.

"I want you there, Luce. Trust me, I spend most of the time we're apart worrying about what the hell you're doing." I hugged an arm around her stiff shoulders, mindful of her wings. "But your power is too strong now that your pixie side is unlocked. They'll swarm us on Dronish. It's more dangerous for all of us if you're there," my voice was low, "so stay, enjoy a few days with Colt ... have a break, meet your father. You've lots to be sorting in your own world."

I met the light blue eyes of her mate over her shoulder. His white-blond hair was falling messily over his features. It used to be longer and he'd worn it tied at the nape of his neck, but now it was too short for that. His current length was just enough to be sexy.

Thank you, he mouthed to me, his relief apparent. Of course it was. For once he didn't have to be the bad guy.

"Fine." Lucy finally relented. "I'll wait here, like the poor little pixie, but you all better get your asses back here, like tomorrow."

Her eyes took in all five of us. And I wasn't the only one to flinch a little at the hardness of her gaze.

Okay, well it was mainly me and Talina. The other three were unfazed.

"If you're bored, or need something to do, you can help Jedi research," I said to Lucy and Colton. "He told me he's found some important texts on the conduit and the prison. It might be crucial information for us to lock away the Seventine for good."

Lucy's solemn expression did not waver, but she nodded decisively. "We can do that."

I gave her one last hug before she turned and left with her wolf-Walker. I watched as their familiar visages disappeared across the green field. I hadn't been to any of these worlds without Lucy and I felt uneasy leaving her behind. As if we were growing away from each other, moving in different directions. Which was not okay with me.

I forced myself to focus by turning to Fury. "Did you check on Dune?"

She nodded, her white hair flying around her face. "Yes, I traced back just before and he's holed up observing the zone we're worried about. But all is quiet at the moment ..." She trailed off.

"After we find the sixth girl, I'll come with you to Crais," I said, and then turned to face Talina. "And we can go to Spurn also. I'll see if I can sense anything on either world."

I was particularly tuned in to the Seventine. Apparently there was a bond between me and the first. And I had that stubborn, niggling feeling in my gut, the one I used to get on Earth when a ganger was about to ambush me. Something big was going down on one of these worlds, and I wasn't sure we'd get there in time to stop it. It was hard to know which of the tasks was the most urgent. Gathering the half-Walkers was always the top spot, but sometimes other things could be equally important. Especially when it came to the Seventine.

Delane's wings stretched a little as she shifted on the spot. "What do we need before we travel to Dronish?" Her tone was low and serious. "Do you know the terrain? Weather? Will we be able to breathe?"

I blinked at her a few times. Damn, I could have used her on some of the other planets. We mainly just popped along and hoped for the best. Of course, for most of the worlds I'd had Brace with me. Walkers had so much information at their disposal, and I had none.

"I think maybe we need some facts about Dronish before we go there," Delane finished.

She had her left eyebrow raised in that way where I knew she was mentally calling me a moron. It was an expression she had down to an art.

Lina and Cerberus wandered up to us and stood to the side.

I glanced at my faithful hound. "What's up, Cere? Are you two planning on coming to Dronish with us?"

Both of his heads nodded at me while his four eyes locked in with that intensity which I was coming to see was all animal.

"But won't they feel your energy?" I said, looking from the hellhound to the unicorn.

And then, I swear they looked at each other and started laughing. They didn't really make a noise. It was more about how their heads jerked around and snorts emerged.

"Are they laughing at you?" Fury said as she stepped forward. "That's freaking awesome."

I couldn't help my own smile. Even though at times they were ferocious beasts, they were also pretty adorable. "I think we better gather some information on our animals also."

Josian was supposed to have helped us, but he was busy at the moment.

As a group we wandered across the grassed area and into the wide open entrance of the Doreen war council tent. I was having some trouble with the fact that my father was no longer the princeps. I wasn't sure what this new leader was going to demand of his people. I hoped he wasn't the same sort of crazy dictator as Que, but to think that someone thought they had the power to control me was ... well, crazy. I was no one's sheep. I would not cow down to anyone. If you wanted to lead me, you needed to gain my respect. I didn't know this new leader, so for now I would lead myself, utilizing the wise council of my friends and family.

Okay, I wasn't great with authority.

Five men and three women were in the room. They were scattered between two tables, scrolls and maps and parchments spread out in every direction. A board was erected at the back of the space, with images and information pinned to it.

Eight pairs of eyes locked on us when we entered. The largest of the men, who had been standing near the board, narrowed his eyes at me.

He straightened and stepped closer, stopping about three feet from us. "Don't bother to announce yourselves. Just stroll right on in." His tone was hard, biting as it washed over me. And straight away it had my energy roiling inside. "Now get out of the tent and follow protocol."

"I'm sorry, what?" Fury said. "Did I just hear you correctly?"

She turned astonished gray eyes onto my face, but before I could verbalize my own version of 'what the eff?', Cerberus was suddenly huge, filling the tent, and both of his heads were doing that ominous growl which reverberated along the ground and had every hair on my body standing on end.

Guess he didn't like rude-ass Walkers either.

The man, who had dark-red hair, not as potent as my own but in the same shade, took a step back. I knew it was Gerry. I could feel the mantle of leadership on him now, even though there hadn't been time for an official ceremony. Besides, who else would think they could come at us so aggressively?

"Cere." My voice was calm as I laid a gentle hand on his leg. He was filling most of the space in the tent. Luckily the ceiling was high or he'd have knocked it down on top of us. "It's okay, no need to eat him just yet." I settled my eyes – which I'm sure were as hard as the emerald stones they mimicked – on the arrogant man.

"I'm not sure what you think your role in our life is, but I'm ... we're not one of your subjects." I let some of my power leak into the room as I spoke, and I wasn't the only one. Tendrils of fire, water, earth, and air trickled along with my own. "We're original powers, half-Walkers with a far bigger responsibility than princeps of a Walker clan. You will show us respect, or I'll do everything in my power to remove you from leadership."

And I would.

Rightfully it should be Josian here. Due to unfortunate circumstances I was stuck with this unknown leader during a time of war. Which was a right old pain in the ass.

He swallowed hard. His breathing increased for a few moments as he debated what he was going to say. I knew he wanted to slam me down, put me in what he thought was my rightful place, but ... he was hesitating. Which told me everything. He wasn't sure he could take us on. I could guarantee he was no match.

"Why have you come here?" he finally said. "I mean, what can we help you with?"

Much better. I exchanged a glance with Fury. She was grinning from ear to ear.

Ria was the one to answer. "We need information on Dronish and on the sacred animals."

I had no problem with the Regali half stepping in. I wasn't the leader of the half-Walkers; we were a team. I might have called some of the shots in the past, but we were all powerful in our own right. And I respected the hell out of every single one of my friends.

Gerry's lips thinned as he gathered a few papers. "I have to leave, but the others will fill you in on any information you need."

He edged past Cerberus and strode out of the tent opening, no doubt the only action he had right then to take a little bit of power back. The moment he disappeared from sight my hellhound shrunk back to his horse size and took his place beside Lina.

A beautiful woman who had been standing near the largest table dropped the papers in her hands. "Sorry about Gerry," she said as she started to move. The light filtering through the tent highlighted the purple streaks in her black hair. "I'm Heidi, and I'm happy to fill you in on both the sacred animals and Dronish."

Striding over to us, the long-legged female Walker indicated we should exit the tent. It was time to gather some information.

6

We were standing in the shade of the large temporary shelter. We had to watch our words, as there were many milling around in hearing range. Not that any of this information was classified, but still, we erred on the side of caution.

Heidi wasted no time. Her mild accent was easy to understand even with the rapid chatter she seemed fond of. "The sacred animals are built of original energies. They'll bond with each of you half-Walkers and they'll be a source of protection. They're each strong, powerful, and absolutely lethal if you wrong them." She glanced at our two beautiful creatures. "Don't underestimate them because they stand here looking domesticated. They're the very definition of wild and won't hesitate to deliver swift and brutal death to any that threaten their Walker."

"Can they come to Dronish with us?" Delane asked. "Or will their energy be detected?"

The edges of Heidi's lips curved into the slightest grin. "They'll not be detected unless they want to be. You don't have to worry. They can be whatever you need them to be. Take them with you wherever you go now. They can hold their own even against the Seventine. They're a gift and it's only by the grace of the mother that they've come back to us."

It was probably in response to the lalunas overstepping their place in the star system.

I wondered why Cerberus had never left pixie land. I had no doubt now that there had not been enough power to hold him there, so why had he stayed? Was there a reason we were yet to uncover? Or had he been waiting for me? It couldn't be a coincidence that it was only after I found him that the other animals started to appear.

"What are the other sacred animals?" Fury asked.

And I could just see that she was hoping she'd get something big and badass as a companion. Probably a dragon, knowing her. A match for Dune's dragoona.

"I can't tell you. They change shape and structure over the years. What they were at the beginning isn't what they'll be in the end."

Helpful.

"And Dronish; not a lot is known of this world anymore. Walkers can't occupy their world for too long or we're mobbed by literally thousands of the inhabitants. They're vampires of a sort. They drain the life-energy of others to survive. Parasitic in nature, when their hunger overcomes them they lose all reason."

Talina's emerald hair wrapped comfortingly around her as she entered the conversation. "What is the climate of the world? What do we need to prepare ourselves?"

"They've drained the energy of all but one moon," Heidi said. "So it's dark, freezing and there's not much oxygen, but you'll have enough initially and your bodies will adjust quickly enough. The inhabitants – Drones – are ... different. You'll be immediately recognizable as aliens."

"What do you mean: different?" I narrowed my eyes at her.

They weren't going to be real vampires, right? With fangs. Surely that had been created on Earth.

Heidi shook her head. "They have only one eye, and a long sucker which extends out from their mouths and attaches to whatever they're draining."

Great, I'd prefer the fangs. And could I have a minute here to say ... what the eff?

"I would recommend using a hood or cloak that hides your faces. Since they're a secretive and sneaky race, they won't find this odd."

And it would help with the cold.

"How're we going to find this half?" Talina's brown eyes were so wide they looked huge. "This world sounds like it's going to be the most difficult."

"Actually," I said, "I have a bit of a plan this time. When I tether to all of you I can feel the other unknown girls there. I think that if I'm close enough I might be able to trace where the power is coming from. So providing we don't get mobbed and captured ..."

I trailed off, and Heidi jumped in to speak again.

"I've seen you all use your power together once – very impressive, by the way – and that type of energy will be felt by every Drone in no time. I would make sure you're not too close to the main city, and don't stay tethered for long."

Delane interrupted. "The most time-efficient path

would be for us to call all of these ... Drones by using our power. Then when we have them all there, we'll easily find the half-Walker. She'll look different."

Fury threw her hands in the air. "Yes, but how do you plan on getting her to leave without us all being suckered by their little ... sucker things? We need time to explain everything to her, convince her that she needs to help us."

"And hope like hell she's not as difficult as Fury was," Talina snorted.

Fury flipped her off but didn't argue. She knew she'd been an asshat.

I wasn't sure what way to go with finding the Dronish half. This was the sort of thing that I usually decided on the spot. I was a bit of a 'wing it and hope for the best' kind of Walker. Which was not something that sat easily with Delane or Ria. They were strategic ... planners. Talina and Fury were different again. The Spurnian was flexible, go-with-the-flow, and she trusted me implicitly. The Crais half was hotheaded. She always threw herself in without thought.

"I'm sorry, I've no idea how to help you with that decision," Heidi said. "But I wish you all the luck. We'll continue the fight back here."

I reached out and halted her before she left. "What's Gerry's problem? He should have no grief with us yet."

She pursed her lips, her eyes roaming my features. Finally she answered. "He doesn't feel that he rightfully earned the mantle of Princeps. Gaining the leadership in this manner, especially from someone like Josian, who's so beloved, well, it's made him overcompensate in trying to bring all of Doreen under his command." She rubbed at her forehead in a rapid movement. "He hasn't said anything, of course, but my guess is that he's afraid that no one will take him seriously, respect him. So he's kind of going off the deep end."

She turned her head to take us all in again. "And you five are really outside of any command. We all know that in the end you trump us, which he's fighting against."

She shrugged and there was so much written in that movement, so many unspoken words.

"Good luck. I wish you the best on this voyage." She went back into the tent.

"Well," Ria said, looking around, "looks like we're going to need some coats."

I loved the way they voiced no further concerns about the new Doreen princeps. I could feel that the half-Walkers agreed with Heidi. He did not control us. No one controlled us. I just had to make sure our masses of power never went to our heads. We couldn't lose our good intentions; we had to stay grounded. Which, considering the level of power each half-Walker added to our group, was going to get harder in the next little while.

LESS THAN AN HOUR later we were ready to leave again. We'd procured very long, thick, heavily insulated hooded coats. And also gloves, boots and thermal underclothes. Right then, on First World, I was sweating my butt off, but apparently even with all the layers we'd still be cold on Dronish. On top of that we were strapped down with weapons. Which was Delane's contribution to the outfits. Apparently you can never have enough weapons.

I glanced at the other four. "You all ready?" I could

not make out their faces buried deep in the heavy hoods, but the nods answered my question.

Cerberus and Lina both let loose their calls: one was a bark, the other like a horse's whinny. I took that as agreement that they were ready too.

I retrieved the mental image that had been gifted to me earlier by Brace. Arotia, the last city of Dronish. This was where all the surviving Drones should be, our best bet to find the half. I called a doorway and it appeared before us. The dark, scary vortex was familiar territory now, and as a group we stepped forward to traverse the vacuum. I didn't hesitate to make the final leap out into the unknown. Dronish. The vampire planet.

Here we come.

ON THE OTHER side it took a few moments for my senses to adjust. It was so cold that it literally felt like there was no warmth at all in this land. The air was heavy and musty, and on top of that it was so dark that at first I couldn't see anything. But eventually my eyes adjusted – Walkers could adapt to anything – and I started to see the world before us. I had opened the doorway just off to the side of Brace's image of Arotia. It was a strange-looking town, small and circular with a large wall surrounding it in a protective manner.

From our vantage point – outside and up on a slight incline – there looked to be only ten or eleven large buildings inside the barriers. They towered high into the air, similar to the skyscrapers that had once dominated New York City. Cerberus trotted next to me, and just as I was about to reach out and pat him, he started to shrink. He continued, getting smaller than I'd ever seen him go before ... smaller than a normal-size dog ... then smaller than a kitten.

Eventually he stopped; he was about the size of a little bird. Crouching down, I held out a hand to him, and he ran up my arm and rested inside my coat on my shoulder. Sort of snuggled into the crook of my neck. Hidden by the huge hood.

"Unbelievable." Fury's voice sounded from a cloak to my right. "He's undetectable now."

I glanced over at Delane. Lina was no longer at her side; she must have shrunk too. No wonder Heidi wasn't worried about our animals going with us. These creatures were even more adaptable than Walkers.

Ria's voice was shaky as she stumbled closer to me. "This world is more than cold. There's almost no plant life here. I want to call them to me, but I barely feel an iota of a living environment."

"I'm guessing they need more warmth and sustenance than that sliver of moon is providing." Talina pointed toward the smallest speck of moon.

We spun around as Delane took off to the side. In a flash of movement she had her sword in her hand. As we started to follow her, I pulled my own samurai-style sword free, a weapon I was proficient in but had never had much training.

Delane was fast, pulling ahead.

We continued to follow as she cleared a few of the planes and came up on the side of a mountain. It was here that she dropped down and started to move on her forearms and knees. Army-style crawl. The dark cloak blended her right into the ground.

The four of us followed, getting low to the dehydrated ground also. I knew I wasn't the only one wondering what the hell the Angelica was doing. But as I continued climb-crawling and my head rose over the top of the crest, it all became startlingly clear.

Shit.

Delane had ears like a goddamn eagle. She'd heard the sounds of battle that none of us had even remotely picked up. The Drones were at war, and I mean majorly at war. There seemed to be a mass of fighting going on. It was weird, though. They didn't have any weapons, instead they were ...

"Oh, my freaking giddy Earon." Talina burst out. "What the hell is that thing that just came out of its mouth?"

We could see them quite well from where we were positioned. Some of them drifted close to our spot as they fought amongst each other. Heidi's description of them was all too clear, but despite knowing of the sucker and single eye, seeing it was an entirely different thing.

Of any of the planets, the inhabitants of Dronish were the strangest I'd seen, and that included the Spurnian fish people. The Drones were tall and thin, that ultra, ultra thin, without one ounce of shape, muscle or tone. Almost as if they were just skin draped over a piece of cardboard. They wore long shapeless sheets over their bodies, leaving their heads and arms exposed.

Their skin was translucent, which meant I could see there wasn't much beneath it in the way of blood or organs. Some – I guessed they were the males – had weird stones embedded into their bald heads. The other more feminine ones had these random tufts of hair on their heads. Oh, and they had just one large, blood-red eye. But the final and most disturbing piece of the freakish cake was the tongue-like projection which extended from their mouths. When they attacked, this sucker would attach to whoever they were battling. That was how they fought, with their tongues.

Gross! And on top of gross: what the eff?

I held my breath as I watched one such attachment scene right in front of us. Within moments the one who had the tongue attached stopped struggling, before fading right out and collapsing into nothing. Pretty much disappearing right into the black sheet. The other one, who was rolling his 'tongue' back into his mouth, was suddenly flush and full of life. Slicks of oil seem to roll right off its weird-ass face. Right, well the vampire name was starting to make sense, but I guessed it wasn't blood these suckers were after. Energy.

Fury crawled across to my side. Her hood shifted left to right as she followed the action in front of us. "Can you connect and find the female?"

I knew which of the girls was which from their energy. Their elements gave them distinct power.

"She shouldn't be hard to recognize if we can move in the general direction ... I mean, if she has two eyes and all." I didn't care if she had one, two or six eyes; it wasn't important.

And in fact the single eye was large enough that it actually didn't even look that weird. Okay, it was a little weird.

I gestured for the girls to move closer to me. We snuggled together.

"I'm going to tether to you all. We'll probably find

ourselves with a little too much attention, but if you all don't mind a bit of battle, well, who am I to argue?"

Delane shifted to her side, turning her hood in my direction. "I was born ready to battle."

No doubts at all about warrior-Walker. I was sure I could hear Lina whinnying in agreement.

There were nods all round, so without pause I flung my golden cord. It split and extended, connecting to the other four girls. I took a deep, satisfying breath as the energy flooded through me. The different texture, scent and feel of each girl was unique, but they blended seamlessly with each other. Like the air blew the fire toward the earth, which was nourished by the water. And back the other way, but in a different order.

I focused on the two transparent tethers. They were weaker, unknown. One was so slight, I could barely even feel the energy; the other was much stronger. The Dronish half was close.

Instead of speaking mentally as we usually did, I spoke out loud. "We all set?"

"Ye ... Yes." Fury stuttered her word a little. "You know it's a little hard to force the words through the energy, but once I start it gets easier."

"M .. me ... me too," Talina agreed.

"Okay, follow me."

I got to my feet, my outward senses blinded as I searched for the last girl. I could see the cord now. It was faint, but there was a path I could follow. The other four around me had their weapons held aloft, but I wasn't sure any of them, besides Delane, were much use in battle. The Angelica and I seemed to be the only two with fight training.

Thankfully the cord seemed to lead away from the city, back toward the Walker doorway. I followed the thread, secure in the knowledge that the others had my back. I knew they couldn't use their power. I was the one in control right then, but they could physically attack. Or at least give me some warning of an ambush.

The unknown cord was just starting to darken, the gold definitely less translucent, when we were set upon by a group of eight Dronish inhabitants.

Fury roared at me. "Abby, attack!"

I pulled my senses from the cord and back to our immediate surroundings. It took Delane no more than a minute to take out five of them, her sword cutting through the darkness in flashes of steel and death.

One had managed to attach onto Talina, its sucker extending into her hood.

Gathering energy, I sent a wave of power toward the Spurn half. In seconds the Drone was surrounded in a whirlpool of water, the torrent flinging the lithe form far into the distance. Another went the same way from Fury's fire, burned to a cinder within moments. The last was strung up in Ria's hair vines.

I flinched at the thought of killing these alien creatures, but there wasn't much I could do while they were attacking us. Thankfully, we had a reprieve after this ambush, managing to camouflage our movements behind some rocky mountains. That lasted only about a minute before we were back crossing some open plains.

It was clear, even in the semi-darkness, that this land was leeched of life, just like on Crais. Although here it was the icy cold and lack of sun. The gravity felt a little heavier than First World's, and the air was pretty musty.

There looked to be very little life in this land. No trees or grass, just weird rock-style formations and mountainous planes. The cord continued leading us around the back of the city wall, and out into a darkened and flat plain.

Fury grumbled, "I ... I hope this cord isn't leading us into the middle of nowhere. Supes seems a little off her game since Josian."

The cloak hid my eye-roll.

"Abby knows what she's doing." Talina, my most loyal half-Walker.

There was some truth to what Fury had said. It wasn't just Josian, although that had thrown me off balance. But being unmelded to Brace had definitely weakened me. Which was why the laluna was determined that we would stay that way. It was also clear that the longer I was without Brace, the weaker I was becoming. As if something inside me was fading away without my mate.

Using gloved hands, I rubbed my temples as that thought assaulted me. Was I losing something by not being with Brace? Surely I could be strong on my own? Surely I didn't *need* a man to define me? It was nice to have his strength to lean on, but I wanted to be able to stand on my own also. It didn't seem as if Brace was weakened without me. I'd certainly never noticed anything.

My thoughts were cut off as a shadow rose beyond us. A structure in the distance. It took us a few more steps before the shape came into focus. It was a cave system, or some sort of large rock overhang. I couldn't tell if there was an opening or not – it was far too dark – but we'd see soon enough.

I don't like the feel of this. Ria had reverted to mental

speak, her hood swishing as she glanced left and right. *Anyone get the feeling that we're being watched or followed?*

I couldn't sense anything specific; I was too flooded with all of our energies. But I had a similar awareness going on. A tingle at the back of my neck that was slowly trickling down my spine.

Maybe it's the Dronish half, I said. *I'll just keep following the golden cord.*

The cord of the unknown sixth half was solidifying further. It was almost the same density as the ones connected to the girls by my side. Cerberus snuggled closer to my neck, distracting me, and by the time I glanced up again we were almost at the entrance to the tunnel.

And a blur of shadow, which looked a lot like a foot, was coming straight at my face.

Instinct and training kicked in. I hit the ground a second before my nose would have been foot mush. As I landed, Cerberus was up and off me, and he was massive again.

I heard a shriek and the blur was gone. I broke the tethers to the other girls. Our visible energy dissipated.

"Did you see it?" Delane asked.

Lina hadn't appeared, so she must still be on Delane's shoulder.

"It was a shadow, but there seemed to be a shape inside it." The Angelica had her sword held aloft, steady in her capable hand.

"It might be the half-Walker or something that can lead us to her. Don't kill the shadow," I warned as we walked into the cave.

It was darker in there, but our eyes were already

adjusted to see in low light. We crept along the path. As we moved further in I noted there were small glowing circles dotted high on the wall.

"Just like Crais," Fury murmured.

This place definitely gave the same vibe as the underground area of Fury's home world. I heard weird scraping and thudding noises as we rounded the corner and came upon an open area. The space was sparse, just a few padded mats and what looked like black sheets scattered around.

Cerberus started to growl low at my side. I took his warning seriously, lifting my hands in preparation. I'd sheathed my sword; I wouldn't risk killing the half.

I felt the air whoosh first, before noticing a shadow which flew from my right. My head snapped back as a hard object landed solidly on the fleshy part of my cheek. Most definitely a fist. I felt every single knuckle as I hit the deck.

Holy eff, how was I going to fight a shadow? More movement caught my attention, and I swung out blindly from my spot on the floor. My fist grazed something solid. Okay, so it was not really a shadow. Just, uh ... wearing a shadow.

This had to be my half-Walker.

Shadow was one of the seven original powers that Jedi had mentioned, and the fact that Cerberus was not tearing the shadow a new ... um, shadow ... well, that told me it wasn't really an enemy. I threw my hood back and gestured to the others to do the same. Then I jumped to my feet.

"Stop fighting us," I yelled. "We're not your enemies; we're here to help you –"

My words were cut off by another smack in the face, my lip this time. It split instantly and blood poured out in a gush. Damn these prickly half-Walkers. Thankfully, the wound was healed within moments, although the metallic taste in my mouth lingered a little longer.

"I don't know whether to laugh or cry." Fury was standing with the others.

They were all fidgeting on the spot, looking torn about jumping in.

"Abby's getting her ass handed to her by a freaking shadow."

"Stay back," I said, my words mostly for Delane.

The Angelica had that look in her eye; she'd gone into warrior mode.

"I think it's the half-Walker. Remember, shadow is one of our abilities."

A blur of movement came at my side again, but this time I was ready. I'd tuned in to the way she fought. For some reason she continued to come at me from the side. The shifting of air alerted me that I was about to get hit again.

I flung my head to the side and at the same time I spun out my right leg and collided with something solid.

The shadowy figure fell to the ground.

I jumped on her before she could move. It was weird. When I started looking for the person in the shadow, I could see her, but before that she'd been nothing more than a blur. If she hadn't attacked me, I would never have noticed her.

The thin yet solid shape thrashed and fought beneath me, but I was stronger. In fact, she felt so light and frail under me that I was worried about crushing her.

Although, I knew I wouldn't kill a half-Walker by squashing her. After three minutes of struggling she started speaking or spluttering out random words. Some were English, others not.

"Marl," she shrieked over and over.

"Who is Marl?" I asked her, keeping my voice calm.

Her body bucked beneath mine again. She was not giving up. "What have you done with Marl? I'll kill you."

She made her point perfectly clear as her nails raked across my exposed skin.

"You need to calm down. We're not here to hurt you, and we don't know any Marl."

The shadow girl did not calm.

I held her down the best I could and hoped she'd give up soon. It took a long time. I think in the end she only slowed because she tired herself out. I pulled my weight back a little, both hands still wrapped tightly around her forearms.

Talina stood over my back. "I think Abbs has gotten a little more ruthless." Her voice held laughter. "She never tried to wrestle and hog-tie any of us."

"I think she came close with me." Fury was also laughing.

"Nah," I said. "I was going to knock you out."

Fury and Talina lost it then, falling down on each other.

"We had shadow beasts on Nephilius," the always serious Delane said. The sword had not left her hand, and she was also very close to me. "They were nearly impossible to kill. We had to wait until they morphed out of shadow and back to solid."

I glanced down at the very definite image of a female

under my hands. The shadows still mostly cloaked her, but I could see her outline. And then right as I was squinting to see her better, she appeared, in all her fascinating glory.

She spat words at me. "I don't become a shadow. I use them to hide me only." Her English was heavily accented, hard to understand.

We all stared at her for long moments. She was amazingly interesting. She had two eyes and they were the color of blood, before fading out to something golden on the outside. Her hair was purple, a deep rich midnight purple. It was long and wavy, caressing her very delicate but sharp features.

I could see the Drone in her. She was more angular than any Walker could hope to be, but somehow it worked. Her skin was dark, the color of rich soil, but it seemed to lighten and darken at will. She had glittery stones, similar to those which had adorned the Drones outside, around her eyes. This half was quite spectacular.

I released her arms, holding my hands out in front of me for a few seconds so she could see I did not mean her harm. I got to my feet, my movements slow. Everything about her screamed flight risk. We needed to move slowly to try to earn her trust.

She followed my movements and stood too. She was tall, at least six feet, very thin, and was wearing the sheet thing like the rest of the Dronish inhabitants. Her skin looked sort of shiny, like oil. I rubbed my hands together but no oil coated them from when I'd held her.

"What are you?" She blinked her red eyes a few times, looking from one of us to the other. She lingered extra-long on Cerberus and Delane. Which was understandable: two heads and wings were certainly worth the additional stare. Delane would have to get her wings tucked back into her coat before we left here.

Ria stepped forward. "We're the same thing you are." The Regali half was full of diplomacy. "Half-breeds, born of Walker father and a mother from our home planets." Her hands opened in a warm and enticing motion. "This is why we all look different and yet are the same."

Ria had been quiet since we'd arrived here, the lack of plant life throwing her off balance, but as always the queen in her rose to the surface when needed.

The female continued watching us, her wariness never falling from her scrunched features. "I'm not sure what to make of you all, but right now I need to find my Marl. He is missing."

"What is a Marl?" I asked.

"He's a Drone," she answered readily. "I left to observe the fighting, and when I returned he was gone."

"We can help you search?" Talina offered, her emerald hair moving around her slowly, but looking quite limp in the dry and frigid Dronish air.

"No." She was firm. "How could you help? You immediately stand out, and we will be mobbed. I can call the shadows to hide me while I search."

"What's your name?" I asked her.

She stared at me blankly.

I tried again. "What do they call you here?"

A flash of something sparked across her eyes. "My mother called me Sapha, and Marl does also."

Sapha.

"Great, Sapha." I smiled. "Well, we have a lot to tell you. There're events happening outside of Dronish, star-system battles which could spell the end of every single world. Including yours." I gestured to us girls. "We're half-Walkers. There're only seven of us in existence, one from each planet. We're the ones to stand and fight. To save everyone. We need you to join us, help in the battle." I glanced behind me. "I understand you won't want to leave until we find Marl, but we really need you to listen to our story."

Sapha simply stared at me for an extended moment. Before shaking her head. "Dronish is already dying. What do I care for saving other worlds? I have accepted this fate, and am fine with the end."

Great! She didn't care about dying or the fact her world was already on its way out. Those were my *big* selling points. Before I could say anything more, she pulled the shadows around herself and took off.

Shit.

"Well, that went well." Fury flipped me a grin.

I groaned. "I know. We better follow her." Cerberus had shrunk again, so I picked him up and he settled into my shoulder groove.

As we started to run we pulled our hoods up. Delane's wings were flat against her back again, hidden from view. I knew I could tether to Sapha now, but I didn't want to disable her while she was in the center of that fighting chaos. Walker vision allowed me to see the spark of her essence – even while she wore her shadows – as she darted across that open plain. We followed her right up to the back of a huge fence, a barrier which seemed to be made of stone or even bones. It towered high in the air.

"This is where her shadow disappeared, right?"

Delane was looking left and right, her weapon waving as she turned.

In a smooth motion Lina flew off Delane. We jumped back as all of a sudden a massive unicorn filled the space. Striding forward, the sacred animal used her horn and shifted this strange covering to reveal a decent-sized hole in the fence. Thank the gods for Lina. The hole had been cleverly disguised. I very much doubted we would have found it on our own. The unicorn returned to Delane, leaving us to crawl through one at a time.

Once we were all on the other side we stepped cautiously toward the noise of battle. It was so much louder within the barrier. It didn't take long before we reached what seemed to be the center of Arotia. The ten or so skyscrapers which appeared to make up the town were circled around a large area. The battling Drones paid us no attention. At that moment we were safe, covered by cloaks, our powers contained.

"The area doesn't look too large. We should see if we can spot Sapha. Last resort, we'll connect again," I murmured loud enough so the girls could hear me.

The Drones were involved in major battles. I had one hand on my sword, which was strapped into a back scabbard, but I hadn't drawn it yet. Delane had sheathed her massive sword and now held her favorites, the tomahawks. I could just see the tips. Most of the handles were hidden up her sleeves. How many weapons did warrior-Walker have on her?

We stayed to the outer areas, creeping slowly and avoiding direct contact with any of the fighting, energy-sucking creatures. There were lumps and dark shapes littering the ground, mostly made up of the sheets the

Drones wore. If they lost the energy battle there wasn't much besides skin left.

A scream echoed across the space, which drew our attention, mostly because there had been no yells or shouts previously. The prevalent noise had consisted of running, falling, and collisions as the Drones fought. I turned toward the scream and ground to a halt, before taking off again at a sprint.

Sapha was no longer cloaked in shadows. Oh, hell no. Now she was cloaked in all kinds of pissed-off, and she was bringing the smack down to some female Drone.

"How could you kill, Marl." Her shrieking noises became words as we got closer. "He was all I had. You should have killed me long ago, Mother, because now it's my turn to hunt you."

Mother? Oh, holy eff.

7

Sapha's mother was on the ground, hands held in front of her as she tried to fend off the mad-as-hell half-Walker. The shadows were going nuts, rising high above our heads and starting to swirl in a mass of angry and tumultuous swirls. This was going to be bad, so very, very bad. I knew it.

"We have to do something, Abbs." Talina pushed her hood back so I could see her stricken features. "She's going to kill them all, and I know she'll regret that. We're not killers, not for no reason."

Delane also lowered her hood. "I'll stop her," she said, already marching toward the Dronish half.

Uh, shit.

Fury's voice came from a cloaked figure about three feet from me. "Great, now you have to stop Delane and Sapha." The Crais half hooked her thumb in the hood to push it back, the dark material perfectly framing her red skin and white hair. "I'll draw the Drones and leave the Walkers to you, Supes."

And before I could ask her to clarify this amazing plan she'd just pulled from her butt, she was surrounded in her flames. The surge of power blasted across the space and thousands of ... single eyes ... turned in her direction.

It was freaking eerie.

They didn't rush her. Instead it was as if her power had enthralled them. The Drones started to stride slowly in smooth movements toward Fury.

I didn't wait around. I needed to do something now before she was overwhelmed. We could fight a few of them, but thousands ... no hope.

Delane was almost at Sapha. The Dronish half was still screaming in agonized shrieks, over and over, her pain spilling more and more power into the air. I was worried the mass of shadows was going to hit us before we could reach her. I needed to project something from a distance, to slow Sapha's release of power.

There was only one thing I could think of that might work. My dream energy.

Gathering tendrils of power from my core, I reached for the part of me which was linked to Lallielle. The dream weaver. I sent that energy straight in the direction of Delane and Sapha. I was still running, only stumbling a little as every living entity before me stopped what they were doing, freezing into battling statues. It hadn't affected those behind. I wasn't strong enough to halt all tens of thousands of them, but still I'd subdued a large portion of the Drones and my two half-Walkers.

"Talli! Fury! Ria!" I screamed as I ran toward Delane, just in case they hadn't noticed my plan.

I had to dodge the frozen Drones or push them aside when there was not enough space.

Finally, I made it to my statue-like half-Walkers. I scooped up the Nephilius half. Damn, she was heavier than she looked. All that solid muscle. She flopped over the opposite shoulder to where Cerberus rested – thankfully no weapons stabbed into me – as I plowed toward Sapha. I was just going to have to go with the whole knock-her-out-and-convince-her ploy. We were heading back to First World. We had no choice.

I could hear pounding steps behind and relief flooded me to see Ria scoop up Sapha. At least we weren't at risk from the shadows any longer. The moment I'd projected the dream energy, the shadows had dissipated. Clearly they needed Sapha's conscious energy.

"Hurry," I shouted again. "Hold onto me; I'll trace us."

Ria used her free hand to latch onto my wrist, and Talina was right there also. So we were just waiting on Fury.

"Move your butt, fire-girl," I yelled.

She was moving, but something had woken in the Drones. Their snail impression was over. They were now high-tailing it after her. If they reached her before she got to us, we were in so much freaking trouble. I threw my tethers out then, letting the power of six flow through me.

Holy. Shit. Balls.

Six was like ... wow. We were gods or something. It was intense and almost too much for me to handle. I wanted to go crazy, shoot fireworks into the sky and smash every single Drone into pieces. Cerberus nudged me, one of his heads licking up my neck. With this movement, and trickles of his ancient-feeling energy, a sense of self and clarity came back to me. I was Abigail, not a god, and not someone who had the right to choose life and death for any creature.

But I could distract the Drones long enough for Fury to make it to us. Let's hope I didn't have a fighting, kicking and screaming shadow-Sapha on my hands by then.

I sent out plumes of power in different directions. Water went one way, fire another, wind started to swirl in the darkness and from someplace far away I could feel the plants responding. There was life here, just buried deep. And then, for the first time, shadow filled our combined power. It was graceful, like air, but with a sense of heaviness, as if there was more there: secrets, darkness. It was interesting and eerie all at the same time. And it clicked into place another piece of our puzzle.

My plan sort of worked. The Drones all split into different directions, following the power. I knew that Fury could trace herself back, but I was not leaving without knowing she was safe, and this way we'd all end up in the same place. The girls still faltered sometimes with their tracing ability.

"Go, Abbs. I'll trace myself back to the beach house," Fury shouted as she ran.

I shook my head. "I'm not leaving you ..."

My loud words trailed off as Fury closed her eyes and disappeared. Okay, she'd decided to save the back and forth arguing. I hoped she would make it to First World. Closing my eyes, I found a tether close to the front of my house and, reaching out for the glittery strand, I took the rest of us to safety.

As I hit the ground running, the others let go of me,

and I struggled to hold the suddenly shifting Angelica over my shoulder.

Knowing her level of discipline, I hoped Delane would quickly orientate herself.

Shit! Lina.

I hadn't even stopped to think of the sacred animal. Cerberus nudged me then, and as I glanced down at him I noticed Lina was tucked into my hood. Thank the gods she hadn't been squished by Delane.

I lowered the Angelica to the ground. Her eyes were half open, the black irises darting left and right. Ria gently placed Sapha next to her. At that point the sacred animals bounced off my shoulder and within seconds were large again. They took a step back, as if they were leaving us to our little girl-fight.

Fury's voice distracted me. "She's going to be so pissed off at you."

I was relieved to see her emerging from the front door of my house.

"We'll need to do major damage control just to get her to listen," Fury continued.

Talina, who must have ducked into the ocean to refresh, ran up to me. She threw droplets of water around. "Should we tie her up?"

I bit my lip. "Something tells me she'd appreciate that even less than the kidnapping."

Ria's plant life was surrounding her again and she looked much more content as vines twirled around her arms and legs. "Maybe this will be fine," she said. "We'll use reason and logic to convince her that she must help us."

Delane had both eyes wide open now. Talina reached

Dronish

out and offered her hand to the Nephilius half, but the warrior got to her feet without any assistance. She wasn't rude about it, though, bestowing Talina with the semblance of a smile. All of us stood around Sapha.

I stared at the flickering eyelids of the Dronish half, the jewels embedded in her dark skin sparkling in the sunlight. I just knew she was going to be the toughest half-Walker to bring into the fold.

She came awake in a fast motion, her eyes fluttering open right before she slammed both hands over them and started to scream.

"What's that light?" She repeated the words over and over. "Burns. I can't see."

Talina was wringing her hands together. "We need to move her inside. The sun's too bright for her eyes."

I was moving toward her when Ria stepped in. "I can help with that."

With a flick of her wrists the Regali queen raised her hands above her head and vines started to rise and swirl around us. The sacred animals stepped back even further. They had obviously decided to wait on the outside of whatever Ria was creating.

I swallowed loudly; a cage of greenery swirled and twirled up, surrounding us in a dome. Darkness descended as the plants interlocked, blocking most of the light. The space inside was thankfully not that small. There was plenty of room between us and the edges of the ever moving wall of green. But still, it kind of felt like being eaten alive. I paused at the sounds of growls rocking through the air around us. The moment I was cut off from his sight, Cerberus wasn't happy.

"I'm okay, Cere," I said loudly.

The low rumbles slowed before dying off all together.

Unable to stop myself, I reached out and caressed one of the vines, and then turned to the Regali half. "You have a wicked power." I let the smallest of grins cross my lips, and she returned my gesture.

"I know."

Sapha's shrieks had ceased the moment the vines had enclosed us, but she continued to breathe in long ragged draws. And she hadn't opened her eyes again.

I crouched down closer to her. "We've blocked the sun, Sapha." My voice was low; I was trying not to startle her. "Breathing will get easier. There's more oxygen here, but the lightheadedness will fade soon."

Her Walker side would kick in and adjust her vitals so that she was no longer disoriented. Eventually she seemed to calm. Her inhalations and exhalations smoothed out. She removed the hand from over her eyes. Her pupils darted around, taking in the cage above our heads.

Finally she locked onto my face. "Where have you brought me?" Her clipped, accented words were sharp, and she used them like weapons, flinging them at me. "How could you steal me away from Dronish? I need to avenge Marl, kill my mother, and put an end to that vampiric race once and for all."

Fury cleared her throat and tilted her head to the side. "You want to kill every single one? But they're your people; you're half Drone."

At this point we were met with twin beams of red, her anger spilling over as she captured each one of our gazes. She got to her feet, her disorientation disappearing under pure rage.

"They are nothing to me. Nothing!" she shrieked. "My mother tried to kill me. They would all have killed me for my energy. They need to be destroyed for their own good, and the good of anything innocent that crosses their path."

I took a step closer, getting in her face a bit. "That might be true. Possibly they're of no use in this star system. But what makes you think that's your decision to make? If they're not supposed to exist, then they won't; that's how the great balance works. It's not your job or mine – we don't have the right or the power." I wasn't sure what words to use to make her understand.

Her lips thinned out, her hands clenching into fists at her side.

"Are you trying to tell me that, if the Drones are supposed to die, time will simply take care of that problem? That this war they're in will most probably destroy them?" She'd understood the most important part. "I don't accept that."

Okay, maybe not.

"What about Marl?" Ria took over the negotiations.

Sapha snarled, an actual animal snarl. "He's dead."

Ria's beautiful features softened. "I know he is, but there must be so many young like him, young who are pretty innocent. You would damn them all?"

Sapha's eyes squished tightly closed, and her swallow was audible.

"Are the Drones innately bad?" Fury asked.

Great. Seemed as if now we were going to have the bluntest person, besides Lucy, trying to convince her.

"What do you mean?" Sapha's expression was blank again now.

"I mean, you seem to be hell-bent on punishing them for something that's simply their nature. They have to consume energy to live. It doesn't seem as if they try to be evil. They're surviving. It's their nature."

Sapha blinked a few times in rapid succession. And I could tell that she had never thought of it in that manner before. Score one for blunt.

"Stop talking!" she finally shrieked, clutching her head.

"Lower the vines," I said to Ria.

She raised her hands and, reversing her previous actions, started to retract the cage above our heads. Slowly, the sunlight filtered through the gaps.

As the beams of light washed through our group, Sapha was distracted from her outrage. Then, the stunning ocean came into view, the tranquil blues and greens of the water mixing with the white wash of waves.

Sapha almost fell to her knees, her gaze locked out into the distance. As she stumbled I caught her, my hands sliding across the dampness of her skin. Her head swung around and the stricken expression told me everything. She was so far out of her depth. She'd lived in darkness, alone. She did not know how to handle the emotion.

"There is so much power here. Life forces are so strong." Her lithe frame shook.

"You don't have to be alone any longer," I said and, with instinct driving me, I gently encircled her with my arms.

Sapha resisted the hug at first. I could actually feel the warring inside her. She wanted to shove me away, but despite the tension, she did not move from my arms. It took her quite a few minutes, but with a whoosh of air

Dronish

she relaxed and pretty much fell into me. I held her tighter.

Walkers crave touch. We cherish the strength of another's energy, using it to recharge our own. And something told me, in the world of Drones trying to kill her, Sapha had never had much love or touch. I let her decide when the hug would end, even though it went more than a few beats over uncomfortable for me.

Cerberus nudged my side and I knew the hound wanted to get in on the action. I reached out and patted his closest head. Sapha pulled back at that point. She didn't seem thrown by a dog with two heads. Although she kept wary eyes on him as she stepped back.

Her eyes continued to be drawn to the ocean, even as she started talking again. "I think maybe you need to tell me everything, from the start, and don't lie to me. I will know."

I exchanged a glance with Talina. Her gentle expression almost creased into laughter, but I knew she would never laugh at another so openly. She was too nice. Fury, on the other hand, was not so much. Attitude was something Walkers had inherently, and it amused us when the half-Walkers got their 'tude on.

I interrupted Fury's chuckling by starting the story.

I explained about my life on Earth, how I found First World, the Seventine, prophecy, seven worlds, and the big battle that was ensuing. I went into a little detail about the lalunas, but left Josian out of it. It didn't really matter to the story, and she was already so untrusting. Each of the half-Walkers had their chance to speak. They told her about their worlds, the destruction they had seen because of the laluna and the Seventine, and described the bond and powers we had together.

Delane finished by explaining about our ability to trace, thankfully not giving her detailed instructions yet. Sapha was already a massive flight risk.

By the end of the conversation, the Drone was still calm. "Show me something," she said. "Something that proves even one point of this story."

I didn't wait for any ideas. I threw out my tethers and connected to the five females standing around me. For the first few moments the rush of our power was almost deafening. It took me a while to orientate myself and come back from the power high. I wasn't even sure what it would be like when all seven of us came together. Probably we'd explode from sheer energy.

We're connected, I said. *And in this form I can control the power, elevate all of our gifts, or just an individual one.*

I sent power along the line to each girl, one after another.

I'm fire, Fury said as the blue flames rocketed into the sky.

Water. Talina was next, her whirlpools swirling.

Air. Delane's whirly wind was scary.

Earth. Ria didn't really need to demonstrate after the vine cage, but the shooting of greenery all around was still pretty awesome.

I was about to add conduit, but Sapha spoke first.

Shadow. Her mental voice was low and shaky.

I sent energy into her and the dark mass of eerie blackness left her body and swirled above our heads.

Holy mother of all. I was speechless. Our powers were

Dronish

... remarkable. And I still couldn't decide who had the most awesome.

THE SIX OF us spent the rest of the afternoon using our elemental energy. Both separately and tethered together. It amazed me that the more we used our gifts, the faster and stronger we became. Like a muscle that needed to be exercised, we were building strength and force.

"Enough!" Fury finally bellowed, collapsing back onto the sand. "I'm starving. Feed me now, Supes."

I laughed, and clutched at my own stomach as it too growled in protest. I raised my eyes to meet Sapha's gaze. The Dronish half was still standoffish, prickly. Although, her pleasure when her power was elevated had been clear. Not to mention, there was something else brewing in her red eyes, something she was pondering.

"Using our powers requires us to increase our sustenance intake. You must be starving, Sapha?" I softened my gaze. "Do you want some food?"

She stared at me blankly, the stones around her eyes flashing in the sunlight of First World.

"What's food?" She blinked a few times.

Everyone in the clearing stopped dead. I opened and closed my mouth a few times. Sapha hadn't been kidding us. She stood there, her expression expectant, waiting for our answer.

Finally I recovered. "How do you recharge your energy?"

I took a step closer, which caused her to take a step back. Okay, still didn't want me in her personal space.

Her eyes flicked between my face and Fury's – who'd

come to stand beside me – as she tried to answer. "I use the energy in this land. The sun, the ground, every grain of this rough dirt ..." She kicked out at the sand. "I am so full of energy I need for nothing else."

"Well, shut the freaking door," Fury snorted. "Now I'm officially jealous. Sapha's self-sustaining."

Sapha's eyes widened, showcasing every facet of their unusual color. "Are you saying that you all need something more than the abundance of energy in your land?"

A wicked grin crossed my face. Seemed it was time to demonstrate the amazing power of chocolate.

AN HOUR later we had reached the conclusion that food was not Sapha's thing. The rest of us ate everything that wasn't tied down in Lallielle's kitchen, but no matter what the Drone tried, it ended up coming back out of her mouth.

Cerberus and Lina had abandoned the house and were outside on the beach again. I think it was all of the gagging from Sapha which had caused their exodus. I sort of wanted to join them.

"I don't understand." Sapha's dark skin was a strange khaki shade now. It was chameleon-like, changing color at her will. "If I should be able to eat, why does my body reject it?"

Delane – who held a plain bread roll in her hand – reached inside, past her stoic warrior, and found some empathy. "Take your time. You'll adjust. We didn't eat on Nephilius – my home planet – either. The clouds sustained us through prolonged contact with bare feet. But I've had to adjust since joining with Abby." She shrugged. "I don't love food the way the others seem to, but it has its appeals."

"It took me a long time too." Talina waved an apple-like-fruit around. "We don't eat much on Spurn and initially the First World food was too much for my stomach. But now, I love the variety."

And she did, despite still preferring her cucreamer fruit and krillonia, the shrimplike planktonic crustacean from her home. Each of the half-Walkers ate a variety of food, but for the most part preferred that which was closest to what came from their home planets. Ria, for example, was very big into fruit and root-like plants. Even though she was all about nature, she accepted that this was part of the great cycle; she needed to eat to survive.

Sapha's dark features paled further. The green was distinct now. She stared down at the foods littering the dining table. "I think it is going to take me a long time to adjust to this. I don't feel any urge to eat."

And she probably wouldn't feel the urge, since she didn't actually need the food for energy.

"Do you have a sucker thing, like the other Drones?" This was something I'd been wondering since first seeing her.

Sapha shook back her purple hair. It was so straight and silky, not one fly-around strand. Something to thank our half-Walker genes for. "No, I have no need for their archaic way of energy transference. My very skin works in the same manner."

Fury leaned across the table. "Well, that's good. That little thing was seriously freaky." Her lack of tact was in full force today. "I'm going to have nightmares thinking about one of those coming at me."

Sapha narrowed her eyes, and I wanted to kick Fury under the table. Did she have to insult the girl's home world? We were already on a knife edge keeping her with us. As a distraction I pushed back my chair and stood.

"Come with me, Sapha, there's something I want to show you."

She continued to glare at the Crais half, but did rise to her feet with the others. The five girls followed me into the large front hall bathroom. Reaching out, I gently touched the dark material on Sapha's shoulders. She jumped, but before she could pull away I guided her across the space, letting her go in front of the mirror. Sapha gasped as our reflections flashed back at her.

"What is this witchery?" She clutched her face, her eyes widening as she noticed the way her reflection mimicked every move she made.

"This is a mirror," I said. "It echoes back exactly what's in front of it." Reaching down, I flicked open the clasp on my necklace. It was time to find out her clan. "And this is the Walker mark I was telling you about, the same as I wear, but yours will only be visible in the light of moonstale."

Sapha had never even mentioned my permanent marks, but since she and the Drones had stones and such littering their faces ... she probably didn't think they were strange.

"Supes having permanent marks is decidedly unfair," Fury grumbled. She'd been lamenting this since the moment she'd found out she was half-Walker.

As the yellow light splashed around the room, marks emerged across all the faces in the mirror. Black tribal on Talina, gray swirls on Fury, purple square patterns on Ria, golden sunbeams on Delane and, as we stared at Sapha, white dots started to scatter across her dark skin. A stunning contrast with her coloring.

"Gai," I breathed. "You're from the Walker clan of Gai. Your princeps is Jedi."

Which reminded me that I needed to find the dark-skinned princeps. He was off doing research and trying to find facts about the lalunas and the origin of the Walkers. I was hoping he had discovered something which could help us in this battle.

Sapha was staring at herself. Just staring. She hadn't said anything, but that look she'd had before, calculating, was still in her eyes.

"Will you stay and help us in this battle?" I decided to go with blunt again. I had a lot of things to do and no time to baby these half-Walkers. "We're the only thing that stands between the destruction of seven worlds and billions of inhabitants."

She reached up and rubbed at her face, as if she could remove the white dots littering it. There was no immediate answer, but finally she spoke. "I will stay with you for now, but I promise nothing. I have never trusted anyone besides Marl, and he is dead. So now I trust only myself."

I forced myself not to curse. Why were these freaking Walkers so freaking stubborn? Frig! Knowing there was nothing I could do to force her hand, I simply nodded.

"Thank you. I would appreciate it if you did stick around, help us develop our powers, and I believe you'll come to trust us."

"We're a family." Talina smiled, her emerald hair flowing around her. "The only half-Walkers in existence, connected at a cellular level. And we're so very happy that you're one of us."

Sapha tilted her head to the side, her features softening as if something Talina had said resonated with her. Something more than any of the previous information we'd imparted to her.

Delane straightened, her expression unchanging, her stance rigid and uncomfortable. "I think we should get back to the war council. We need updates, and to check in with the training."

Delane was taking her warrior-Walker role seriously. Which was why she was so fundamentally important to our battle plans. And I agreed: it was time to get back to the war council and see what had been happening.

8

Sapha was a quiet, watchful type of individual. She didn't ask questions. Instead she just observed with those ruby-toned eyes. She showed no surprise when I opened a doorway and everyone, including Cerberus and Lina, marched through. She didn't even ask about the animals, and I knew they had to be odd to her. She would most probably get her own sacred guide soon. I wondered if that would help or hinder us in getting her to stay. I'd impart this piece of information to her later. I didn't want to overwhelm her with too many details.

As we traversed the doorway, I wondered if she would freak out inside the vacuum of the Walker paths. Nope, not even one flicker of unease on her face. Either she was unfazed by everything, or she was an expert at masking her true feelings.

The door exited us onto the edge of the war council field. As I straightened and my gaze washed over the scene, my eyes widened, lips falling open. The area had changed dramatically in the time we'd been gone. I could see at least ... fifteen distinct areas – zones that had been set up. I knew seven would be for the Walker clans, one for pixies, one for faeries, and another for the woodland sprites. There was an area for Lucas and his First World royal guardians. But I wasn't sure who else was here.

Fury halted me at the edge of the chaos. "How long are you going to be in the camp, Supes? Can you come with me to Crais? We need to look at that area."

I nodded a few times. "I just need to check in with Josian and Jedi. After that, I'm all yours."

I was also hoping to see Brace, but I wouldn't hold my breath. Being without him was moving past pain to some sort of extra level of torture. If I saw him again, I wasn't sure I could stop myself from reforming the bond.

Unexpectedly Fury leaned in and kissed my cheek. I blinked at her a few times.

She grinned at my surprise. "You're doing a great job, my friend. Tether to me when you're free to leave. I'm going to see if I can track down my father and ask a few new questions I've thought of."

I managed to give her a half-wave as she disappeared into the crowd.

Talina was also blinking at the retreating Crais half. "Okay, who the heck was that?" she finally said as she turned wide brown eyes in my direction. "Do you think Fury's been replaced by a doppelganger?"

I nodded my head more than once. "I have no freaking idea. But I'm not going to question a good thing."

Talina chuckled a few times. "Are you okay with me heading back to Spurn soon? I know you're super busy, but I'd love it if you could pop over there too. We can check those few areas Ladre is worried about."

"No problem," I said. I didn't have much time, but I'd find it for Fury and Talina.

She grinned broadly. "Great! I'll wait by the lake, near the Doreen area." With those words, Talina was gone.

That left me with Delane, Ria, and Sapha.

Sapha looked around with interest. There were many milling around us and she appeared to be observing each very closely. "So somewhere in this crowd is my patriarch?"

It took me a moment to understand what she'd said; sometimes her accent was heavy.

"Possibly." I pushed back a few of my curls. "The man who fathered you will be from the clan of Gai." I pointed across the field to where the banner of Gai was high and waving in the light, cool breeze. "I have to head to that clan to speak with their princeps. I'll introduce you."

I expected her to protest, but to my surprise she simply nodded her head.

"What about you two?" I shifted my gaze to the Nephilius and Regali halves.

Delane straightened, her hands dropping to the twin axes she wore crossed over her armor. We'd dumped the cloaks long ago, which was part of the reason that I was feeling so chilly all of a sudden. First World was rarely cold, but the breeze had a bite to it that day.

"I'm heading to the main tent. It was set up for the leaders of the different races and clans to convene and discuss the impending war. I need to know what's happened in our absence." Delane leveled her gaze on me. "I expect you to come for an update before this day is out."

I sucked in a deep, but slightly ragged breath. The days were getting too short for the list of obligations I had.

"I'll do my best, Delane. Thanks for keeping on top of the battle plans."

With a salute she left us, her stunning unicorn following close behind. I reached out and rested both hands and my head against Cerberus' neck. My faithful hellhound gave me his strength for a moment, allowed me to center my thoughts. I was starting to see that I couldn't be everywhere, and it was good to have trusted people that I could send out in my place. Finally I straightened – received a lick up the side of the face – and turned to the last two.

Ria was shifting from foot to foot, looking a little more agitated than usual. The vines that emerged from the ivy print across her hair were starting to spring free, which mostly only happened when she was worried. Furrowing my brow, I reached out and gripped her hand. She returned the squeeze.

"I need to head back to Regali." Her voice was low and urgent. "Call it queen's intuition or something more but ... I have a bad feeling."

I worried at my lip. "Go, Ria, make sure Artwon is okay. It's probably time for you to check in on the progress of the sacred tree death and give them some of your energy anyways. It's important not to abandon your people."

I didn't need her right then, and we all knew I could

call as soon as anything happened. The beauty of tracing was that we could be in another place instantly.

"Thank you, Abby. Tether to me as soon as you move out again. Or if the Seventine attack."

I knew she had not forgotten the way the Seventine had possessed those humanoids and severed the tether to her sacred tree on Regali. Now her beloved forest was dying and the only way to reverse that was to lock away the Seventine again.

After Ria had left it was just Sapha, Cerberus, and me.

"Stay close," I warned her. I was not keen on her disappearing on me.

We set off into the main part of the field. There were so many mingling around that there was no clear path. It was just getting difficult to cross when Cerberus let out a frustrated growl and moved in front of us. Within two leaps he was at his huge size again. I worked hard to hide my grin as those lingering around dived out of his way. It was that or be squished by a ton of puppy.

Cerberus had that twinkle in his dark eyes as he plowed a path through the crowds. He enjoyed his ability to part a mass. And so did I. He led us straight to the front banner of Gai. Clever puppy must have overheard the previous conversation.

There were a few Walkers lingering out the front.

I got a head nod from the first one I stopped in front of.

"Can you tell me where Jedi is?" I asked him.

His reply came without hesitation. "Jedi and Josian are in the research and library zone." His low voice was rough, his accent thick.

He directed my gaze to a massive white tented area. Unlike the other zones, this one had walls securing the perimeter.

"Thank you." I returned his head nod and, using Cerberus' bulk again, we crossed the hundred yards to get to the white tent.

I followed my hellhound around three quarters of the dwelling. So far there had not been a single opening. Going out on a limb, I'd say they didn't want visitors. Finally we stopped at the first possible entrance we'd seen so far: a thick zipper, which was secured all the way to the ground. How secretive. Reaching down, I took the wide silver zipper in my hands and slowly lifted it upwards. Sapha still said nothing. She was so quiet I kept forgetting she was there. In fact, if it wasn't for her particular shadowy power brushing against me, she'd most probably blend right into the scenery and disappear.

Her chameleon nature seemed to make it easy for her to go unnoticed. Sure, her unusual looks had garnered a few glances as we walked around, but it was nothing like the rest of us halves usually received.

The zipper was heavy. I had to yank quite forcefully, but I finally managed to get it almost to the top. I wasn't tall enough to reach any further.

Before I could step through the entrance, a newly shrunk Cerberus nudged me aside and took the first steps into the tented area. Over-protective hound always had to go first.

I followed him in, making sure Sapha's energy never disappeared from my back. Something told me she was considering doing a runner again. As the sacred animal moved further inside, the large room he'd been blocking from my line of vision came into view. I paused, confusion rushing through me. I had to blink a few times and make sure I was seeing everything correctly. It was a library, rivaling that of the pixie queen's. The room was well lit – despite the lack of natural light – from a few high-placed energy domes. It was cool and still inside, as if the very air was refined and filtered to keep all these precious books safe.

I started forward, through the high shelves, heading toward the round center that everything else seemed to span out from. There were about a dozen tables and chairs gathered in this section, and camped out at the largest were three familiar Walkers: Jedi, Grantham, and Josian. My father's head shot up the moment we moved into view.

"Baby girl," he boomed, before jumping to his feet, a grin crossing his unusually haggard features.

I ran forward and threw myself into his arms. I really needed some Walker hugs. My lack of melding bond was beating at my shredded heart and soul. The pain was getting a little hard to deal with.

"How are you doing?" I asked as I pulled back a few moments later.

His throat moved as he swallowed loudly. I could see him composing himself before he eventually answered. "Everything's fine, Aribella. I've mended fences with most of the Walker community and the princeps. It's just ... Lalli." His eyes flicked away for a moment. "She won't talk to me and she's blocked me from her mind." A half-grin crossed his face. "Not that I don't deserve her ire."

I was a little surprised that Mom was still so angry

with him. "I'll talk to her, Dad." I hugged him again, just because he needed it.

He kissed my forehead. "No need for you to get in the middle of this." And that was the last he would discuss about Lallielle.

In that moment I remembered Sapha.

I turned back to find her so I could introduce the Dronish half-Walker, but she was nowhere to be seen. My heart rate increased minutely and if it wasn't for the fact that I knew she didn't possess the knowledge yet to trace to Dronish, I'd have been a little more panicky. As it was, I was about to dash back to the entrance, when a shadow movement caught my eye just to the left of where we were standing. I recognized her blur. It was tucked in between two large book shelves. She hadn't run. She was cloaking herself again.

I strode across and, as I neared her hiding spot, her shadowy energy called to mine. Even though no one else could sense half-Walker energy, I often felt the girl's powers. I stopped right in front of her and, like last time, the moment I searched for her in the shadows, I could make out her shape.

I calmed my voice. Already I knew she reacted badly to unexpected noises. "Sapha, you don't have to be afraid. No one will hurt you in this room. And it's time to meet your princeps."

She dropped the shadows. Her rapidly blinking red eyes were the first image to appear, followed by the rest of her cloaked figure. "It is habit that I hide."

The three Walkers were standing where we had left them, their eyes curious, but expressions unreadable as I led Sapha back toward them. We halted at the edge of the large table. I didn't want to overwhelm her by getting too close to the powerful men. Each of them exuded large waves of energy. I was used to the way it buffeted off me when I got too close, but I knew the Drone would be afraid.

"This is Sapha, the half-Walker from Dronish." I didn't touch her, simply swept my hand close to her body. "She's unsure about helping us in this battle. For now she wants to learn and observe." I locked eyes with Jedi's unusual silver-ringed pupils. "And she's from your clan; she's Gai."

A grin crossed his features, perfect white teeth shining at us. "I thought you'd never get around to finding my half," he teased me, his infectious chuckle filling the space.

I wrinkled my nose at him in return. Smartass.

The very dominant male left his side of the table, moving around to stand next to Sapha. His large frame dwarfed her. "Welcome to Gai. I'm Jedi, your princeps, and it's my pleasure to meet you."

Sapha looked terrified, her features frozen. Jedi didn't let that faze him. He still reached out and took her hand. "If you ever need anything, or help – if anyone bothers you, then you can always come to me. I'm here for you at any time."

There Jedi went again with his sensual and shameless flirting. By now I was pretty sure he meant nothing by it. It was just his way.

Sapha pulled her hand free. "I will keep that in mind," she said indifferently, and Grantham couldn't hide his grin.

"About time we found a woman who was immune to Jedi's charms." His voice was loud in the tented room.

Jedi narrowed his dark eyes on the Relli princeps. "I'm starting to get a complex around these half-Walker females."

I rolled my eyes at him before turning back to my father. "What have you discovered? Any information that can help us with the Seventine?"

Josian's features sobered as he sat in his chair again. "Actually, we have found a few interesting facts." He started to shift through the paperwork and books littered across the table. Jedi and Grantham also retook their seats.

I pulled out a chair on the opposite side. Sapha sat next to me. We were about four feet away from the men.

"Alright, hit me with it." I tented my hands in front of me.

We were running out of time, and I knew that finding the last half-Walker was going to be a challenge. Earth was an energy dead zone. I'd be limited in my power and it was a damn big world to hope I stumbled across the human half-Walker.

Jedi spoke first. "Continuing on from our last conversation, I've discovered more information on the origin of Walkers and the first scroll. The original seven and the Seventine were definitely allies, friends, companions – whatever you want to call it. They worked together on many events. Their actions resulted in the first tendrils of life on most of the seven worlds. They were fundamentally important in the creation of the races that govern these planets."

I was still finding this alliance hard to believe. Jedi continued.

"Like the lalunas, it took a long time for the Seventine to lose their way, for their power as gods to corrupt that which should have been incorruptible. And that was when the originals knew that they needed a plan."

A burning of excitement started to flash through my blood.

"If the Seventine can be locked away, the lalunas can too, right?" The words blurted from me, interrupting Jedi as he started to speak again.

All eyes locked on me.

"Yes," Josian said. "In fact, we think we've come up with a plan to lock the lalunas into the very walls of the Seventine prison. If we manage this, it will strengthen that prison so that no one will ever be able to free the Seventine again.

I was really excited now. "Will that mean the last three Seventine can't be released?"

Some of my joy fell as all three shook their heads.

"No, there are cracks in the prison that not even the lalunas will fill," Jedi said. "I mean, if we return all seven of the Seventine back to their prison, and the lalunas are already part of the security, it will be impenetrable for all eternity. Never again will we face this sort of battle."

Okay, I understood a little better now. It would all work only if we could re-imprison those Seventine which were already out, repair the cracks their release had left.

"An impenetrable fortress," Grantham said, "for all of eternity."

I was totally down with that. Yes, yes, and hell yes.

"What do we have to do?" I asked, barely contained excitement in my tone.

I'd shifted my entire body forward and was almost across the table. Not only would we eliminate the stones which held my father captive, and were preventing Brace and me from melding – a bond which was most probably essential to winning the battle with the Seventine – but we were going to make the prison so strong no entity could ever escape it again.

The men paused then, exchanging a few glances before fixing their eyes on me.

Oh no, there was a catch. Dammit, why was there always a catch?

Jedi broke the silence. "The only way I can find at the moment is an exchange of power. Which would mean, to merge the stones with the prison, we would have to free at least one of the Seventine. We would pull the Seventine along a pathway, and in return the lalunas would enter that same path and form one with the prison. They would fuse with the wall and their energy would strengthen the jail."

Shit. Freeing a Seventine was the complete opposite of our goals.

"Are you sure this is the only way?" I huffed. "I'm not sure any plan which involves freeing one of those creatures is a good one. They get so much stronger with each release."

Jedi's eyes dropped for a moment. "You're right, but we have to weigh up the positives versus the negatives of this plan. Yes, we'll be freeing a Seventine, which is a definite step backwards, but Josian is sure that you need to be melded to Brace to have any chance of beating the

Seventine. Not to mention the fact we're securing the prison and ensuring any other plans the laluna might have will be thwarted. In the end, locking them away might be the first step in giving us a fighting chance to win."

I sighed. "So, weighing up the pros and cons, we should be better off even with another Seventine gaining freedom."

There were nods all around, but I saw the doubts also. It was so hard to know. None of us was omnipotent.

"Do we have all the stones yet?" I asked Josian.

He nodded. "Yes, they were relatively easy to find. The three of us spent the last twelve hours gathering them."

"How do you make them stay put?" I asked, meeting his unblinking bronze eyes.

He grinned. "Your laluna is keeping them secured." He gestured to a locked cabinet that I hadn't noticed before, back near the edge of the tent. "All we have to do now is figure out the best way to do this ritual."

I thought of something. "What about Tenni?" Surely they hadn't been able to gather that little hive.

Josian's face fell, his eyes drooping at the corners. He both loved and loathed his laluna, and his heart was still hurting. "All original powers are the same. If you lock enough of them away, the rest will follow. Because we have all the stones except ... mine, the gravitational pull will be strong enough to bring Tenni to us."

Similar to our original plan for the Seventine. Of course, too many of them were free now.

There was still a lot of tension riding the three men.

"What else aren't you telling me?"

Jedi rushed out the next lot of bad news all at once.

"We need the Seventine to agree to this plan. They'll have to join their energy with one of us."

I sank back into my chair, some of the joy and excitement deflating from me.

"Why would they agree?" I asked. "Why would the Seventine risk the odds that the prison becomes any stronger? Would it be worth it for one free brother?"

Jedi shuffled more paper before pulling a sheet free.

"Firstly, they have to be getting desperate. They're running out of time, and a lot of energy is required to free the last three. And secondly, I suggest whoever asks does so in a way where they're sort of hiding the fact that merging the lalunas with the prison will make it the strongest jail in our star system. Instead focus on how it benefits the Seventine, namely by freeing a brother. It shouldn't be that hard. They don't fear the power of the lalunas. In their arrogance, they believe that nothing trumps the Seventine."

I thought of all the times that the first Seventine had found me, contacting me in my head. It had said there was a link between us, which was something I'd always shied far away from. But maybe I could use it to my advantage.

I sighed. "The first Seventine has been trying, for a while, to get me to join them, and the other half-Walker females by default. It says that we're allies and that we should be on the same side."

All eyes were locked on me, including Sapha's. The Drone was probably really confused about then.

"There's some sort of connection between my power and the first's, something from when it possessed Brace and absorbed some of our melding bond." I continued to relay my thoughts aloud. "Can we use this connection? I think I'm the best chance we have to put this into play."

Josian tented his hands under his chin, looking thoughtful. "Yes, I think we can make this work, but we need the plan to be foolproof before we approach them. We'll only have one shot."

"I'll continue this research then." Grantham's exotic green eyes shone with a fire. "We need the ritual words to be correct." He stood abruptly. "I'm going to speak with Nos. He's the visionary. He might have some inherited information for us."

After dropping a hand onto Josian's shoulder, and imparting one last smile around the room, the Relli Walker left the library. I had forgotten that Ria's father was the visionary, which is the soothsayer of the Walker world. He was definitely someone who should have information.

Jedi handed me the piece of parchment that he'd picked up before. I took the yellowed paper, holding it carefully.

"This is the ritual to lock away the Seventine," he said. "I'm a little concerned about the effect this might have on the half-Walkers."

I glanced down, and in a sort of scrawl, cursive version of English, was a list. It detailed the steps needed to draw the Seventine into the prison and lock them away. It read like this:

1. Requires the seven original powers.
2. Connect powers and call on the energy of the ancients and mother to all.
3. Expel power and blood from all seven.

> Requires fifty percent of life blood and equal amounts of power.
> 4. Repeat the words: Terra, ignis, aqua, ventus, spiritus, umbra.
> 5. Lay a seal with your energy, form the circle that will encase the walls and repeat above words followed by: coniungere, carcere, postestas, septum.

I spoke the last words aloud, my head flying up to meet Jedi's concerned gaze. His brows had lowered over his eyes as he watched me in silence.

Josian broke the moment. "All of those words are in the original language. The six elements and the last four represent conduit, power, prison, and finally the Seventine. It will draw in their energy and lock them away again."

I stared down at the paper. "So the only thing stopping us now is that we don't have the seven half-Walkers?"

Jedi and Josian both nodded.

My father spoke again. "Pretty much, and it'll be much harder and require a lot more of your blood and power if all seven of them are free. If we can perform this ritual before they're fully released ... well, that's a much better option."

Sapha shifted in her chair. For the first time since we'd sat down, she spoke. "I think what you are saying is that, to perform this ritual after all of these ... Seventy things ... are released, will cost us half-Walkers our lives. All of our power and blood. But if we can do it before their final release, we have a chance to survive, correct?"

It was in that moment I realized how much she truly observed in her quiet little pose. Quiet didn't mean stupid. Sapha took in every piece of information and, in typical Walker fashion, her brain worked superfast and arranged the pieces in logical order.

Jedi's lips straightened into a scowl of sorts. "Yes, unfortunately it looks that way. Which is why the original seven were no longer able to hold their Walker forms. They poured much into the prison, and the rest of their energy scattered in the star-system."

Scattered until it became part of us seven half-Walkers.

Sapha didn't say anything, but we did lock eyes for a moment, and I saw plenty unsaid in those red depths. This was probably not the conversation we should be having with someone a little unsure about joining our cause. I was about to say something reassuring when a familiar tapping sensation caressed my shielded head.

Brace. I dropped the barrier without hesitation.

Hey, Red.

I let out a relieved sigh, not caring if everyone else in the room thought I was a freak.

What's happening, Princeps? I did my best to keep my tone light.

Missing you, and kicking the shit out of my faithful subjects to keep myself sane.

I was almost ninety percent sure he was kidding. I let out a few chuckles. He continued speaking.

I've found out something interesting about the lalunas. Not only are Tenni and the rest of her little faeries connected, but the fourteen stones are also each connected. If we trap in the majority, the rest will be pulled along.

I smiled; we were all on the same track. *Yep, Dad has collected the thirteen stones. We're holding them here, and Grantham is off determining the exact ritual we need.*

Brace paused. I could sense his brain ticking over. *What's your plan then, to contain the thirteen until the ritual?*

At the moment my laluna has them all tied down here – I broke off, sending my senses outward for a second.

Jedi had started to speak again.

I halted him by holding up my hand to indicate I was busy right then. He frowned but paused.

I returned my attention to Brace. *After we get them to the mountain we're going to trap them in the walls of the Seventines' prison. Jedi and Josian have been researching and, if we do that, then their prison will be virtually unbreakable. Never again will the Seventine be freed ...* I trailed off.

Brace picked up on my unease. *I sense a 'but' in there. What's the catch?*

The man knew me way too well. *We're going to need the Seventines' help, and one of them will be freed in exchange.*

He was quiet for a few moments, before answering. *That's a risk worth taking, in my opinion.*

After hearing the princeps explain the pros and cons, I agreed too, but still I worried that we were making a mistake. To be fair, Brace and I weren't the most unbiased in this situation.

I have to go, baby. Brace's voice lowered. *My men are searching for ... this room in Que's house. They think they might have found something.*

Be careful. I miss you. I wanted to add more but kept it short.

Miss you too, Red. We're going to fix this, I swear it to you. I love you. He faded out of my mind.

Dronish

I tightened the barriers again. They were so much weaker now that I was unmelded to Brace. I had to work hard to keep myself shielded all the time.

I was about to rejoin the conversation in the room when another tapping sounded on my barrier. Cool, watery energy washed over me.

Talina.

I dropped the barriers.

Abbs, I need you at the lake right now!

She sounded frantic, and then she was gone from my head. I jumped to my feet and that instant Cerberus – who'd been asleep beside the table – was at my side.

"I have to go," I said to the room. "Talina needs me at the lake."

Josian and Jedi were also on their feet. Sapha didn't move.

"Come on." I attempted to lessen my bluntness, but when I was worried, I lacked tact.

With unnecessary slowness she stood. I turned away. Trusting that the Dronish half would keep up, I took off. Cerberus stayed by my side, his bulk useful as we plowed through the crowds toward the Doreen area. I needed to get to the lake.

I entered under the banner, and crossed through the tents and along the eating zones. My heart rate slowed a little as long emerald hair came into sight. Talina was standing, as still as a statue, on the edge of the crystal-clear lake. She didn't seem hurt and no one was around her. Water streamed off her as if she'd just exited the lake.

It wasn't until I reached her side and she turned large brown eyes in my direction that I noticed the trickle of what looked like tears trailing down her pink cheeks.

"You should have told me how amazing it was," she said, her voice no more than a whisper.

I furrowed my brow, staring around trying to figure out what she was talking about.

Sapha, Josian, and Jedi fell in next to Cerberus. Everyone had followed me.

Then I saw it.

Rising from the depths of the lake, silver and emerald sparkles reflecting brightly in the First World sun, a scaled form ascended slowly, and I finally deduced what had happened. Talina had found her sacred animal. As the tip of its head broke the water, I raised a hand to cover my open mouth. Unbelievable.

"He came to me when I was under the water." Talina stepped closer, as if she were being drawn to the creature. "I'm not going to lie, I freaked out at first and reached for you ... but then he touched me and I knew the gift."

As majestic as the other sacred animals, Talina's bonded one was a water dragon. He was massive, his shadowed form in the water the size of a huge elephant, but longer and svelte. He moved toward us without pause. His head was sleek, with a large jaw filled with razor-sharp teeth. His neck was long, sharp fin-like protrusions emerging all the way down to where his body disappeared under the water.

"It's Apollo." Josian sounded both astonished and delighted. "He's often in the dragon-lizard variety. Seems he chose a water version this time to complement Talina."

"Apollo," Talina breathed. "Perfect."

It took no time at all for the water dragon to cross the expanse of lake. As the land beneath him tapered up to shallow ground, more of his body emerged from the water. On either side of the fins, at the join between his neck and powerful front legs, he had small wings. These translucent appendages were definitely not for flying; they were far too delicate. They looked like they'd work as fins, to offer gliding assistance in the water.

The body was long, lizard-like, with fins all the way to his spiked tail. He was in shades of silver, blue, and emerald green. Hues of the ocean and strangely in tune with Talina. Stunning and deadly.

I resisted the urge to step back when he placed his large, clawed front feet onto dry land.

He had an energy similar to Lina and Cerberus', but different somehow. Sort of a little more alien or reptile-like. There was no hesitation as the colossal creature pulled himself from the water. He was downwind from where we stood, and started to head straight for us. Or, more specifically, Talina. The Spurn half-Walker also moved, as if she unable to stand still a moment longer. She met Apollo mid-way.

They stared at each other for a few brief moments, and then she reached out and, in a manner similar to Delane's, placed her hands on his long, broad, scaled snout. I knew she had said he'd touched her in the water, but this must have been their first proper contact.

Energy flared between them. Talina's emerald hair flew around her head in a graceful arc, before coming back to rest against her back. I wondered in some ways why Cerberus and I had not had such a dramatic connection. Don't get me wrong: I'd felt the bond form, but there had been no crazy energy show. Maybe it had something to do with being in pixie land. Power had definitely behaved strangely in that little prison dimension.

Once the bond was sealed, Talina and Apollo turned to make their way to us. The water dragon was shrinking as he moved, becoming less dinosaur and more horse-size. Around the same size as my hellhound.

And speaking of, Cerberus took off in a graceful gallop, both heads lolling around. He circled Apollo a few times, before pausing near the water dragon's head. Their snouts came close, and they appeared to be greeting each other. I felt a deep and strong emotion to see the sacred animals interacting with each other. There was something more there, something special that bonded them.

The same as with the half-Walker girls.

9

Sapha was fascinated by Apollo, more so than she'd been with the other two animals. I think seeing the bond form had awoken something inside her. A need she worked hard to conceal.

"So, I will get my own animal? If I stay with you," she asked as she stared and stared some more at the scaled creature.

He was as nimble on land as he'd been in the water. His large claw-tipped feet were wide and evenly balanced.

"Yes," Jedi answered her. He seemed to have taken her under his wing. "They'll come soon. I expect the next four are on their way right now."

White hair burst into our line of sight. It was Fury, and she was dragging a very reluctant Walker behind her. Her father. She must have heard Jedi's last statement.

"Oh, my god, I cannot wait until I get my animal," she said. "It's going to be something ferocious, like a dragoona or a griffin."

The girls and I had gone through many of the mythical creatures I knew from Earth. We had guessed which of them might end up being the actual sacred animals.

Lukalien's already grim features fell even more. "Don't get your hopes too high. Sometimes what we think is the best thing is sometimes the worst. The universe gives us what we need, not necessarily what we want."

Fury rolled her eyes at me. "He's full of philosophical crap like that. I'm actually not sure he is my sire after all."

Her father didn't look offended. If anything, his daughter seemed to amuse him. Oh, well, if anyone was to get him out of his shell, it would be Fury.

"You ready to go to Crais, Supes?" Fury turned to me. "I'm not sure I can be away from Dune for too much longer. I'm starting to get all cry-me-a-river on the inside."

I couldn't contain my chuckle. But I felt her pain. I was all cry-me-a-freaking-ocean on my inside.

"I just want to check on Lucy," I said. "I'll meet you back here in twenty minutes."

I knew my pixie friend was off trying to discover her faerie side, but I missed her and I wanted to make sure she was okay.

Fury nodded. "Yeah, I saw her heading into faerie land." She confirmed my thoughts. "I'll wait here and see if my animal shows up in the next little bit." She started to look around expectantly.

"I'll stay here also," Sapha said. "I would like to get to know the other females." She was edging closer to Jedi. "And I would like to learn about my Walker clan from the princeps."

Those two had bonded awfully fast, considering she was as jumpy as hell.

Dronish

Jedi's grin was hard to miss. "It's my honor to help you understand the Walker world." His tone was reassuring. He flicked his eyes from Sapha to me. "After we're finished here, I'll be back in the library."

I narrowed my eyes on him for a moment before turning to Sapha. "Just know there's no point in running. You've no idea where to go, and I can find you with our connection." It didn't hurt to remind her of these facts.

She sighed. "I won't lie, I'm a little nervous still. And I need to go back to Dronish; I need to kill my mother. But for now, I know that I have little choice, so we must learn to trust each other."

I angled my head to the side as I watched her expression morph from sad to fearful to thoughtful, and even an iota of contentment. Her expressions weren't the only things to morph either; her face also wheeled through a range of angular shapes and colors. I don't even think she realized that she did that. Transitioning through slightly different versions of herself.

I graced her with a smile. "I can agree to some of that. Trust must be earned. Neither of us should be expected to instantly have it."

Fury interrupted then. "I don't trust many people," she declared. "But Supes has a way of worming under your skin. Don't be surprised if you start thinking of her as the sister you never had."

Ah, the Crais half was always such a sweet-talker. I gave her a hug before I turned and walked away, leaving the dazzled Talina with her Apollo, and the equally dazzled Jedi with his new little half-Walker. Seemed 'dazzled' was the word of the day. Cerberus also decided to stay behind. If I had to guess, he was in the middle of an intense discussion with Apollo.

Josian fell into step with me.

"How are you doing, Dad?" I asked him again, with more seriousness to my tone this time.

He dropped some of the jovial act he'd been projecting. "I'm angry with myself and I miss your mother. Other than that, I'm fine, baby girl. I've been through worse things in my long life, and I still have all of my family alive and safe. As I said before, I'll never complain if that's the case."

"Go find Mom." I stopped under the bannered entrance to Doreen. "Never give up; never stop trying until she understands. She's hurt and feels partly responsible for not knowing what was going on."

Josian grinned then, showcasing his unblemished teeth. "Oh, baby girl, you have no idea. I'm just giving her a little breathing room for the moment, but pretty soon she's not going to know what's hit her. My determination to win back her love and trust ... well, let's say an eternity could pass and I would not cease my efforts."

I stood on tiptoes and he ducked his head so I could land a kiss on his cheek. "That's the father I know and love. Good luck, I'm off to find a little pixie."

"I should be wishing you luck then," he muttered.

I wrinkled my nose at him before turning to head across the field, away from the library area and toward the fey zone. Despite their protests, all of the fey were in the same general area, although they had separate zones, and it seemed the woodland sprites had drawn the short straw and were the neutral ground between the pixies and the faeries.

Dronish

Refis was out the front of the pixie area as I strolled past. He inclined his head. I paused for a moment, noticing he was whittling something with his trusty little dagger. Some sort of figurine was emerging from the piece of wood.

"Good day, Lady Aribella." His bland, generic voice still kind of surprised me. But I was getting used to it.

The newfound respect was a little harder to accept, though. He'd been so disdainful of me during our first few meetings, but since I was blood-bonded to his sister, he seemed to have elevated my position from that of lowly Walker.

"Hi, Refis, what's happening?" I inclined my head to the right, trying to see his carving better. "What you whittling?"

He held out the small figurine and from my new angle the visage was familiar.

"Malisna." I bobbed my head a few times. "That's a pretty great likeness."

He lowered those multi-colored rainbow eyes. "She's a little down again. Lucy has been speaking with ... the faerie." His voice dropped, his anger seeping through. "I don't want her to fall back into a depression ... I don't think I could survive that again."

I wanted to comfort him. Malisna was the only mother he'd known and she had pretty much ignored him for twenty years after Lucy, her child, had been stolen from her and dumped on Earth. It had damaged something inside him, you could see from the pain in his eyes all the way down to the break in his heart. It must be his worst nightmare to think that might happen again.

"Lucy's just curious." I tried to inflect my voice toward

sympathetic, but I wasn't sure I had achieved it. "She won't choose sides, but this doesn't mean she doesn't love Malisna. Luce and I spent most of our lives wishing for our mothers. Trust me, we won't be giving them up now."

By the time I left, Refis' mood seemed to have lifted from drown-himself-in-the-bath to watch-sappy-movies-and-cry. Throw in a bit of chocolate and he'd have a right old pity-party. Poor little pixie. Guess I hadn't been very convincing.

I continued across the grassed field, noticing that the king of the sprites was at the front of his area. I wanted to stop and quiz the handsome and lithe leader, mostly about his feelings for Malisna. But I knew neither of the monarchs would appreciate my interference, so instead I gave him a wave and continued on my journey.

The faerie banner was the strangest of all that I'd passed. Words written in bizarre foreign text and symbols. Colors that started at a dark green and shimmered along to end in a deep rich maroon. The transitioning seemed to be magical in nature; the colors were not solid but transient. Moving at will.

Faeries were eerie creatures.

I stepped across the threshold and immediately an energy encased me, taking hold and freezing me to the spot. Of course, I was stupid to think they would have no magical security or protection. The Walker areas even had alerts in place in case those from different clans crossed their territory threshold.

But just because I wasn't surprised by the security didn't mean I appreciated being held immobile. In fact my claustrophobia, which only spiked on occasions now, started to press in on me. Just tiny little trickles of unease, along with the need to wiggle and scream like a moron until freed. I was strong enough to control the panic. Just.

A few faeries emerged from whatever rock they'd been hiding under, moving in to form a circle around me. Their expressions were unchanging. They watched with little to no obvious curiosity.

My anger tipped over. Screw this, I was not powerless and I would not be made to feel as if I was.

I drew on my endless pit of energy, gathering it up into a large wave of power. With a deep breath I sent my wave of energy outwards, in one single motion of destructive light. It whooshed away, and every being in close proximity was smacked to the ground. I'd seen my father, and Brace, perform this nifty little trick before, but never thought it would be me on the end of an energy strong enough to knock others to the ground.

And yet, I was still trapped.

I was missing something here.

Power wasn't the key to freeing myself; it had to be something more. I ceased the expulsion of energy, slowing the trickle until it stopped altogether.

At this point the scattered fairies started to pull themselves up. Their previously blank expressions now ranged from fearful to full-blown pissed-off.

I was happy to note that despite my little power show, I wasn't feeling depleted. Which was a nice bonus. From all the practicing with the girls, I was stronger. I continued wiggling, trying to loosen the faerie-magic hold on me. It was frustrating. I had no more than half an inch to move within this spell. I expanded my senses, sending them from my body, to try to *see* what held me.

It was an energy cage.

A crisscrossing of power coated my body. I followed the lines as they intersected. They were long, with lots of intricate twists and turns, but finally I found a tiny little loose end. I focused my power on that section and, treating it like a tether, managed to connect my golden cord. The two ends intertwined, and suddenly I could feel every part of the foreign energy that was making up this cage. It was cold, metallic. Very different to the strong heat and earthiness of Walker power.

Without thought I sucked the power into me, filling up my well. The foreign coldness did not want to mix with my Walker power. Instead, as more of it trickled into my center, it formed its own little bubble inside me. A bubble that attached to the wall of the well.

It was a strange sensation, almost as if my energy area had turned into a filing cabinet, and the faerie magic was sitting in its own little indexed space. I knew I could grab onto it again if I needed to, but for now it was stored in its spot. I fell to the ground as the cage disappeared. I was free.

I lay face-down for a moment, trying to figure out what had just happened. That was freaking weird. Could I gather other energies and keep them stored inside for future need? Was this what I needed to do with the other original powers? Store them. But how was I supposed to find these other powers?

My thoughts were interrupted by the sound of approach. Lifting my head, I locked eyes with my favorite blond pixie.

"Abbs!" Lucy was fluttering her wings rapidly as she came toward me. Followed closely by Colton and Latinti.

I flipped over onto my back.

"Are you okay?" my best friend asked as she dropped gracefully to my side.

"Never better," I groaned, running a hand through my loose curls.

I needed to get in the habit of braiding it again, anything to help with all the grass, leaves and sticks that seemed to lodge themselves in the red depths.

I pulled myself up to stand. The gathered group pressed in closer to me. We were drawing a little too much attention, but a few hard looks from their prince had them backing up again. I was still fascinated by their varied appearance, and the obviously curious but guarded nature of their species.

"Apologies for the binding, Aribella, daughter of Josian and blood-bonded of my Lucy." Latinti was all formal as he crossed his arms across his lithely muscled chest. His dark gray silk shirt strained against the movement. "We needed additional security after Malisna decided to declare war on my testicles."

I blinked a few times in rapid succession, biting the edge of my lip to stop the broad grin that wanted to spread across. He'd said that so matter-of-factly that I'd almost wondered if I'd misheard. But no, clearly the ancient-looking man before me had a sense of humor.

"I'm starting to see the family resemblance." I raised my brows at Latinti's equally smartass daughter, Lucy.

Her smirk said it all. "We haven't progressed to father-daughter terms yet, but he's growing on me slowly."

"You should go and reassure your mother that you're okay." The faerie, who showed no displeasure at Lucy's words, inclined his head. "I can feel her sorrow from here."

I followed his line of sight across to the air space above the pixie zone. I stilled. Okay, clearly sorrow wasn't the only emotion Malisna was experiencing. Heavy, angry dark clouds had formed in a small spot above her area. She had called energy and this storm was the result. All fey were in touch with elemental powers, and right then Malisna was unhappy – yeah, let's go with that understatement of the year.

Colton hadn't said much. He was doing his usual staunch arm-cross, I'm-a-badass-wolf-Walker thing that he had down. From the first moment I'd met him, when he'd wandered into the Angelisian beach house, he'd been cool, calm, and confident.

Not much had changed. Walkers were pretty unchanging with the times. Although his pixie was known to fire him up on occasion and his hair was much shorter. It used to be shoulder length, tied back in platinum locks at the nape of his neck, but now he'd gone for shorter on the sides and a little length on top falling over his masculine features. He said it was easier to manage and, strangely enough, he was less shaggy in wolf form now too.

"Did you find the half-Walker?" Colton's words reminded me that Lucy and I had been apart longer than usual and she knew none of the happenings of the last few hours.

I quickly launched into the story of Dronish and the standoffish Sapha.

"Still sounds like a step up from Fury." Lucy flicked her curls over her shoulder.

She seemed to have gotten used to the huge increase

in hair length after coming into her pixie powers. Which reminded me of something.

"Did you unlock your faerie side?" I wasn't too nervous to ask since she was before me looking safe and healthy.

She exchanged a glance with Colton. It was quick, but I caught the flash of amusement. "No, we all decided that right now is not the time to be unlocking new abilities."

Translation: Colton was going to kick the faerie prince's ass if he touched Lucy in any way geared toward violence.

"And I don't know how the new energy will react since I'm bonded to Colt now," Lucy finished.

"Good point."

They already had pixie, Walker, and wolf joined together. Add faerie into the mix and it could be an energy disaster.

Lucy's eyes flicked to the pixie area. "I have to go and see Mother." She leaned in and gave me a hard hug. "Where are you going?"

My heart hurt a little in that moment. Lucy and I had once been so inseparable; we had no one but each other. Now we seemed to be heading in different directions. I supposed it was inevitable. We both had so many new responsibilities and families, but I wasn't cool with this. Not cool at all.

"Promise me that we won't drift too far apart," I whispered as I held her tighter. "No matter what direction life takes us, we have to make time to be with each other."

Lucy pulled back from me, her expression sending a slight trill of fear through me.

She was pissed. "Abigail Swish. How could you think

for even a second that you could get rid of me? Never. Ever. Ever. Going to happen." She emphasized each word with a stamp of her tiny foot. "I'm your guide; I keep you from doing stupid shit like this."

I couldn't help the chuckle that escaped. "I just meant that we have new lives and responsibilities. We'll probably end up spending a lot of time apart in the coming months ... we need to make more effort."

She sniffed, her eyebrows bunching together. "I already have it all worked out. This is how it's going to go ... lots of crap will happen, blah, blah, big battle and in the end we'll imprison the lalunas and the Seventine. Then you and I will live next door to each other on Abernath. Neighbors and sisters for life."

Her words filled me with a hope and joy that had been sadly missing of late.

"Did your powers of premonition tell you that?"

Latinti shifted in a strange manner then. "Premonition ... sounds as if you have some faerie abilities already."

We all faced him. I was surprised Lucy hadn't asked this already.

"So these little flashes of the future I have on occasion, these are from the faeries?" she asked, eyes wide as she looked up at the imposing male.

Josian had planted some of the major prophecies, courtesy of his bonkers laluna. But Lucy still had an affinity for seeing the future, just small glimpses. Malisna had explained that was not a pixie power. We'd guessed it was faerie, and now it was confirmed.

Latinti reached out and took his daughter's hand. His fingers were long and delicate, like an artist's. I wasn't sure manual labor was part of the faerie philosophy.

"It's a facet of the power in our royal line. Most do not possess this ability. We are special."

I managed not to snort out my laughter. Lucy was special all right.

"Shut it, Abbs," she said, clearly reading my mind.

I waved a hand at her. "Anyways, I have to bail now. Fury needs my help with something on Crais, and then I have to get to Earth and find the next half-Walker – like immediately."

At their confused look I quickly detailed the information we'd found in the library, the timeframe and rituals which required all of the half-Walkers or original powers. I wasn't sure the faeries understood everything of my rapid babble, but Lucy would definitely have followed along. We'd had a lot of years of babbling – we were experienced.

The last sight, as I bade them goodbye and walked back toward the Doreen area, was a range of heavy and worried faces. Lucy especially looked torn between finding Malisna or following me. In the end I think it was only because it was more strain for me to shield extra people on Crais that stopped her coming along.

As I walked away I rubbed the spot right above my heart. My chest felt tight. I hated when people were upset. I should start demanding everyone be positive and happy at all times, because it was hard for me to stay sane and optimistic when their worries piled in on me too.

I ignored the curious looks which followed me across the field. I was used to it. Especially from the Abernaths. They all remembered now that I was bonded to their princeps, that they had sent energy into me during the initiation ceremony. But since Brace and I were currently ... whatever we were ... they didn't know how to approach or address me. I needed to deal with that as well. Sigh. Add it to the list.

Fury pounced on me the moment I walked back into our zone, and Cerberus licked the side of my face. My hellhound looked happy after his time with Apollo. I quickly explained to the massive puppy that Fury and I were going to Crais, and that it was harsh there and I'd be back soon. Of course, like all the others in my life, he completely ignored me, shrinking himself back to tiny size and bounding along my arm and up onto my shoulder. Okay, apparently he was not staying behind.

"Ready?" Fury held out her hand. She'd be tracing since she knew where to go.

I nodded. "Do we need to shield?"

"Nope, I'll take us into the cave that borders the area."

Sounded good to me.

I closed my eyes and held on to her arm tightly. It was strange not being in control. I'd never been traced by someone else. I had no idea how it felt. Surprisingly enough, it was very similar, just a little jolt and we were there.

The stifling heat hit me hard. We were definitely back on Crais.

I opened my eyes, shaking my head as I tried to adjust to the air. It was like breathing in heavy dirt. The taste and texture was not pleasant.

Fury sighed. "I'm starting to think I could never live here again." She was uncharacteristically somber as we started to move through the hot cave.

The red rock walls seemed familiar, but everything on Crais looked the same. It could be any of the cave systems.

"Living with this heat, the disgusting air, the inability to run in the sun." She shook out her white mane. "I know, deep down, Dune wants to be here, with Cleo. It's not the same for him. This land rejuvenates him."

I reached out and squeezed her hand. It didn't matter which couple, we were all facing our obstacles.

"The fact that you can instantly trace to and from a place ... well, that should alleviate some of the barriers to wanting to live on different worlds." I tried to find a silver lining for them.

Sure, because it's always simple like that.

Her dark gray eyes met mine. "I hope we can reach some sort of compromise, but in the end I won't be without Dune. So maybe I'll live here, and just trace for some girl-time visits with you guys."

The emotions hit me hard. I hadn't really thought ahead to the moment when I would no longer be fighting the Seventine. But I completely hated the thought that the half-Walkers and I would live on different worlds. We felt like family, and while we didn't need to exist in each other's pockets, residing on the same world would be nice.

I was going with positive thoughts on this one. "I have faith that after we finish this battle and prevent the complete destruction of the worlds ... well, things will fall into place." I nodded decisively.

"I like your confidence, Supes."

We were moving pretty rapidly through the tunnel. I used my shield a few times to clear the soot from my lungs. I wondered at first how deep we were going, but then as the light appeared across the way, I realized we were heading straight through to the other side. The brightness became more blinding as we moved closer.

"Shield time, Supes."

Fury winked at me, and I threw out the barrier that would not only protect us from the heat but also keep viable the small amounts of oxygen available, you know, just so we could breathe. Well, so I could breathe; Fury was adapted to this world. Stepping free of the doorway, I used my hand to shield my eyes from the brightness. The heat seeped into my boots from the cracked red ground beneath us. If anything, the intensity of the two suns seemed even stronger than the last time I had been here. I hoped the soles of my shoes weren't going to melt. Just to be sure, I slipped a layer of the shield under our feet. I hadn't done that the last time, afraid I wouldn't have the strength to complete our task. Today my energy was a hundredfold stronger than it had been all those months ago. I could have shielded us for days. I barely even felt the strain.

Fury spoke in a rapid succession of words. "Dune is close by. I can feel the nomads scattered around, but they're staying clear of this area. I can't use my power unless I want them all over my ass, but your energy seems to be okay ... undetectable." Her point was loud and clear: if things went to crap in a can, it was up to me to take care of it.

Yeah, I could totally do that. She didn't call me Super Abby for nothing.

The land of Crais was unchanging as we crossed the long unbroken expanse of red dirt. There were still craggy, mountainous overhangs scattered around, large rocky cliffs, and a few scraggly trees, but all in all it was a depressing expanse of red. Under the suns – which were halfway up, on opposite sides of the sky – Fury's hair looked whiter, her skin redder, and I wasn't sure if she realized it, but vitality poured off her in waves. Her half nature was showing itself.

My thoughts were cut off as we started to move closer to what was a widespread series of cliffs. I'd thought they were a very long way away from us, but in actual fact they were just smaller than most of the others. As we moved closer the first slivers of disturbance could be felt in the land. There was definitely something going on here. We were about a hundred yards away when I sensed the Seventines' presence.

"The Seventine are here," I told Fury. "I can feel the first, and he's going to know I'm here now."

Sure enough, as we moved into the shade of the cliff, from a small opening emerged four nomads. But they weren't just nomads. The energy gave them away first, followed closely by the fine fissures spanning the red skin of the poor possessed souls.

The first stepped forward. "Hello, ancient one." The puppet he was possessing started to talk. "We've been waiting for you."

Oh, hell, this was going to be bad.

10

Fury and I were unmoving as we watched the Seventine span the entrance. I wouldn't make the initial move toward them. We couldn't do anything to stop the Seventine right then. They could sever tethers and possess anyone, and there was no way to halt them until we could trap them back in the prison.

I clenched my fists against the feeling of powerlessness. The pain from my nails brought some clarity, clearing the waves of anger that had flooded me.

For now we just needed to figure out what their plan was for Crais. Because they were running out of time to free their brothers and desperation was a scary mother.

"We're so glad you're here," the first waved one hand in an arc, "I wanted to show you our power again, the tethers which are ours to possess. You've arrived just in time."

One of the other Seventine stepped forward then. "We have the energy at hand now to free the last of our brothers and end this little dance. In a few short hours, all seven of us will be released from our prison and we're going to rain destruction and desolation on the seven worlds."

Another spoke. "None will stand before us."

Finally the fourth of the group finished their gloating. "None will survive. We have no more mercy. Our power has been contained for too long."

I cut to the chase. "How are you going to find enough energy here to free the last three?" It was my understanding that they would need an exorbitant level of power for these last Seventine prisoners.

The first grinned and unease swirled through every cell of my body, from the blood right to the bone marrow.

"Greed needs to be punished. This world has two of something. Why do they have two, when they only need one?"

Great, he was a freaking poet now.

Fury and I exchanged a single, holy-shit-balls look, before turning back to the Seventine. Were they talking about the suns?

"We can't let them take the energy," I murmured to her.

If they freed the three before I found the last half-Walker, it was all over; we would never catch up in time. They would start unraveling the worlds, continuing on to the convergence. Then the end would come for all of us.

Fury angled her low words toward me. "Dunc is on his way, with distractions."

The powerful thrusts of the winds were the first indication of his arrival. I didn't want to take my eyes from the four evil beings before me, but the need to see what was coming up behind my back was too strong. I lifted my chin and shifted my gaze over my right shoulder. The sight pretty much took my breath away.

A large group of dragoonas filled the sky.

"I've never seen a pandemonium of dragoonas." Fury's voice rose into an excited crescendo as the beasts moved closer to us.

A pandemonium ... I liked that.

Most of them were in dark colors: reds, blacks, grays, with a few other shades scattered amongst them. Cleo was still the only green one, and there were one or two bluey purples. I could see clearer as they closed in, the brightness of the red sky and dual suns fueling their descent toward us. There were at least fifty magnificent and utterly scary dragon animals heading in our direction. Varying in size and color they were, but each brought the same sharp teeth and flames.

I spun my eyes back to the Seventine. They were still in the same spot, looking a little mesmerized by the pandemonium.

Fury raised her hands, as if she could embrace the beasts. "They're amazingly resistant to magic, energy manipulations, and Walker attacks."

"How do you know?" I asked.

Fury stepped a little closer to the male who had just dropped down off the only green dragoona. Dune. I extended the shield so she could continue stepping closer to him. It was as if there were a magnet between those two, something intangible that drew them toward each other. It was a magical quality, possessed only by those of us with true mates.

Despite her 'Dune' distraction, she still answered. "My father told me. He explained many of the things he learned about the mixing of our cultures. He said the dragoonas were most probably descended from the Walker sacred animals."

Apollo, most likely.

Her words reminded me of Cerberus, who was still curled up in the crook of my neck. I had completely forgotten he was there. Damn, he could be so still and quiet when the situation warranted it. Still, it gave me a moment's relief to know that he was with me. He had my back, and since the Walker guides were filled to the brim with ancient energies, they could definitely help against the Seventine. If it came to that, of course.

The first sneered. "You can't stop us. This show of intimidation is laughable." He sounded calm, unruffled and definitely amused. Insufferable bastard. "We've been searching for many eclipses, and finally we found the center of this world."

"What's the center?" Fury barked the words at him, hands on her hips.

Although her irate look lessened as Dune finally reached her side. He entered my protective shield and wrapped his arms around Fury. Her tension immediately lessened. Leaning down, the nomad murmured a few words, which brought a true smile to the Crais half-Walker's face.

"What's the center?" I repeated her question.

The first leveled its gaze on me. Well, the gaze of the poor nomad who'd involuntarily become a living bomb. "You're lucky that the energy of the originals runs within you ... which we find useful. Otherwise the minuscule years you have lived and the tiny pockets of information you contain would be ... intolerable."

A vision of me punching him fair in the face was a nice little reprieve from the arrogance.

"Every one of the seven worlds is built on tethers, and during the convergence all of these will join to allow us an easy, one-step severing."

I already knew that; must be included in my tiny pocket of information.

"But within the individual worlds are lines of energy. They interconnect and link across the globes. The center line is the most important. It's the tether to the suns, moons, and orbiting stars of that world. It's the life force of the planet."

I had a horrible feeling that I knew where this little conversation was going. We'd guessed at it before …

"You're going to take one of the suns?" My question was blunt.

Fury and Dune exchanged a glanced filled with disbelief and fear.

It had to be the suns. They'd referred to Crais having two of something that they felt should only have one. What else could it be that would have enough energy to free the remaining Seventine?

The first grinned. The ivory teeth common to this world flashed in the bright sunlight. "Finally some of the originals' intelligence shines through."

He gave me a slight dip of his head. Then the four of them turned on the spot and, using their hosts to move, fled back into the mountain.

The three of us exchanged a wide-eyed look. There was no way in the world we could let this happen. But how the hell did you stop something like that?

"The dragoonas can't follow us into the mountain,"

Dune said, "but they will wait here in case we need them."

He was right. As we moved toward the entrance, I could see the gap was way too small for even the tiniest of the scaled beasts. I jumped as Cerberus yelped close to my ear. For the first time since arriving on Crais, he was shifting on my neck.

I stopped moving forward. I could sense he was about to jump free. Sure enough, he was off me and huge within my next breath of stale air. I peered around his bulk, trying to determine what had initiated the menacing growls coming from his muscled figure. Something not fun was heading toward us.

Sure enough, before we could escape the intense suns into the cave, shadows rose out of the entrance and burst out. As more of the forms poured free, we moved backwards in a rapid series of steps. My eyes were cataloguing the features of those coming at us, but my brain hadn't caught up with what I was seeing.

What. The. Eff? What the hell were these things?

"I'm extending the barrier," I said. "Something tells me that we're going to need the space." Understatement.

"We need weapons." Fury's voice was higher than usual.

I shook my head. "You don't need a weapon. They're freaking ... trees. Just burn them down. I don't think it's time to worry about the nomads."

Her eyes widened, before she nodded decisively.

I had no idea what the Seventine had done, but somehow walking in our direction was a forest of six-foot animated trees. They looked ancient, but without any leaves or greenery. Just the knotted, aged trunks. Not to mention they walked on root-shaped legs and had twiggy arms. The eeriest part was the complete lack of visible faces.

Okay, so Fury was her own flame thrower, but I needed a weapon. Damn, it wasn't like I could magically materialize a sword like Delane could do from the clouds on Nephilius.

Wait a minute.

Thinking of Nephilius gave me an idea. I had done something for the first time I was there; I'd traced the half-Walkers toward me. Could I do the same thing with a weapon? Only one way to find out.

It didn't seem advisable to shut my eyes right then, what with the forest closing in, so I just mentally pictured the weapons' room in the beach house. Josian had it well stocked; there was a lot to choose from.

Hoping this would work, I sent out my golden tether toward the sharpest blade in there. Something that would have no trouble slicing through wood. My golden cord ended up hovering over a long sword with a thick and razor-sharp blade. It was a little heavier than I liked to use, but I'd be okay for a good thirty minutes. Let's hope the fight didn't last longer than that.

It took me a minute to realize it was much harder to connect to inanimate objects. They still had tethers, of course, but their ties were not searching back for me, as they were when I connected to the girls. I had to do all the work. My golden cord finally intertwined with the glittering cord of the sword. I took a deep breath and reached into my energy well.

I brushed back the foreign faerie energy which was still situated inside and reached for the same energy I'd used on Nephilius. As with the half-Walker females, I had to will the object to come to me.

Excitement jumped inside me. It worked. A sword was suddenly in my hand, my fingers closing around the smooth handle, its weight solid in my grip. A grin ripped across my face. Hell, yeah! That was awesome.

Fury turned and her jaw actually dropped when she finally noticed my new attachment.

"That is freaking awesome." She repeated my thoughts as she fist-pumped her excitement into the air.

Cerberus gave a bark of agreement, but that was the end of our celebrations.

Suddenly the trees were moving again, their rooty legs reaching us in a matter of moments.

It was time to battle.

They moved toward us in a regimented unit, and when they were no more than a few feet away I stared really hard, trying to determine if there was a face hidden in the bark. They seriously just looked like dead trees. If you discounted the fact they were walking.

I was wondering how they were dangerous; they didn't have any weapons. Then I was given a first-hand experience of their skills. I was completely unprepared when branches shot off and wrapped themselves around my center, squeezing the life from me. My sword flew to the side, breath was crushed from me, and within seconds my insides were one big aching mass.

My energy rose to the surface to try to counteract the massive strength and power of the branches. I could feel the blood running down my side as the wood cut into my arms. I knew if my inner strength had not been so huge, I'd have been cut in two by this creature.

Luckily, I hadn't dropped the shield around Fury and me yet, so we weren't burning lumps on the red parched ground.

Cerberus barked once before bounding across to me. He severed the branches with a well-placed swipe of his massive claws. The branches unraveled from my body, falling to the burning hot ground in a lump. I followed suit, landing next to them. I flinched as my skin sizzled against the scorching ground. Now I could add burns to my injuries.

I gasped in air as rapidly as I could, exhaling just as fast. I was trying to fill my lungs. All the while my body still screamed from the crushing pains. I forced myself up from the red earth. Cerberus lent me his bulk to lean on. My cuts, burns, and red welts started to heal immediately, and within a few minutes I was ready to fight.

Fury scurried to my side. "You okay, Supes?" As I nodded she glanced behind her. "Note to self: don't let them give you a hug."

She called her power. The blue flames surrounded her. The heat was suddenly more intense in the protective shield. I knew the nomads would be on our asses soon. Hopefully they were busy with whatever the Seventine were currently up to.

Fury ran forward. I gasped as she left the barrier, before remembering that she could walk under the suns while covered in her flames. I pulled back my shield so it just surrounded me now. Cerberus had long ago left. The massive hound was in combat with some forest folk.

Fury raised her hands and shot blue energy at the large tree closest to her. It started to burn, but not rapidly like that of a normal dead tree. I could feel that she had to push more and more power to knock it down. I lost sight of her then, as I had to step up and battle.

I'd retrieved my sword from the ground, and swung it around in a few strong arcs before I moved to Cerberus' side. Branches were flying at us again. I jumped to the left, swiping through and cutting them down. Plenty more came at us, but the sword made quick work of them.

Together my hellhound and I managed to dispatch two of the tree men. They started to fan out, surrounding us from all sides, but then the advantage was ours again as the dragoonas flew in to join the fight.

Some attacked from the air, landing on the trees and snatching the trunks up into the sky. Suddenly we had a path right into the mountain.

"I'm going to try and make it into the cave," I shouted to Fury and Dune. "We have to stop the Seventine."

There was nothing more important.

Of course, I had no idea how I was going to stop them, but I'd cross that mountain when it came up.

Flinging my heavy sword away I wasted no more time, ducking around the last of the trees, Cerberus right on my heels. The hound had to shrink quickly to fit through the doorway. I dropped the shield as soon as I was a decent way into the cave, wrinkling my nose at the disgusting air, but managing to breathe without too much drama.

The tunnel was long, thin, and winding. Dark enough that without a small energy ball I'd be running blind. I was trying to calm my nerves, but facing the Seventine was not something to take lightly. I knew they wanted me to join them, but they could just as easily turn on me if I became a nuisance.

And I hadn't forgotten that we needed their help. I had to make sure they couldn't get this energy so they'd have no option but to agree to the laluna plan. So my goals: stop them stealing the sun, and get them to agree to lock away the lalunas in exchange for the release of their fifth brother. Should be easy as.

I reached the end of the tunnel. There was a crossroad, and I had to choose to go left or right. I paused, unsure what to do.

"Do you know the right way, Cere?" I looked over my shoulder.

Both of his heads started to drift left and right, before finally, with a short bark, he indicated we should turn left.

Trusting his judgment, I sent my light ball in that direction and we started to move again. It took a while, but as we traveled through this arterial, I started to feel the Seventine. And along with their massive power was something else. Something strong and ancient. Something that gave me chills and had the hair on the back of my neck standing up. I was guessing this was the center line, the one which was allegedly part of the tethering of the suns.

The air cooled and cleared as we traversed further inside. My heart rate increased as the power level around us rose. No point lying about it: I was freaking scared. I wasn't a warrior. I'd been thrust into this life, with only the basics of training from my time on Earth. Running on the streets with the gangers had taught me skills, but the Seventine were leagues above in evil.

Dronish

Thank the gods for Cerberus. Just having him by my side gave me the courage to keep powering ahead. That and the fact that I couldn't let my friends and family die.

In the end, I'd rather be the one who was killed than the one who stood aside and let my loved ones be destroyed. I inhaled a lungful of dirty air as we neared what looked to be the hub of this mountain. It was time now to suck it up and stop these guys.

Cerberus pushed me to the side, taking the lead for the first time. It was a tight fit in this tunnel, so I was a little plastered to the wall, rocks littering around me as the hellhound squished his bulk in front of me.

Yep, buddy, you've made your point abundantly clear. You protect me.

I totally loved this puppy.

My ball of light was suddenly useless as we rounded a corner, and the tunnel was flooded with both heat and intense brightness. I threw my shield around myself again, before gasping and slowing when I reached the edge of the center line.

It wasn't the suns. Instead the light was from a glowing beam that shot upwards through the rocks. I dropped my shield as I stepped closer. The four Seventine stood around the beam, their hands linked as they poured power into the stone.

"No!" I screamed, pushing forward.

Cerberus tried to stop me, but I ignored that.

"You can't do this; you'll destroy Crais. I have another offer for you."

They didn't halt their actions but the four faces, with their fissured skin, turned toward me.

I held both hands in front of me. "The lalunas plan to

imprison you again after you sever the last tether. They won't let you be free in the rebuilding of the worlds. I want your help to lock them in the prison. In exchange, we'll free the fifth of your brothers."

God, I hated making this offer. I did not want to free the fifth. I had to keep reminding myself that the pros outweighed the cons of our plan.

With a sigh, I looked from one to the other. "It's in your best interests to help us. If the lalunas are gone, you will be the most powerful."

I could see that they were considering this as they exchanged glances. Mulling over my words. Just when a sliver of hope entered my heart, it was dashed by the first shaking his head.

"Normally, I would take you up on that offer. We do not like the control of the lalunas; we want them gone. But we can free all of our brothers with the energy from this sun."

One of the others laughed. "And there is no stopping the severing of this center line. We have already started the process."

I'd seen them sever the tethers to the sacred tree on Regali, but the sun was a much larger and more powerful object. It powered an entire world. I had no idea what I could do to stop them. I gathered masses of energy and shot it toward the closest Seventine. But the energy just rebounded at me. They were in some sort of protective ring, which was trapping all of the power around us. I needed something else. I needed the girls.

I threw out my mental tethers and connected to the five other half-Walkers.

The Seventine are severing the tether which connects to

one of the Crais suns. I need your help to stop them. My words were fast and furious.

Just a little warning to the girls before I yanked all of the tethers straight toward me. Thankfully, the five of them landed in a tumble in the tunnel behind Cerberus and me. There wasn't much space in there.

Jumping to their feet, they all crowded into me immediately. Sapha was the only one who seemed scared or unsure. Of course, she had no idea how she'd just appeared on Crais.

The Seventines' energy ring was starting to move higher up the glowing cord. They were getting closer to the rock above us.

"Join with me!" I shouted. "Let's shoot every bit of force we have at them."

I had no idea what else we could do. The girls didn't hesitate, even Sapha. One by one they called their element: fire, water, wind, earth, and shadow. I threw out my tether and their powers flowed through and into me. I didn't hesitate to blast a shot right at the four nomad-shells in front of me. The color of our blast was a mix of blues, reds, blacks, and greens. Swirls of our elemental energies and, of course, the gold of the conduit threading all.

As the point of our blast hit the Seventine, my eyes were forced closed by the explosion of light.

After a minute or so, I drew back to see what had happened.

I couldn't believe it. The four of them were laid out on the floor. We had knocked them down. Unfortunately, they seemed to be right about stopping the severing of the cord. The glow was still rising without their ring of energy.

As the power continued to rise, the rock above our heads started to break apart. All of us were pushed into the ground as the cracked dirt started to shake under us. The bonds between us broke as we fought against the strength of the energy which was ricocheting outwards.

Ria screamed, "What's happening?"

"This is the center line. The tether to one of the suns is about to be severed." My words were muffled, my face pressed into the rock. "With this energy, they'll be able to free the remaining Seventine."

Delane started pushing against the energy, trying to force her body up. "We have to stop them."

None of us could stand. I was making no ground in gaining traction. This was a power beyond anything I'd felt before.

Talina reiterated my thoughts. "Even the Seventine are unable to stand." Her eyes shifted toward the four inert bodies that were scattered away from us.

I managed to twist my head enough to see them better, and I knew immediately that they were now just dead nomads, their split skins lifeless. There was no spark left.

"The Seventine are gone," I choked out.

Brace! I screamed for him, projecting my energy.

Red. His voice was in my head, and suddenly it got a little easier to breathe. His power was immense, counteracting some of the energy holding us. *Do you need me?*

Yes. I didn't wait for his compliance. Instead I traced him straight to me.

Brace resisted at first; I'd taken him unawares. He

started to fight my pull, but then realized what was happening. I think he had the power to stop my trace, but thankfully he released the hold and allowed me to pull him from Abernath and into Crais.

He landed beside me, and within moments the winds started to build up. He was morphing into his secondary power, which is in many ways a lot like Delane's. A whirlwind, cyclonic force that lifted all of us half-Walkers and allowed us to stand back on our feet. As his power surrounded us, the energy from the tether severing was eased.

"I need to find the Seventine," I shouted at Brace.

I could barely see him, my hair flying around my face, blinding me with the masses of red curls.

Brace leaned his head backward, following the path of the breaking rock above us. "They're following the center line. Once the junction between this world and First World is reached, they'll be able to take the power from the sun."

I could just make out Brace through his tornado.

"Hang on," he said.

Wait, what? Hang on to what exactly?

Then I started to lift in the air. I swallowed my shriek as my feet left the ground. I managed to keep it together by wrapping my arms around myself, as if that would keep me safe. I was now the one following the path of the center line. As the rock continued to crumble apart, crashing down to the floor below, the middle of the mountain opened right up. I pulled my shield around myself as the first rays of light beat down.

From what I could see, squinting through the whirl of wind, there was only one single sun visible, with a strange shadow of the second behind it. Crais' day had reached the point where the larger but weaker sun crossed over the front of the other. And circling this eclipse were the four shadows of the Seventine.

You're too late. The first was in my head again.

I didn't reject him this time. Instead I used his voice to pull me closer. The tie between us was a real thing. A tangible link. Something I'd fought against and ignored, but right then, I needed it. If I could get close enough to break their link to the center line, I could stop them absorbing the energy. Or so I hoped.

Brace's power continued to stay with me. Either he was in my head, or I had a certain control over the whirly wind. It was weird to fly like this, but also quite exhilarating. The Seventines' power rocked against me as I joined their little circle. I was right next to one of them, no idea which, but I guessed it was not the first, since the connection between us was still a little stretched.

The untethering was almost complete. I could tell by the rising energy: it was almost at the two suns. And so were we. I could feel the pressure on my shield. This close the heat was so much more intense, and it was taking a real effort to maintain my bubble.

Then, as the last of that energy released from the Seventine hit the suns, the world stood still ... before dissolving beneath us. A howling scream cut through my eardrums: the sound of the land of Crais shattering. Then the larger sun drained before my eyes. The metallic taste of blood filled my mouth as my teeth cut into my lip. I'd bitten down in panic. The Seventine held the end of the tether. I needed to take it back from them. Without

Dronish

thought, I projected my golden thread, the well inside me jumping with excitement.

I didn't stop to think about the fact that I was just one half-Walker. That I was about to absorb the energy of a freaking sun. And that if I managed to wrench this energy from the Seventine it was probably going to kill me.

In that moment the golden cord connected and my heart stopped beating.

11

I'd felt power before. The half-Walker females were intensely powerful in their own right, and together we packed a mammoth punch. But all of that was nothing compared to the energy from the Crais sun. My well filled, overflowed, and then the burning started to char me from the inside out.

Over and over the agonizing pain scorched me, threatening to burst free from my body. I could feel my outer shell straining. My eyes were closed, but I felt the cracks breaking across my skin. I was going to resemble one of the Seventines' victims.

I felt myself hit the rock-hard ground. Even in my pained state I somehow knew I was back on the surface. But I had no idea how I had got there. Probably Brace.

"Abby!"

Screaming surrounded me, but there was too much going on inside for me to take in the outer world.

"Connect to us."

Most of these words were lost in the swelling of heat

that filled me. Instinctively I knew I was dying. My body was reaching the end of its capabilities to take the pressure. It was too much, and the destructive force when it blew from me was going to be phenomenal. My only fear was that I would kill everyone around me with the explosion.

"Red."

Brace reached me like no other ever could. My eyes flew open and, judging from the shock and horror on the faces around me, I looked exactly how I felt. Bad. Very bad.

"Connect to the half-Walkers; share the power."

I finally understood what they'd been saying. I gritted my teeth and, reaching through the burning, found my tether and flung it free. The connection was as easy as always. It was as if we were designed to share power. Voices flooded my head, and there was a slight ease on my shell. Some of the burning shifted around, spreading into the others. But it was still too much for us. One by one they started to scream. Even the stoic warrior Delane couldn't contain herself.

Great! Now, instead of killing only me, I was going to destroy us all. I needed to pull it back, but I couldn't sever the cords. The strength of the power between us was too much. It had molded a strong powerful bond that would be broken by no one.

You have to release the power, Sapha moaned in between her shrieks. *Send it back.*

Could I do that? Send it back into the sun. I needed to talk to Brace, I needed him in my head. But there was no way right then. I couldn't speak; the power rode me too hard. How could I ask him what I needed? A thought filtered into my head. There was one way where communication was effortless.

The melding bond.

My hand trembled as I lifted it to the globe that hung on my necklace. I was damning my father by doing this, but if I didn't we were all going to die, and then I was damning everyone in all the worlds. I needed Brace's help, and this was the only way to do this.

Brace was at my side. Well, as close as he could be without my inner sun energy crisping him.

"Red, what are you doing ..." His words trailed off as I flicked the clasp and let the moonstale light flood free.

I don't know if it was because so much power filled me, or if it was my memory of the last melding bond, but the force of our connection dropped me to my knees. Something that the freaking energy of a sun hadn't done.

The rush of Brace's signature power smashed into me, his energy washing along the walls of every part of my body. Every cell responded, my heart and lungs swelled, as if for the first time they were beating and breathing again. Until this moment I hadn't realized the true extent of my inner fatigue; the strength of gods and warriors flooded my being.

The bond had been broken for long enough now that I'd become used to the sensation of being half myself, half a soul, half a power. It wasn't until we joined again that I realized the loss I'd had, the intense strength of a soul complete.

Red. Baby ... Brace's voice broke. *I've missed you. Damn, I've missed you.*

There was no time for a real reunion right then, but later, if we survived this moment, I was going to relive this force of emotion. Examine every single memory of our re-melding. Right then I might have cracks littering my skin, but on the inside the cracks were gone. I was whole again. Of course, now we had to all not die so I had time to remember these moments.

The shrieks of the other half-Walkers eased slightly as Brace absorbed a little more of the sun's energy. In fact, his strength almost equaled that of all of us half-Walkers. The man was intensely powerful.

Can I shoot this power back into the Crais sun? I asked him rapidly.

He hesitated slightly before answering. *No, the shell of the sun was destroyed when the Seventine ruptured the tether. If you release this amount of energy, we'll most likely rip Crais apart.*

His voice was shaky, the power starting to beat at him. *What do we do then? It's going to kill us all.*

I tried to keep the panic from my voice; I wasn't very successful. My skin stretched again. I could feel more cracks littering across it, and I wasn't the only one. Blood rained down from all of the girls, spattering from the fissures on our skins. Time was running out.

What about Dronish? Sapha was the one who spoke up, and I realized then that the half-Walker girls could hear my conversations with Brace. It was as if he were part of our tethering now.

Her words resonated through all of us. *We still have a sun and moons that are in need of power. You could bring life to the world again.*

I thought you wanted it destroyed, Fury barked out.

Sapha laughed without humor. *I'm not so selfish that I would see two worlds fall when we could save both. Whether it is the Walker half of me that feels this way, I need to be a better individual than my mother and the rest of the Drones. I need to do something that matters.*

If I hadn't been about to be ripped into a gazillion pieces I'd have been proud right then. But all my energy was focused on surviving the next ten minutes of this life.

How will we get to Dronish? Ria asked. *I can't concentrate long enough to find a tether.*

I'll open a doorway and take you all. Brace's power washed over me. *But that means I'll have to pull back some of the energy that's sharing the sun's burden.*

There was more than one groan at those words. Right then I wondered if we could survive the loss of his presence. We were barely hanging on even with Brace's help.

I sucked in deeply, tension and panic riding me as I waited. His presence left us. The screams started in earnest. And yes, I was totally one of the ones shrieking my head off. The pain was intense as my well continued to filter the power around.

"Hang on, girls." Brace was close. "Stay with me, baby Red," he whispered.

I would have replied, but I was too busy dying.

I barely noticed as my feet left the ground, and then we were in a doorway. Somehow, inside the vacuum the energy of the sun lessened, as if the lack of gravity was lifting the power from us also. Lending a helping hand in carrying the burden.

Then we were on the other side. The darkness and cold bit into my bare skin, but with a sun heating us from the inside out, it would be impossible to freeze. Brace connected with me again, and the relief was instant as the energy diversified.

Okay, now we need to find the center line of Dronish. Which would be almost impossible in normal circumstances, but carrying this energy will lead us right there.

It had taken the Seventine a long time to find the center on Crais. But I still wasn't sure how this was going to be different.

Send your golden tether out. Search for the coldest place on Dronish. Brace was talking and his instructions didn't fill me with confidence.

I decided to simply try. No harm in that. Unless of course I took too long. Then we'd all be dead.

No pressure.

My golden cord was filled with the power of the sun. I mentally sent it from my body, willing it to find the coldest spot that needed the warmth. It zoomed away, and we struggled to hold on while we waited. It seemed to take forever, and then even longer as it weaved, swerved, and seeped into the nooks of Dronish. One by one we fell to our knees, except for Brace, but judging by the pale nature of his normally tawny skin, he was struggling. I ended up on my hands and knees. If the tether didn't find something soon, my face would be pressed into the parched and rocky ground.

It's not working. I was starting to get desperate. *I'm just going to release the energy into Dronish and hope that it'll fill those places which are dead or dying from lack of power.*

Brace answered immediately. *If you can give it any more time, Red, you need to hold on. What you propose will most likely blow this world apart and kill everyone. Energy needs a direction; it needs to know where to go, and on this scale I've no idea what that undirected power will do.*

I knew what he was telling me: it could destroy more

than just Dronish. It could tear apart the fabric of this entire star-system.

I wish we'd been able to use this power to lock away the Seventine or Ialunas, Delane said, and it was the exact thought I'd had more than once. But it had happened too rapidly. There'd been no time to think or plan. At that thought my tether started to slow. How strange. I could tell that it was like a gazillion miles away from me, but it seemed as if it was still beside me.

Its movements continued to slow. Something had captured its attention. I decided now was the time to follow its length. Without pause, I brought our group to the tether. It was easy, instantaneous. We had so much power within us that without any effort I moved seven people. Most probably I could have traced us to Dronish earlier, but I'd been unable to form a clear picture in my head, so we might have ended up somewhere we didn't want to go.

You found it, Abby. Brace's love wrapped around me, his warmth adding to the heat already baking my insides. *The center line is here, but shit ... what's happened to it?*

I opened my senses, the same way I had on Crais, and could see the line running high into the black sky. The very sky which was devoid of stars, suns, and with only a sliver of moon. The Crais line had been solid, thick, and strong. Dronish's was weak and tattered, similar to the tethers of the dark mountains. As if so much damage had ripped through this world that it was close to dying itself. Dronish was a land on its last hope.

Do I just direct the energy toward the line? I hoped Brace had a clue.

I don't know. This is the domain of the conduit, and only you can make this happen.

Not helpful, thanks. Oh, well, I can't expect him to know everything.

I sucked in deeply, pushing past the pain and exhaustion. All of us were still on our hands and knees, unable to stand or fight against the power any longer.

I swear this is what dying a slow, painful death by torture feels like. Fury's voice held an ounce of its usual strong and bold presence.

I couldn't blast the power from us – there was too much, spread around all seven of us. And the pain too great. Instead I started at a slow trickle, urging the power into the tattered line. It moved in small increments, but somehow as it gathered momentum, more and more started to burst free.

It still took a long agonizing time, and I hoped like hell we never had to do anything like this again. As the well inside me emptied, I reached for more of the hot, burning power, sucking it from the girls.

Last was Brace. He wouldn't let me take his share until everyone else was depleted, so he was the one to suffer the longest. Not that I could tell. He wore a stoic face that even Que would have been proud of, and the former Abernath princeps had been a crazy-ass-megalomaniac-sociopath.

Eventually my mate opened the bond between us, and let the last of the burning energy free.

Thank you, Brace.

I relished the fact I could speak in his head again. It was as if I'd been cut off from all of my senses and hadn't even realized. Now I was whole again. The pain which had plagued my ragged soul was finally lifted.

I love you, Red. I. Love. You.

He said it over and over. I knew he was also overwhelmed by the emotion between us and, as the last of that power drained from me, I dragged myself over to him and fell into his arms.

"I love you too." I was crying, the tears leaving tracks along my skin and falling to the parched ground.

I wasn't the only one.

From where I lay in my mate's arms, I could see the half-Walker girls. Most of them had more emotion on their faces than I'd ever seen before. Even Delane and Sapha. Fury and Talina were full-on bawling. I'd have laughed, but I was too overwhelmed.

"You guys are like the golden couple, literally," Fury choked out between sobs.

The golden tethers that were part of our sacred melding had shot all around the place again, lighting up the freezing darkness that was Dronish.

I'd forgotten about the center line, completely consumed with the love around me. So I wasn't paying attention to what was happening to the sky and world around us.

Light started a slow ebbing stream across the blackness that had been the sky. Tendrils started from the center line and flowed through the air. I wasn't cold, wrapped in the arms of my hot-ass man, but I'd noticed the other girls shivering. Then, as the warmth followed the light, their shivers subsided. The cracks on our skin started to slowly fill in again, taking longer than usual, but thankfully still healing. I barely noticed the pain, but the slow heal was like an itchy sandpaper coating my skin.

Sapha's red eyes were wide. "I can't believe it." She spun in circles, trying to see everything in one go. "The energy has returned to Dronish. The sun burns and the moons live."

She was right. There was now a very large and hot sun sitting to the left of the sky. And six moons scattered in the foreground of the sun's path, only just visible in the bright light.

Is it too much to ask that we have five minutes to focus on the bond? Brace's words were a cross between resigned and pissed-off.

Five? I teased. *I'm going to need longer than five minutes to focus on this bond.*

Not only were emotions flooding through me, but there was this tingly heat which had started at the top of my head and was slowly working its way down my body. A tingly heat that had everything to do with the bond and everything to do with the hard planes of muscle and warm skin that was pressed to me. It had been a long time without Brace, and I wanted all of him right then.

He laughed. *Stop thinking about that, Red, or you and I will be secluded in our snow cabin for days, weeks ... maybe months. And the worlds can fix them damn selves.*

I sucked in a deep breath. He was right. I needed to focus. We needed to finish this with the lalunas, because I couldn't leave Josian as their prisoner. Who knew what was happening in there, how they were messing with his mind? I had to save my dad.

You have no idea how much it pisses me off that we can't just hole up right now. I pushed back my curls.

Sometimes I wanted to stamp my feet and curse at the world for everything it was taking from me.

It's almost over, baby. And then we'll have so much time, an eternity.

I knew Brace was right, but it didn't annoy me any less. Plus there was this teeny, tiny part of me that worried we wouldn't win. I was confident, but not stupid. The Seventine were damn powerful, and there were so many factors leading up to the convergence; well, who the hell knew which way it would go?

I was distracted from these thoughts as I finally focused on the land laid out before us. Dronish. A world which had been dark, cold, and dying. Now it was alive again. But it was strange to observe an environment almost completely devoid of life. It was as if a lava field had flowed across the land, coating and covering everything. The shapes of life were still there: mountains, trees, houses. But it was petrified into large black blobs. Blobs which were rock-hard now. It was almost a land of statues, a frozen moment of a world that used to exist.

Sapha rushed to my side.

I'd noticed earlier that she'd been watching Brace and me with more than curiosity in her gaze. It seemed as if the driving emotion in the depthless red eyes was longing. Desire. She wanted what we had here. True love. A bond greater than anything that had or would ever exist in these worlds.

Right then she was dancing on the spot next to us, clearly not wanting to interrupt, but something had driven her to cross the space and stand at our side.

I pulled away from the Abernath princeps. Reluctantly. Very, very reluctantly. I could hear his chuckle in my head, and just having him back where he belonged was better than any gift.

"What's up, Sapha?"

Her eyes widened at my choice of words. I guessed she didn't understand the context.

"Sorry, I mean, is something wrong? Are you okay?"

She nodded a few times. "We need to go to Arotia. The Drones are in danger."

I didn't question her. I trusted my half-Walker girls, and I knew the reason would be important. I held out my hand and she barely even hesitated before placing hers into the open palm. We were making progress. Brace linked to my other side and the rest of the females fell in line. Without hesitation I traced our large group to the outer region of the barrier-lined city.

The screams were the first thing that registered in my brain. My eyes took a few more seconds to catch up. Drones were everywhere, curled up, crouching under any cover they could find. It was lucky they mostly wore thick sheets, because, clearly, the sun hurt them.

Ria had her hands threaded through her gorgeous chestnut hair. "What's wrong with them?" Vines were starting to spring free, as she swung her head from side to side, and for the first time I noticed the small black dots which flew off her hair plants.

Were they seeds? Was Ria actually creating new life-growth? Maybe her power could help to restore some of that which had been lost from Dronish.

Sapha started to run, yelling as she went. "Drones are night dwellers. The sun burns them."

There were at least fifty of her people outside of the gates, and as we followed her path I gasped at the angry red burns littering their translucent skin. Basically any place where they weren't covered by their black sheets had been severely toasted.

"They're very much like the vampire legend." I said it out loud, but no one besides Brace understood my reference.

We'd once joked about Josian being a vampire, rocking out his red eyes. I'd definitely have to tell Lucy. If she forgave me for abandoning her so much at the moment.

"Combine power with me, Red." Brace reached out and linked our hands.

You just want to touch me, I teased him.

He grinned that wicked, badass, full-perfect-teeth smile, and before I even realized what he was planning he kissed me on the mouth. Hard, passionate, and absolutely delicious.

Our power responded inside us, rolling together with a strength that surpassed the half-Walker females. Our lips still locked, Brace called some of that energy. Truth be told, I was too distracted to do anything more than keep kissing him.

You have to stop, Abigail. I'm not going to be able to help these Drones if you keep distracting me.

Good to know I wasn't the only one enthralled.

Reluctantly I pulled away, and as I turned my head my jaw dropped a little. Brace had elevated those prone Drones, lifting them free of the hard dirt and, as one large mass, they were ferried toward the city of Arotia. We ran after them. I could feel a small amount of energy draining from Brace and me, but we seemed to have plenty left to go around. This activity wasn't even tiring me out. We used the back entrance into Arotia, Sapha's little fence hole.

Once we were inside the girls took off in all directions. No one hesitated. They started to drag the screaming, burning Drones out of the light and into the tall, skyscraper-style buildings around us. Brace and I deposited our fifty into the bottom level of an undercover building. Thankfully, many of the inhabitants were already holed up in their homes. But still thousands littered the open streets of Arotia.

The scent of burning flesh was prominent. But still more subtle than that of burning human or animal that I'd smelled before.

Sapha looked exhausted. For someone who'd wanted her entire world to die, well, she was tireless in trying to save those left.

I caught her eye as we rushed past each other with more victims.

"We have a chance now." Her voice shook. "Dronish has a chance to survive. We know better; we are better now."

I wasn't sure she actually believed that. Had her people evolved enough to learn from past mistakes? Or, like humans, were they doomed to continue repeating the sins which had destroyed their world in the first place? I gave her a nod and a smile. I hoped for her sake that her words were true. At least we'd given them more time, rather than the slow torturous starving-to-death thing they had been doing.

I was reminded then of the fact that we'd taken away a sun from Crais. Again, this was another world which had learned to adapt to their harsh and extreme environment. What sort of changes had we wrought? Would there be suffering and death prevailing there at the moment? Fury must be worried sick, especially about Dune. I was worried about Cerberus, but I knew he could move between the worlds, so I hoped he was back on First World.

I had to focus on the current problem. It took a long time, but finally we seemed to have found all the exposed Drones and dragged them to safety. Brace took off for a quick circumnavigation of the area, ferreting out any we'd missed. It had taken many hours to gather them. By the time we were done, the sun had shifted across the sky. It was close to setting, allowing the six moons to appear in their bright, blue glory.

I was next to Sapha now. We were trying to space out the victims in the largest of the skyscraper buildings.

"Are they going to be okay?" I asked her.

She would have the best idea whether these burns were life-threatening.

"Yes. I will gather the mineralines. They will be fully charged with more than enough energy to replenish the Drones. The crystals will replace the oils which should naturally coat our skin. These liquids are healing and protective. Previously the lack of energy limited these protections, but we will have more than enough now."

Creeping out of the shadows and listening to her words were many of the Drones who'd been safe inside. I left Sapha then. She was explaining to all of those present what had happened and also recruiting their help with sharing the mineralines around.

We'd stashed Drones everywhere, in every building, so Sapha was going to have to repeat this little speech more than once. At least she didn't seem to be dwelling on her friend, Marl. Being back on Dronish would probably bring those painful memories to the surface again. Right then she had more important things to deal with. I just hoped she didn't run into her mother.

I found Fury in the chaos. I could tell by the look of relief on her face that she'd been searching for me too. "I'm tracing back to Crais." Her words fell over each other. "I need to check on Dune and Cleo."

I nodded once. "Will the world survive now without two suns?"

Fine lines creased the corners of her round eyes. "Honestly, Supes, I have no idea." She rubbed at her temples in a tired manner. "The dragoona and nomads rely on the energy, so it will depend if there's enough strength in the sun left." I gave her a commiserating look, and then she disappeared.

12

In the hours that followed we helped Sapha gather the mineralines. She seemed astonished by how many the priest guy, Kan, had holed up in his temple. Seemed as if the people here had been getting royally screwed by those in authority. Again. Most of First World's youngling planets were quite advanced and fair to their people. Earth and Dronish seemed to be the worst of the lot. I knew that many of the negative traits of these worlds had been accelerated after the release of the Seventine. The balance had been thrown off.

The mineraline crystals were lit up – fully charged for the first time in years – and I could feel the energy bleeding off them. With help from thousands of uninjured Drones, they were distributed around. I watched in fascination as the injured opened their mouths and those snake-like protrusions emerged. The mouth ends would attach to the stone and then energy infused into the host. Burns disappeared, cracked skin smoothed out, lifeless muscle sprang to life, filling out the almost nonexistent frames. As the oils sloshed across the skin, their eye morphed from this sickly yellow to a blood-red. In that moment they would stand, the picture of health, when only moments before they'd looked at death's door.

"The sun will rise again in a little while." Talina was stationed near the entrance to the building we were in. "But I think they'll be okay now."

She was probably right. They seemed to have recovered enough that the rest would come along in time. Then they would rebuild their lives. It was time for us to go. We'd delayed long enough. I needed to deal with the lalunas and Josian. Which meant I had to find the Seventine again. I wandered across to Sapha, who was crouched beside a small, child-sized Drone. Her eyes lifted to meet my gaze.

"We have to go," I started without preamble. "The countdown is on and there was no point saving these two worlds only to let the Seventine destroy them."

Her eyes examined me, roaming across my face. Abruptly she leaned down and whispered something to the child, and then stood in a smooth motion.

"You have saved my world, my people. I will help you. But ..." She held up a hand. "I still do not trust you, nor the other females. That will take time. In my experience, nothing comes without strings. No one does anything without expecting ten times more in return. So, for now, I reserve judgment."

Damn, she was prickly. "No problem."

We needed her and she knew it. The power which came along with this knowledge was always scary. Who knew what she might demand from us in the future? For now she'd been nothing but great, so I wouldn't stress too much.

Brace had not been far from my mind. I'd been keeping track of him as he zoomed around doing ten times the work load of the rest of us. I could sense his presence as he moved closer to me. I wasn't surprised when arms came around me and a kiss dropped onto my cheek.

"We need to get back to the war council." His voice was strong and commanding.

But then there were those soft words he whispered in our shared bond. I forced myself to focus, and to halt the flood of blush that wanted to coat my entire body. Oh, Brace, he was a keeper for sure. Images of our nights in the snow cabin continued to float through my mind, not to mention our time on Abernath. He was turning me into one of those girls.

I sort of liked it.

The half-Walkers, minus Fury, gathered around us. We left the building and moved out into the open space of the town of Arotia.

Brace paused suddenly. "Something's happening at the dark mountains." He twined our hands together as we crossed the center of town. "It looks as if the Seventines' dark creatures have started to emerge."

He was either in contact with the other princeps or his Abernath council. His words were definitely worrying, but right then my focus was on Josian. We had to imprison the lalunas, strengthen the prison, and save my father. I was still very stressed about the thought of releasing a Seventine, but I had to trust the other princeps. They seemed very sure this was the best way.

I raised my chin to meet Brace's eyes. "I'm going to have to make a deal with the Seventine."

I had no other option; I was going to have to find the first again. Only problem was that melded to Brace once more made me too strong for it to get in my head.

I sighed. "Can you please remove yourself as much as possible from my mind?" Even I could hear the reluctance in my tone.

Brace stared at me strangely for only a heartbeat before his genius mind caught up. "You want to try and contact the Seventine."

Then just like that I felt him withdraw. He still occupied a small section of my head, but mostly his presence was undetectable.

I hated even this minute distance between us. I fought the urge to start chasing the Seventine right then. I didn't want to seem too eager. I was going to wait and see if they came to me. Without the power of the Crais sun, they really couldn't waste the opportunity to release the next of their brothers. They were running out of time.

Everyone linked hands, so I traced all of us back to the edge of the battlefield. My feet moved forward without pause, when suddenly my eyes caught up to the scene. I ground to a screeching halt. What the hell was going on here?

It was not the chaos I expected. Instead I was staring at a plethora of large regimented groups. Each distinct and separate. I could tell the different Walker clans, not to mention the other species and fey which were here to help also. The way everyone was lined up, standing motionless, it was clear they were waiting for something.

Delane had her weapons in her hands again. "They're

mobilizing to the dark mountains," she said. "We were discussing the logistics of this when you pulled me to Crais."

I turned to Brace. "Do you know what's happening in the mountains?"

"The Seventine are trying to bring it all down. If they destroy the structure of their prison, it'll weaken the entire area and its tethers. They'll have to expend less power to release the brothers, and we won't have anywhere to lock them away."

"So the strength of their prison lies, in part, with the actual mountain range itself?" My eyes darted around, trying to take in everything.

Brace pulled me a little closer. "Yes, strength is woven into each and every tether on the dark mountain. With each freed Seventine, they've lessened the security and frayed the tethers. It's weak now. When we lock them away again, or even when we secure the lalunas into the walls, the tethers will find strength."

I remembered the frail, tattered nature of the mountain tethers. We needed to hurry with the lalunas. I couldn't let the Seventine destroy the prison. It had been chosen by the original Walkers as the strongest place to confine them.

"Do you think they'll still take the deal, even though they're trying to destroy the mountain tethers?"

Brace nodded. "Yes, the creatures they've released are mainly there to disable our forces and to weaken the mountain's ties. Probably bring down parts of the prison. But they still need to free the fifth. If they don't soon, they'll run out of time."

I had a feeling then I was going to find the Seventine

Dronish

at the dark mountains. They'd obviously gone straight there after Crais and started to release their minions.

I reached out and gripped Brace's shirt, pulling him closer. "Can you check that the lalunas are on their way to the mountain?"

He didn't hesitate, kissing me solidly before dashing off through the masses. Watching his broad shoulders disappear, my heart only ached a little. Being melded meant that he always felt close to me, even when he was far away.

Ria distracted me. "What's our next move?"

I explained to all of them what was happening. We were going to follow our allies to the dark mountains. We needed to fight, and the half-Walkers would be frontline in this war. I'd be going to Earth very soon, but I had to deal with the lalunas and Josian first.

"Aribella!"

The scream had me spinning around, my heart rate picking up as I scanned for the source. Long black hair caught my eye first. It was Lallielle, her flawless features scrunched as she pushed her way through the Abernath contingent.

"Baby girl!" The frantic nature of her words was increasing.

I turned to the girls again. "Follow Delane, go to the dark mountains, find out what's happening, and I'll meet you there soon." I sucked in deeply. "And keep an eye out for our animals. They're probably there waiting for us." I really freaking hoped so, anyway. I had the impression from the other Walkers that the sacred guides were pretty indestructible. I held on to that thought.

The different groups were starting to disperse

through a few large Walker doorways that had been opened. The half-Walkers would follow the crowd. Talina gave me a hard hug. "Be careful, see you soon."

I could feel the tension under her cool, pink skin.

"I'll be there," I promised her, hoping it was true.

I took off then, across the field toward my mother. I'd only heard that tone from her once before, and that was when she'd lost everyone in the dark mountains. I was alternating between needing to know what was wrong, and hoping she wasn't going to tell me something that would tear my world apart.

She was still struggling to make her way through the masses. I hit the edge of the Abernaths and started to weave my way through. Luckily, as soon as they noticed it was me, the soldiers moved. They were still so disciplined from their time under Que. Things had improved during Brace's administration, but a few months does not undo thousands of years of servitude.

"Princeps." A man, his hair the color of ash, nodded his head and lowered expressive eyes, his entire being the picture of respect.

I stumbled a little and he caught my arm.

"Thank you," I said, my lips trembling as I pulled my arm free.

I'd forgotten that I was part of their leadership now. That I held the energy of these people as well as that of Doreen. I was, as always, split between two worlds.

In that moment Lallielle slammed into me. Her slender arms were around my neck in the same heartbeat.

"He's gone, baby girl." Her sobs had her shuddering

against my shoulder. "Josian, I can't feel him anymore, and I've looked everywhere. He's gone."

She continued to mumble, but the words were lost. Shit, she didn't realize that Brace and I had reformed the bond. She didn't know Tenni probably held Josian captive right now and was blocking all access to him. To her it was as if he was dead. I believed the laluna when she said she would never kill her bonded one. But, as I'd known it would, it still felt like he was dead

"No, Mom!" I had to shout so she could hear me over her pain. "Dad's okay. His laluna has him, but we're going to get him back." My voice was firm. I was focused right then.

Men and women still marched around us, but the crowd was starting to thin. I continued to search for Lucy and Colton in the mass. I was worried about my friend. Since it seemed as if the still sobbing Lallielle was going to be incoherent for quite a few moments while she released her fear and worry, I reached out for the one person who'd know how Lucy was.

Colt. I mentally projected to the blond wolf-Walker. I hit his barrier, and it took a moment before he let me through.

Hey, Abby. Everything okay?

Just checking in on you and Luce. Are you heading to the dark mountains?

His mental energy disappeared for a moment, and I figured he was letting Lucy know.

Hey, Abbs. Her sweet pixie tones washed through the connection. Lucy had inserted herself into Colt's head so she could chat too. *We're just with Malisna and the pixies.*

We're going to the dark mountains right now. What about you?

I quickly explained about Josian and the lalunas. That was where my focus would be for the next little while.

Okay, well stay safe and in contact with us, she ordered. *We'll probably see you at the mountain. If not, make sure you don't head to Earth without us.*

I'll let you know, I assured her, and then with a few last words I withdrew from the connection.

My energy shield wrapped around my mind again, more solid than ever before. My previous struggles to stay shielded had been a hundred percent about the broken melding bond. I was relieved that so far everything seemed to be back to normal. I hadn't noticed any changes in the connection between Brace and me. I was keeping my fingers crossed that would remain.

Lallielle pulled me closer. She had her head buried in my neck as she continued sobbing her heart out. She hadn't ceased her breakdown since dashing across the field. I sympathized and empathized with her whole-heartedly. I knew her emotions. I'd felt her pain. It was even worse that she'd been fighting with Dad too. She was probably wracked with guilt.

"Mom." I tried again, gentler this time. "He's okay. Tenni has him because Brace and I reformed the bond. It was an accident. We had the energy of the Crais sun and were going to die. I needed Brace's help."

Slowly my words penetrated. She started to quiet a little, the occasional gasping sob still shuddering her frame.

"I was so horrible to him." I could barely hear her.

"He tried to explain, he begged, apologized and I ... I ignored him. I walked away!" The last part was shouted as she lifted her head from my shoulder.

Her face was ravaged ... haggard, and for the first time she looked like a woman in her thirties. "I don't deserve him. I couldn't stand by him when he needed me most."

Shit, she had to pull herself together.

"Stop!" I shouted at her. "Stop blaming yourself and let's just figure out how to get him back." I felt terrible, but I didn't know what else to do to snap her out of this downward spiral of depression.

Surprisingly enough, my outburst worked. She visibly calmed. Her wide green eyes met mine. I gentled my tone.

"You were hurt; you reacted as anyone would who had received such a shock." I took a deep breath. "And we know you were blaming yourself just as much. You projected that guilt into extra doses of anger toward Dad." I reached out and took her hand, squeezing it tight. "But now we have to pull ourselves together. We have one shot at getting him back. Just one. We have to go to the dark mountain, and we have to lock the lalunas away."

Her long lashes fanned across high cheek bones as she fought for composure. Finally she lifted her eyes and met my gaze, determination shaping her features now. Here was my strong mother, the one who had made difficult decisions and was mated to an imposing red-head Walker. Momma bear was back.

"How do we lock them away?" she asked as she straightened her clothes.

"Some sort of energy exchange with the fifth Seventine. Grantham knows the exact wording and ritual."

Well, I hoped he did by now. "We need the Seventine to agree. They have to clear the path to their brother. The lalunas power will strengthen the prison and tethers of the mountain, which is something we have to conceal from the Seventine. We have to make this deal appealing; we need their help."

Lallielle flicked her eyes to the right. I knew who had caught her attention; I'd already felt him coming. That distinct heating of my blood and flittering of energy was all Brace. I could feel his power as it blasted around us. The last of the Abernath group moved aside to let their princeps stride through.

I couldn't stop myself from moving toward him; his pull was magnetic. "The lalunas secured?"

He brushed his hand along my cheek, a smile curling up the corners of his lips. "Yes, they're being held in the dark mountain. At the prison. Grantham is there. He has the ritual, so all we need now is the Seventines' cooperation."

Easier said than done. "And once we send in the thirteen stones, the fourteenth – Tenni – will be pulled in?" I hoped this was the case, because there was no way for us to get into Josian's world. It would be locked down.

Brace's features tightened. "That's the plan. We just have to hope it'll work. Imprisoning lalunas has never happened before, so we've had to guess and adapt some of the ritual to suit this situation."

Lallielle stood taller. "What are we waiting for? Let's go now."

The last of the army was moving through the doorways, so we decided to just follow along. Easier than trying to figure out a safe place to trace. There would be too many groups situated in the dark zone at that moment. I paused about ten feet from the doorway. Something on the edge of the field caught my attention. White hair glittered in the sunlight. Fury. She was dashing in our direction, Dune by her side. I breathed a sigh of relief. Thank the gods they were okay.

Strands of silver flashed in her hair as she neared us, her footsteps slowing. I lifted a hand in the air and waved to attract her attention. It took a few minutes but finally she noticed me. Her hands linked with her mate as she dragged him across the space that separated us.

"Supes ... Badass ... Momma-bear," she greeted us when she was in speaking distance. "What's happening?"

"We really need to find a nickname for you." I shook my head at her.

"Already have one. I'm the bitch."

I snorted. "Yeah, but we don't call you that to your face."

Dune and Brace exchanged one of those manly grins. I don't care what anyone says, these men enjoyed our banter.

Fury winked in my direction, her prickliness only surface deep as always. Her attention was drawn to the remaining groups of our army entering the doorways. "So, I'm guessing this evacuation is something to do with the Seventine."

I worried at my bottom lip. "Yes, apparently there're a plethora of creatures arising around the dark mountains. The Seventine are trying to weaken the area and the prison, so that when they free their last brothers, we'll never be able to imprison them again."

We started walking again, catching up to the end of our group. We were almost at one of the large doorways.

"But we plan on locking the lalunas into the prison walls. It'll free us from Josian's crazy little faeries, and it'll strengthen the prison. But we can't let the Seventine know; they have to assist us. We'll exchange one of them for the stones."

Fury snorted. "That's a shitty plan, Supes. Let's hope the Seventine forgot their commonsense and brains today. Because I can't imagine why they'd agree to this."

Brace reached out and took my hand just before we stepped into the doorway. "They've no choice. If they don't start freeing their brothers, time will run out. Right now, we're their best bet for the fifth."

Thank the gods we had stopped them from stealing the sun's energy. We'd backed them into a corner. Our conversation was cut off as we stepped into the vacuum. Traversing through to the other side was quick. The mountain was not far from the war council fields. The doorways exited us right near the entrance to the dark mountain. The various groups looked to have spread out across the black and deadened plains. I craned my neck to try to see beyond our people toward the forest. Where were these dark creatures that we were fighting against?

I sensed the Seventines' energy moments before the first's voice entered my head.

Hello, my ancient friend. I've been waiting for you.

This was the very reason I'd asked Brace to withdraw from my mind. I'd hoped that once we reached this area and were close to the imprisoned brothers that the first would find me. He always did.

Are you ready to make a deal? I didn't bother with

small-talk, there was no time. I needed this done now so I could get my father back.

We will agree to the exchange, but we want something else from you.

My skin crawled at those words, which I took as a bad sign.

The last time I made a deal with you, you conveniently forgot to tell me everything I was creating. You're evil. I don't negotiate with you anymore.

I could feel his emotions now: anger, sadness, and a sort of respect which it had never shown me before.

If you do not agree, we will not aid you. Without our guidance you won't find the path to the fifth of our brothers.

I snorted. *And without us, you'll never gather enough energy to free the last three. We've thwarted you on Crais, and such a short amount of time remains.* They had two months left at most now. *There's no tether left with enough energy. You can't take another world's sun because you'll destroy that planet. And the mother of all will right your wrongs if you throw off the balance too much.*

That was why they needed to wait until the convergence to sever major tethers. If they tried to strip the energy of the worlds too quickly, the balance would step in. Crais had worked because it had two suns. Taking one would not destroy the planet.

The pause was extended between us, but the Seventine's presence was still there. I didn't push. There was no way I could let on how much we needed this. But I did have every finger crossed and even some toes.

Meet us at the prison.

I breathed a sigh of relief as the presence disappeared. I leaned in closer to my family.

"The Seventine are in." I kept my voice low.

I could tell by the widening of eyes and clenching of fists that I wasn't the only one excited. Lallielle especially had a look of determination that, frankly, scared me a little.

"We need to get inside to the prison," I said.

Brace started moving.

The rest of us fell in with him.

"Grantham is already in there. He has the lalunas," Brace said.

Something was bothering me. "Why are the lalunas okay with this?" I scratched at my side. This stupid shirt was itchy. "I understand that my particular one is helping us, and Josian's one is crazy – freaking crazy – but what about the other twelve? Surely they don't want to be locked away."

Darkness descended around us as we crossed into the entrance.

Brace sent out an energy ball of light at the same time as he answered me. "For the most part the lalunas are not sentient. I know it's confusing – especially after seeing Tenni – but the stones are really just stones. They contain *original* powers, but unless they decided to become sentient, they're only stones."

Fury nodded like that made perfect sense. "So that's how Supes' stone is keeping the rest of the lalunas under control. They're unaware of what's going on around them."

Brace nodded. "Yes, the first step to sentient thought is to find a Walker to bond with. Which is beyond rare. If their bonded one is destroyed they'll revert back to their previous inanimate state."

Fury laughed. "Well, sounds like we should just off Josian. All our problems would drift away in the breeze ..." Her words trailed off as Lallielle and I leveled our very best glares in her direction. Fury's hands flew up, and Dune sort of sidled his way between us and his half-Walker mate. "Just kidding, don't blow me up or anything."

I forced myself not to roll my eyes, or smile. She really was funny, when she wasn't being a bitch-face. The path toward the prison was familiar now. We never hesitated or broke formation. Grantham's figure came into our line of sight. He was just outside the round room which housed the remaining Seventine.

He gave me a hug. "Are we ready to go?" he asked, pulling back. "Where's Jos?"

I blinked a few times. His gruff but jovial manner reminded me so much of my father, and I really missed him right then. "The lalunas have him, so this has to work."

Grantham's green eyes flashed and his features tightened, but his voice was calm as he replied. "Don't worry, I've spoken with Nos and he's confirmed the exchange ritual."

Swirls of energy filtered in around us and Brace stepped closer to me. Even without that I still knew the Seventine were now present.

What do you need us to do?

The first was in my head again. I lifted my chin and turned my face to the left, meeting Grantham's gaze.

"I need to know the ritual now."

The Relli princeps led our group into the round room. The white light was glowing from the many stones littering the walls of the prison. Twice I'd bled my life-force into those walls. The first time I'd unknowingly released the third, the second we'd tried the ritual of the fourth. And failed. Thanks to Tenni. But this time I was determined to win; third time lucky, right?

"Do we need the other half-Walkers?" I asked, my voice low. This room was always eerie.

Grantham shook out his mass of hair. "No, anyone could perform this, as long as a Seventine is present." His pause was extended. "First step, one of them will have to possess one of us."

13

The silence that descended after Grantham's statement hung heavy in the air. I could feel the dark direction of many thoughts.

I decided to break the quiet. "Does it matter which Seventine?" Somehow I knew it was going to matter.

"It has to be the first. He's the strongest, and he has more control over the other six."

I closed my eyes for a moment, before lifting them again. "I'll do it. He won't destroy me."

He was still in my head. *You won't destroy me and you will leave the moment this ritual is complete.*

My mental voice lowered without thought. There was a darkness inside me now. It filled a place that hadn't existed until I'd broken the melding bond with Brace.

Sometimes this crept out through my tone.

Everything that had happened to me over the last year had changed me, and now, on occasion, the blackness deep in my soul seeped out.

As long as the ritual doesn't take more than an hour, you

will suffer no ill effects. And as a show of good faith, I will leave your vessel the moment you finish the ritual.

This is going to tie us together even more, isn't it? He was far too happy about what was going down.

On a level that you will never escape.

My heart raced, that bitter flood of fear inserting itself into my blood. Brace's low tone caught my attention.

"Red will never be possessed by that creature. Never!" In my distracted state I'd missed him positioning himself between me and the rest of the room. His bulk hiding the others from my sight. "It's beyond evil, the very presence corrupting. I'll be the one it possesses, no one else."

Oh, my beautiful, perfect, protective warrior. I reached up and placed a hand on his right bicep. In an instant I had his full attention. His hard features softened as they met my gaze. We stared at each other for many moments, and as he read something in my face his lips thinned.

"It can't possess me, can it?" The hard bite was still there, but it wasn't directed at me.

I shook my head. "I'm sorry, but I made it promise to never possess you again and, as an original power, it can't break those promises."

Brace dropped his head, the black hair reflecting the lights of the room. His fists were clenched and I knew he fought for control.

"It can't be you," he finally bit out. "I don't care who else has to step in, but it can't be you."

Lallielle moved closer to me. "I'll do it. It's my responsibility. Josian, and I, don't want you to take this on, baby girl. You've already had to shoulder more responsibility than any young woman should have to."

You! Only you!

Get out! I shouted at the Seventine.

I called on a little of Brace's strength and expelled its presence. Even with Brace mostly out of my head, we were still strong.

I faced all of the concerned family and friends that were watching us. "It has to be me." My soft words were, for the most part, directed to Brace and Lallielle. "The first will accept no other, and after Brace I'm the strongest. Also –" I cut my mate off before he could object, "I have your strength now. We're one and the same. This will work."

"No!" Brace didn't bother to say anything else.

"Yes." I inserted force into that word. "I can also call on my half-Walker girls, and we've been able to dispel the Seventine's presence before."

"Don't make me watch this, Red. I can't ... I have to fight this." He was struggling against the helplessness that this situation had forced him into.

I shifted my body forward and wrapped my arms around him. I held on tightly, sensing he needed my strength and touch.

"I'm sorry, baby, but there's no other way." I was whispering against his hard chest.

A few shudders ran through him. The power inside was warring; I could feel it. Brace wanted to lose control. Only sheer strength of will kept him from capturing me and stealing me away somewhere where no one would find us.

"It's the same as when I broke the melding bond. Our love doesn't trump the millions of people in the seven worlds. We must think of the greater good."

He pulled back from me and before I could blink he held my chin in his gentle grip. "And I will tell you again, Abigail, that nothing trumps our love. Nothing." He sighed in a long exhalation of breath. "But I need to man up to the words I said to Colton so long ago. I didn't fall in love with all of your strength to try and change you now." His breathing was a little ragged. "It's just that my fear is so strong. If I let it have free rein, this worry churning inside me could very well strip away everything that makes you tough enough to be a warrior and savior." He dropped soft lips down, and I met him halfway. Our kiss was brief; we had an audience. "I don't want to do that."

"Hey, peeps, who threw a party and didn't invite us?" I spun my head to find Lucy and Colton storming into the room. My pixie friend's light-hearted words dispelled some of the tension.

Lucy dashed straight up to me and wedged her way between Brace and me. She snuggled straight in for a hug, and I could tell that she'd missed me. I tightened my arms around her. I'd missed her too. So much.

I pulled away. "What are you doing in here? Weren't you with the pixies?"

She nodded more than once, her long blond curls bouncing. "Yes, there seems to be a standoff out there. Nothing is attacking yet. Plus Brace called for Colt's help, so my man used his instant transmission to get us into this mountain."

I'd forgotten that Colton could shift himself around within the same world. I met Brace's eyes over the top of Lucy's head.

He shrugged. "If you're going to be possessed by the Seventine, I need someone to stop me losing my shit. I'd hate to kill everyone in here right when we're trying to save them all."

I flicked my eyes across to Colton, who'd paused at his best friend's shoulder. They were stunning together. Dark and light. Strength and power oozed from every pore.

"Can Colt do it on his own?" I was still worried.

The wolf-Walker groaned and raised a hand to rest on his chest. "You wound me. Doubting my kickassness like that."

Brace grinned. "He's been wrangling me in for hundreds of years. He knows what he's doing."

I raised my eyebrows. "We'll see."

Lucy snorted, and met my gaze. We cracked up then. It was our job to keep the guys in check.

Grantham broke the moment by stepping forward. "We need to hurry. Every moment that Josian is stuck with Tenni ... well, who knows what's happening."

Those words sobered me immediately. My eyes darted around, and I found Lallielle. She was small, standing back with her arms wrapped around herself.

I crossed over and pulled her tightly against me. "I will get him back, Mom. We'll lock away the lalunas."

Then all we'd have to worry about was the Seventine and the convergence. No big deal.

"Please don't do this, Aribella. Your father wouldn't want you to risk your life ... or your soul."

I could see that she knew about the risks. Letting the first possess me gave him another part of me, another part of my soul. I should be creating distance between us. Letting the Seventine closer was definitely not a great thing.

"We need Dad," I whispered. "I'll sacrifice many

things for these worlds. But I have to draw the line somewhere. I have to take a stand. I won't sacrifice Dad."

She jerked me in tightly again, her soft hair surrounding us like a cloud of silk. "I love you. Do you hear me?" Her voice went all fierce. "I love you more than anything in every world. Your only job is to survive. I dreamed of all the years I would have with you when I finally got you back." Her green eyes flashed at me. "You don't have permission to mess with my dreams."

I grinned. "Yes, ma'am."

Got to love it when her inner warrior-mama perked up. I turned back to the room. Lucy looked much graver than when she had first entered the cave. I could see Brace talking to her and Colton, most probably filling them in on what was going to happen.

I raised my voice. "Let's do this, Grantham."

I didn't want to risk the chance I'd freak out, or that the Seventine would change their minds. They still seemed to be oblivious to the fact that by allowing the lalunas to bond to the walls it would strengthen this prison enough that there was no way for them to destroy it.

Or maybe they knew and didn't care. Maybe they weren't worried about this and felt that freeing their brother was worth the risk. Just as the first couldn't see into my thoughts, I also had no access to his. Most probably, like us, they'd weighed the pros and cons and decided it was worth it. I just wished our part didn't involve freeing a Seventine.

"I'm not cool with this, Abigail Swish." Lucy full-named me, her hands firmly on her hips. "Surely there's a better choice."

"There is no other choice."

She wrinkled her nose, pursing her lips for extra measure. "Remember what happened last time you got into bed with these cretins. Think about what you're risking. They never tell you the truth. What the hell is the catch this time?"

I already knew the catch.

For most decisions I made I used the line I had drawn in the sand. Everything on this side I would do; the other side was where my moral compass would never let me cross. The last time with the Seventine they had manipulated me when I was in an emotional state.

Did I need to take responsibility for my actions? Most definitely; I should have been stronger. But I knew I'd never have made the decision to free the third had I known everything. That decision was on the other side of my sand line. This time I knew what the catch was: strengthening of ties between me and the Seventine, which was unpleasant but not over my moral line. My hope was that once they were imprisoned any and all ties between me and the first would be severed.

"Supes is strong enough." Fury stepped up to my side. We weren't exactly squared off against Lucy and Brace, but it sort of looked that way. "This entire task fell on her shoulders because she was the one who had the strength for the burden. You all need to have some faith in her."

Lucy growled. Crapity crap. Shit was going to get real in five, four, three, two –

"What the eff, Fury? I have all the faith in the world in Abby. I've known her my entire life, but sure, your two and a half seconds of friendship trumps my knowledge." She sniffled a few times and I could see tears forming in the corners of her eyes. "It's not faith I lack, it's the knowledge that I can't exist in a world without Abbs. We're blood-bonded. Best friends. Pixie guide and Walker. Our path has been intrinsically linked since the day we were born."

Her words ran out as her chest heaved; she finished by flipping off the Crais half-Walker. I raised a shaking hand and pressed it to my chest, trying to contain the emotions flooding me.

"I love you too, Lucy. And I promise I have no intention of leaving this world. You and I are together forever, girl."

I blew her a kiss. She glared at me for a moment before sighing and returning the gesture. I couldn't stop from lifting my chin to meet Brace's gaze. He was still tense, fists still clenched at his sides, but he gave me a single nod of acceptance. I felt better having his blessing ... sure, that thought probably just set the feminist movement back a few centuries, but he was my partner. When we disagreed it was as if I fought with myself, the other half of my soul. And it was damn hard to fight with yourself. I let the first back into my head.

Let's do this, and if you touch one thing that you aren't supposed to, I will hurt you.

The first's laughter, maniacal and cold, flittered through my head.

Hold on to your sanity. With me inside, you'll forget who you are.

I wasn't naïve enough to miss the double meaning of his words. I was surprised, though. They seemed sort of sexless, androgynous even, so to have it make a suggestive comment seemed wrong on more levels than just the regular.

Grantham handed the bundle of stones to me. "You'll need to hold the lalunas."

Their heavy weight dropped into my hands, and despite the masses of power flooding the stones, their energy was contained. The cage around them must be masking their power. As I examined it, I finally realized something: my blue stone formed the barrier. It had melted and shaped itself into a box-like container. A container with translucent sides so I could see through to the other stones resting within.

As I thought this, something brushed against my body. The Seventine had started to possess me.

The world stopped spinning for more than one heartbeat. The stones remained clutched tightly in my hands as I dropped to my knees, my body screaming and my brain frozen. It was as if I knew something devastating had just happened, but the rest of me had not caught up yet.

And then the power flooded, slammed, engulfed, and destroyed. Paving a path through my body and reforming and reshaping my cells. It felt as if I should be able to burst apart and be remade into something else.

No!

My scream reverberated through my head. The Seventine was taking me over, squishing its power into all of my nooks and crannies, and I was not okay with that. I would not lose myself.

With that thought, I fought back. The slimy iciness of its power was easy to recognize and, just like the foreign faerie energy, I aimed to lock it away.

It took me a long time. The struggle was very real. I had no idea what everyone around us was doing. I couldn't shift my focus for more than a microsecond.

After many extended moments, I finally won the battle.

This achievement filled me with a sense of self, my relief strong. I could beat the Seventine one on one. Sure, I was still possessed by the first, because I needed its help, but I had it contained in a section of my energy well.

You are strong, ancient warrior. Your energy is from the mother of all. You will be a welcome addition to us when the worlds are reformed.

I didn't even bother to answer. Nothing I said could ever change its views. It was like arguing with a stone: pointless and painful. Besides, if they reformed the worlds, I'd be dead, because I would fight right up until that point.

"Hello, freaky eyes and marks." Fury's words brought my attention back to the room.

I must be sporting the same swirly globes in my face that possessed Brace had done. And probably had purple coloring my red marks.

I focused on the room. "What do I do now?" I flinched a little at how strange my voice sounded. Lower than usual, smooth and hypnotic.

Everything around me was in this amazingly sharp detail. In some ways it was as if I'd never really seen any of my loved ones before, and yet everything was a hundred percent familiar. The lines of stress on Brace's face; the tension in Lucy's body. A million tiny telltale signs that I'd have missed without the power of the first riding along in my body. Even the way the fine hairs

Dronish

stood up on the back of Fury's neck, and the nail marks lining her palms where she'd clenched her fists so tightly.

Grantham captured my attention again. "You need to join your power with the Seventine. Mingle the two energies together and form an arrow-like projection. You'll have to create a pathway into the prison." His deep voice paused for a beat. "And ... blood is required. The creatures who dwell in the walls won't let you pass without an offering of life."

Damn, everything required me bleeding to death.

The Relli Walker produced a sharp knife and took a step toward me. "I'm sorry, Abby, but this must be heart blood, or as close as possible."

What the eff did that mean?

"What the eff does that mean?" Lucy's snarling words matched my inner dialogue.

Grantham's eyes flicked across to Brace. Such a fast, involuntary movement that I wondered if anyone else had noticed. The already tight features of my mate darkened further. I knew Brace had seen that look. He understood what was about to happen.

"The purest of blood is that which has just left the heart chamber. The most potent would be for me to take from the aorta, but ... it's too dangerous. Instead I'll puncture your carotid, taking from the blood bound for your brain."

"You'll cut my throat?" The hypnotic voice I was currently rocking echoed through the chamber.

Grantham nodded.

Lucy gasped, her hands flying to her mouth. Brace stepped toward me, one of his hands raised. Somehow he managed to pull himself together and halt the movements. Colton was instantly at his side, a flat palm resting against the strong, broad shoulder of my mate. The best friends exchanged a glance and I knew Brace was assuring himself that Colton would stop him if he lost his shit.

"After you bleed enough to satisfy the prison, the path will open and you can shoot the combined energy in. The first will find its brother, and then you use the words. *Excrui changen velliuc mectre*. This will join together the energy forces of the lalunas and the Seventine. They will exchange themselves."

"How does it work? Will the lalunas be prisoners in there or are they bound to the walls?"

In essence all of us are bound to the walls. That is where we are imprisoned.

The first answered my question at the same time Grantham explained this to the room. So that meant on top of the regular security the energy of the prisoners also strengthened the prison. Ingenious.

Luckily sentient thought is limited in the walls.

I picked up a stray tidbit of information from the first. I could tell it wasn't directed at me. He'd gone all inner dialogue. Not surprisingly, he had not appreciated his time in the prison walls. I wanted to kick myself hard. I could not be feeling sorry for their crazy asses, for reals? They were going to destroy everything. Kill billions. I was chalking the emotional breakdown up to the fact we were kind of sharing energy at that moment. Nothing else. I needed to move this exchange up fast. I didn't want to share a body any longer than was needed.

"When you have combined energy with the first, tell

me, and I will let free the blood," Grantham said. He stood close to me.

I reached into my energy and started to form a large ball of the golden light. The Seventine's power responded. The darkness that lurked inside it began to expand from the box I'd contained it in, and then our two energies began to mingle. It was like some sort of weird animal mating ceremony. Like these slugs I'd read about in a book once that had both male and female parts but still needed to exchange ... uh, slimy stuff ... to have young. The first and I were right in the middle of exchanging slime and it was grossing me out on a level usually reserved for images of slugs exchanging slime, foot fungus, and gangers.

There was a delicate balance, a dance of sorts that was taking place between us, and by the end our energies were no longer separate. The gold and dark had blended and formed something of a shimmery purple night. It was a complex entity, this new product, something that was a blend of good and evil. Happiness and sadness. But in essence it was all power, and it was strong.

We work.

The first continued his crusade to tempt me to the dark side, but it was easy now to ignore the seductiveness of his words.

I took a deep breath. Time for the pain. Time to bleed.

"We're ready."

Without even noticing, I'd fallen into referring to us as one.

At least Grantham looked pale, as if he was not happy to be cutting my throat. Better than him being a little trigger-happy. He reached out and grasped my hand, leading us closer to the opening of the prison. The white light was extra bright there as it reflected around in its usual power show.

"My apologies for this," he said. "Please stay very still."

I closed my eyes right around the time the growling started behind us. I didn't need to turn and look. I could sense his anger, feel his fear and panic. Brace was about to lose it.

I was distracted from the overwhelming emotions of my protective mate by the cold bite of steel touching my throat. I forced myself not to swallow too vigorously. With a knife that sharp, any exaggerated movement could sever my throat entirely. I took faith in the fact I was Walker and should not die from this cut, even if Grantham's steady hands slipped.

The sliding of steel continued, and I bit back a whimper. It felt as if he was slicing me so slowly. Why the hell was he going so slowly? The knife glided through my skin like a hot knife through butter. The pressure was immediate, but the pain took ten seconds to register each time he moved it down my throat. Which told me he was cutting deep.

"Why is it taking so long to heal?" Lucy's frantic voice reached my ears, despite the buzzing that so much pain had caused to descend over my brain. "She's bleeding everywhere."

Colton didn't answer. He probably had his hands full right then with a tropical cyclone.

Grantham was the one to reply. "This blade is infused

with ancient Walker energy. It always takes us longer to heal wounds caused by our energy."

The growls increased.

"It's better this way. Otherwise I'll have to keep cutting her to produce enough blood."

Roars surrounded me. "It is enough now!"

Winds buffeted us, and the waves of his anger knocked me back a few steps. Luckily the knife had been pulled from my throat seconds before.

"Give me a minute, Brace." Grantham's voice increased in pitch. "Can you hold him another minute, Colton? We're almost done."

"I'm not sure I can hold him another second." The wolf-Walker's voice was strained. "And he's not even fighting me as hard as he could. Let's all be grateful for the amazing strength of will this Walker possesses, or else we'd all be dead – except for Red."

Lucy snorted. "Not the time, babe."

I was starting to feel a little light-headed now, nothing too serious, just where you know that you've lost a little bit of that red stuff which is essential for life.

"You're done." Grantham's voice was very close to my ear. "The path is open."

I felt a hand come up and wrap around my throat, but I didn't panic. I knew it was Brace. I could feel his heat and masculine scent enveloping me. He was going to protect me and stop me from bleeding to death while I finished the ritual. My eyes opened again. I wanted to see what was happening, but I didn't turn to my mate. Right then I had no time to cry, and I knew the fear on his face would bring me to tears.

I focused.

The first and I reached for our energy. We started to shape that sparkling midnight, turn it into a slim-line arrow which could be shot into the prison. The Seventine was much more adept at energy manipulation and soon a gleaming weapon formed between us. It was beautiful and mesmerizing and, judging by the gasps surrounding us, visible to everyone else too.

Do not let go of the end of the energy, the first warned me. *We will need to keep the path open.*

We shot the arrow free. It left in a burst of power, the trails of dark energy following along. I could feel the prison as it descended, the cold power that lined the walls. The many powerful entities which rested within this rock.

As the arrow descended further I started to notice something else: schisms in the power grid. In the beginning it had felt like a solid wall of energy, but now there were these gaps. If my calculations were correct, I was sensing four very large ones. The release of the Seventine had weakened the walls, and it was time for us to fix that.

The stones were still in my hands, their power contained by the cage. I had to wait until the first found his brother before I released them. The arrow continued descending. I had the end firmly clutched in my energy well. Finally, though, we hit the target. I felt the thud, the burst of strength and coldness which coated the tip of the arrow.

Start the exchange.

The lalunas began to glow and burn then. For the first time I could feel them in my hands, and I knew my blue stone was manipulating all of the energy again.

They started to bleed into the line of dark power that

still connected us to the arrow and, as they attached and descended along the path, the midnight purple lit up. It became a symphony of light and color, bursting free and brightening the already well-lit cavern.

At the same time the coldness on the end started to rise. It was as if the fifth Seventine and the lalunas were magnets, drawing toward each other.

I worried what would happen when they collided. It felt as if I were holding a nuclear weapon that was about to explode.

As they closed the distance between each other, the line of energy started to vibrate, starting small and moving up to large racking shakes. I was worried that I'd not be able to hold on to the line if it got much stronger, but I knew if I let go, the ritual would fail. And this was one ritual I couldn't fail at.

Just when I thought I was about to lose my grip, the vibrations eased. Stupidly, I breathed a sigh of relief, thinking that everything was going to be okay.

Little did I realize that this was just the calm before the massive ass-kicking storm.

14

As the energy of the lalunas collided with that of the Seventine, everything around us stilled. This lasted for just a few beats of my racing heart. I was waiting for something to happen. I could feel the level of power along the line was insane, but there was no explosion or anything. Which was weird.

A sucking sensation started to flow around the stone room.

"What's that?" My eyes flicked left and right.

I knew that the power of the Seventine and the lalunas was still contained in our arrow of energy, so it wasn't either of them.

Brace's eyes narrowed as he scanned the space. Then the screaming started. It was high-pitched, and my eardrums began to burn. The pressure built up. Finally the racket died off, and I felt more energy smash into my arrow.

"It's Tenni." Brace was the first one to figure it out.

I'd been a step behind him, understanding what was traveling along the arrow.

"She's being called to her brethren."

Grantham straightened. "The arrogance of the lalunas was enough that she would never have thought for a moment that her brethren were a weakness for her."

It was true. They had believed they were untouchable. I could tell from the way she'd bragged about her plans, the lack of worry or stress she'd exhibited. Of course, we couldn't have achieved this exchange without the help of my laluna.

I grinned. "Arrogance is blinding."

Brace returned that smile. "For some."

I shook my head at him. Silly Walker.

Time to bring my brother home.

I flicked my eyes to Grantham. "Do I say the words now?"

"Is the energy connected?"

I nodded. "Yes, they're intermingling, somewhere about halfway along my arrow line."

"Then yes, it's time for the exchange."

I sucked in deeply. Bringing forth the memory of the words, I opened my mouth and let them fall free. *"Excrui changen velliuc mectre."*

The first joined me in saying the words. Its voice was mental, though, but that didn't seem to matter.

The moment the last of the word *mectre* fell from my lips, energy ricocheted outwards. I hit the ground, and so did everyone else in the room, including Brace, which told me how strong the blast had been. I managed to hold onto my arrow by the speck of will that I still possessed. It was damn close. Rising from the depths, the cold power moved toward us, and again it started to vibrate.

Brace pulled me to my feet.

"The Seventine is coming," I said.

Glorious. The first was still inside me, and I wanted it out, but knew we had to wait to let go of the arrow. The white of the glowing light started to fade out to red, and I knew the Seventine was about to emerge. I prepared myself for more evil to enter the world.

Thank you for your assistance today. You have furthered our plans monumentally, and I will see you again at the convergence.

The first tried to leave. I could feel it bashing against the walls I'd created in my well, the walls of the cage. But it was stuck. I still held power over it. I was feeling a little mean, so I took my time releasing the bond.

In that moment I sensed something new coming from the first. Fear.

What did you do to me?

I had no idea, so I didn't answer. Somehow I could keep it locked inside and it hadn't been able to free itself. It was an exhilarating feeling.

The rushing winds picked up again and the red light spilled across us all. Two shadows zoomed from the prison.

Hang on, what the hell?

Laughter echoed around us. Maniacal laughter.

"What did you do?" I screamed to the swirling mists.

You thought we wouldn't know how powerful the lalunas were? How they were going to strengthen this prison. Of course we knew, but we had the means to free five and six. We took the wager.

No! They had done it to me again, really to all of us. We'd needed this so badly to lock away the lalunas and free Josian. Now five and six were free – holy eff balls. The princeps' plan had not been as great as they'd thought. The cons seemed to be higher than the pros right about then, since only the seventh remained locked in the prison. I should have known that the Seventine would not take a deal which was heavily skewed in our favor.

My blood spattered as I turned to follow the mists. My throat was still bleeding. The pain had faded away though in the ensuing panic.

"What happened, Abbs?" Lucy was tucked under Colton's arm.

He seemed to be supporting her in the energy rushing around us.

"Somehow they released five and six." My voice broke as I explained. I swallowed with difficulty before turning hard eyes on Grantham. "Did you know this would happen?"

He had his hands against the wall, resting his head between them. I wondered what the hell he was doing.

His voice was gruff as he spoke. "The lalunas are now part of this mountain and the prison foundation. They're no longer sentient, but have transformed back to the mineral elements from which they came."

I felt a moment of sadness that I'd never have my little stone drop into my hand again, but it was better this way.

Finally Grantham turned to face us. "They freed two because I underestimated the power you would have after joining to the first. Together you could have done anything." His eyes flicked back to the wall. "As well as checking on the lalunas, I was feeling the vibrations in the stone, talking to the minerals. We were lucky they only pulled the next two free. There was enough energy to free them all, but not enough time. And I'm guessing the Seventine didn't want to risk upsetting the balance too quickly."

My heart was beating rapidly. I snuggled myself closer to Brace, needing the comfort. His long arm swung around me and lifted me into his body. I was hardly even supporting my own weight now.

"Well, that sucks the big one," Fury huffed. "But I'm looking at the silver lining. There's still one imprisoned, and they need a shit ton of power to get it out. Supes will find the last girl and we'll lock them away."

I tried to bring my mind back to the positives, but with the remnants of the first's energy still inside me, I was all out of whack.

As I had this thought Brace released the gates which had been separating our energy from each other, and his presence flowed through me. The heat and signature power load that was Brace washed away the lingering effects of what had happened, and I felt my neck burn a little as the cut finished its healing. My melancholy lifted, and I was able to put a more optimistic spin on everything.

"Okay, so Tenni is no longer a threat and we'll get Josian back, right?" I faced Grantham and he nodded, but there was some hesitation which I did not like. "Not to mention that this prison is now as secure as it will ever be."

As if to reiterate my point, the red light was fading out, but instead of its usual white glow, it shone purple.

The color of the lalunas when they combined with each other.

"Right now we need to finish this up, find the last girl, and get these asshole Seventine locked away."

Colton stood taller. "Are they still in this room?" His features were drawn as he shifted his eyes around.

It always surprised me that others weren't as tied to the Seventine as Brace and I always seemed to be; left over connections from his possession and now my own.

"No, they left straight away." I'd felt their overwhelming excitement; they thought they had this all wrapped up now.

I was going to stop them, no matter what.

"Where is Josian?" Lallielle's voice was stronger. "I still can't feel him, the bond is restricted."

Dad. I mentally reached for him. But for the first time there was nothing, no reply.

"I can't reach him either," Grantham bit out.

Brace straightened, taking me with him, as I was still snuggled against his chest. "We need to go to his world and see what's wrong. The lalunas' power will no longer be controlling him. They're now part of the stone."

So where the hell was my father?

AS WE EXITED the cave I gulped down the lump that had formed in my throat. Outside was exactly how I pictured a war zone. Two sides, patiently staring each other down, waiting to move in for the kill. I could see our side, the Walkers, pixies, faeries, First Worlders and many others, had started setting up camps and shelters. The black ash which coated the ground was shifting in the air. It was not pleasant to breathe, but everyone looked to be dealing. I squinted across the distance as I tried to ascertain exactly what we were facing.

Ahhh, heck, freaking zombies again. And there was also ...

"The same tree things that were on Crais." Fury was also scanning the area. "They're damn hard to destroy."

She wasn't kidding. They'd been practically impervious to her fire. And we didn't have an army of dragoonas at our disposal right then.

My spirits lifted and I let out a joyous cry as a two-headed beast caught my attention. He was galloping across from the other side, clouds of dust raining around him. My feet started moving and I met him halfway, throwing my arms around both heads as best I could.

"Cere," I cried, "I'm so glad you're okay."

I'd known he wasn't dead. The bond between us was solid, but the worry had still been there. It was horrible to think that so much stuff had happened in the past few hours, events which had taken all my time and focus, and had prevented me going back to Crais to look for him. To make sure he was okay.

Cerberus then proceeded to sloppily lick my face, which only made me laugh and cry harder. Lovable beast seemed to have forgiven me.

Fury scowled. "When am I going to get my own ugly-ass dog?" Her hands dropped to her slim hips.

Cerberus gave her a snorting growl, but seemed to take no offence at her insult.

Then, as if she'd summoned the animal by speaking, I noticed something bounding across the center of the battle field. Way out in the open, in the space that separated both sides of the fight. I squinted my eyes, because it was small and fast. Darting, ducking, and diving through the dead plants, dirt, and ash.

Cerberus shifted next to me, letting out a bark when he too noticed the little creature. It didn't stop moving, and it was hard to tell if it was colored black or if it was coated in ash. Finally, my eyes and brain registered what it was.

A kitten. A tiny, fluffy ball of cuteness.

"What's that?" Fury took a step toward the runty-looking cat.

Lucy's blue-and-golden eyes lit up. "Oh, my god, it's a kitty. I always wanted a cat."

Fluff-ball kept moving, disappearing from sight as it entered the masses that were gathered around. It suddenly appeared again and in one last speedy jump landed right in front of Fury. We all fell silent as we stared down, examining the new arrival. It was tiny, no larger than twelve inches tall, and it wasn't dirty. Its coat was a shiny and fluffy black, with especially thick fur around the neck area. Like a mini lion.

Fury's eyes widened then. "No way ... no freaking way in all of Crais hell. You are not my animal."

She wrenched her eyes from the cat, staring upwards into the sky. "Supes, deal with this. It's tiny, and fluffy. No claws. No fangs. It's ... cute." Her voice trailed off in horror.

Lucy cracked up then. I mean laugh out loud, hit the ground, she was that hysterical. "Whoever the Walker gods are, I think I love them," she managed to choke out between her gasping laughter. "Fury got a kitten for her sacred animal." The rest of her words trailed off, indecipherable.

"Supes gets a hellhound, Talina a water dragon, Delane a horse with a goddamned spear on its head." Fury's eyes seemed to be drawn back down toward the innocent little fluff-ball that was sitting so calmly in front of her. "No," she barked at the kitten. "Go away, you are not my animal."

I was worried right then that the Walker guide would be upset by this encounter. I glanced across to Brace to see his reaction. My mate had the smallest of grins, which told me there was no need to worry at that precise moment.

Fury suddenly dropped to her knees, bringing her face very close to the sweet little baby kitty. "What do you want? Food? If I give you something you want, will you go away?"

Brace laughed then, and the sound filled me with absolute joy. I didn't hear his laughter very often. It made him seem younger, less burdened by all his responsibilities.

"That's Crete. He's always some variety of feline, and has the temperament to match," he said to Fury.

I grinned at the Crais half. "Sounds like a perfect pair."

Fury opened her mouth to say something, probably an insult, judging by the narrowing of her eyes, and at that moment Crete leaped at her. She had no option but to hold out her arms and catch him. Her eyes widened as the flood of bond crossed between them. Her white hair whirled before settling into place again. The kitten was so damn cute. He snuggled right into her, dark green eyes wide as they stared up.

"No," Fury said again. "I will not be charmed by your cuteness. I need a monster, a warrior animal. Something that can rip zombies and tear creatures apart with its bare hands."

Crete ignored her ranting, snuggling in further, closing his eyes and starting to purr. Fury just stared down at her new bundle of joy. She eventually staggered to her feet, her mouth continued to open and close, over and over, as if she had no idea what to do or say.

Lucy was still laughing, holding her stomach and wiping away tears. "She's in shock. Fury is never speechless and look at her now. Hysterical."

I couldn't help the snort of laughter that escaped me. I knew Fury would be pissed off that I was laughing at her predicament too, but come on – of all the half-Walkers, it had to be Fury who got the fluff-ball.

Cerberus stepped closer to my side then. His movement drew Fury's gaze. Her features darkened further.

Lucy swallowed the last of her laughter, wiping away the tears still streaming down her face. "I'll take him if you don't want him. He's adorable."

Fury snarled as Lucy stepped closer. "No! You are not Walker."

And there was that arrogance we were so well known for. Fury didn't even seem to notice that she had pulled Crete closer, snuggling him into her chest. Lucy winked at me, and I had the sneaky suspicion that she'd deliberately provoked Fury's possessiveness.

"I can't wait here any longer. Please take me to the

stone world." Lallielle drew my attention by gently grasping my arm.

Shit, she was right. I couldn't wait any longer either.

"Yes, we need to get our Josian back," I said firmly. "You all keep this under control here. Go and find Delane; she'll have the rundown. And make sure Ria and Lucas haven't killed each other yet."

Everyone laughed, except Fury, who was still glaring at Crete.

"I want to go with you." Lucy stomped closer. "You keep running off without me."

I lowered my head and dropped a kiss on her cheek. "Stay here, Lucy Loo. We'll be quick, not worth dragging your butt across the worlds."

She snorted. "You say that, and then you disappear into some weird drama and I get more gray hair worrying about you. Let me tell you, blond, green, and gray do not go well together."

I half-rolled my eyes. Her dramatics were funny. "Okay, fine, you can come with me."

"I will be there." Brace's voice brooked no argument.

Colton stepped in. "And don't even think of leaving me out."

Lallielle flapped her arms, her features tightening. "Yes, everyone is coming, and it's time to move now."

Fury finally lifted her face from the feline that had her sole attention, even though she'd claimed to not want Crete. "See you soon. Be careful."

We stepped away from the crowds, back toward the mountain entrance. Lallielle took one of my hands, Brace the other. Lucy and Colton linked into our group.

Cerberus shrunk down to his tiny size and crawled up onto my shoulder again.

"Ready?" I shifted my head to take them all in. Everyone nodded.

I closed my eyes and reached for a tether. I wanted to go to the main stone living area. My mind expanded and energy rose. I had the image firmly in my head – but there was nothing there. No tethers connected, no glittery strands. Exactly the same as when I'd tried to trace from pixie land. Why was this happening? I replaced the living room image with another, the garden area where Tenni used to be sequestered. Again, there was nothing.

I opened my eyes to find everyone watching me.

Lucy was blunt as always. "I'm guessing by the fact that we haven't zipped across the star-system that there's a problem."

I blinked a few times, trying to get myself under control. I turned to the right and faced my mother. "There're no tethers; his world is gone." The pitch of my voice rose. I was pretty much screeching.

My hands were sweaty. I gripped Brace's harder so that he wouldn't slip away.

"I can't open a doorway either." My mate's voice had me swinging my head around to meet depthless chocolate eyes. "There's no other explanation: the world is gone; its tethers have been severed."

Tears started to pour from my eyes. I couldn't have stopped them if I'd tried. "Does that mean ..." My voice broke and I couldn't continue.

I wouldn't even let my brain comprehend the possibility that he was, that my father no longer ... no! He was alive.

"Tenni clearly planned for this, but Josian is not gone." Lallielle wasn't falling apart. "I can't contact him but the bond still exists."

My eyes darted across her features, trying to ferret out whatever thoughts she was concealing. I felt a glimmer of hope shoot through me.

"So where could he be then? You're his mate. Is there anywhere he could be hidden that you wouldn't feel?"

"Like the dome on Nephilius," Brace suggested.

Colton straightened. "Yes, the lalunas planned for this, probably knowing we would fight them. They stashed Josian somewhere and made sure the power containing him didn't come from them."

So where the hell was my father and how could we possibly find him?

Lallielle pulled her hand from mine. "The rest of you don't have time. We have to beat the Seventine or there's no point to all of this. I'll find him. I'll search the universe."

Grantham stepped up to her side. "You'll need me to open doorways. I think maybe we can use some of the power from the new Doreen princeps to try and find him. Princeps receive a distinct sort of energy from their people. Josian will have remnants of this."

"I want to help." My voice was a growl. "I promised Dad that we wouldn't reform the melding bond, that he wouldn't be a prisoner of those crazy lalunas."

Brace and I had not had much choice. It had been reform the bond or die. But still, Josian had suffered from that decision. Sometimes you don't have any good choices, but you still had a choice. And I had made the choice to reform that bond, so now I needed to clean it up.

Lucy hugged me. "You can't, Abbs. The Seventine and lalunas can't win. We need to find that last girl. We have to go to Earth like now."

I huffed in hard, my lungs burning as if the very air was toxic. Which, considering all of the ash floating around, wasn't farfetched.

"Okay, but I want to know everything you find," I said to Grantham and Lallielle. "Check in with me or Brace. If there's anything serious you might need the half-Walker power for, you have to let me know."

Please don't risk yourselves unnecessarily, I was mentally begging them, but didn't say the words out loud. I swayed a little on my feet.

All of a sudden the blood loss, lack of sleep, stress over Josian and never ending emotionally trying moments were starting to take their toll.

Warmth draped across my shoulders. I blinked a few times, my thick lashes concealing the view for a moment. Brace had removed his long-sleeved ribbed shirt and draped the massive lengths around me. Leaving him in just a simple black shirt. I tried not to swoon or drool. The man was perfection, every single hard plane of him. Sigh, I was blessed to have him as my mate. He'd never had to give me a coat or anything before. This world just wasn't cold, but right then he was as selfless and observant as ever. I had actually been feeling a little cold.

"We'll start with the Doreen camp, and move on from there." Grantham, in his warrior mode, drew my scattered attention. "We'll find him, Aribella."

"I'll come to the Doreen camp." I straightened, my hands reaching up to keep Brace's shirt from falling free.

"No."

The word was not loud or angry, but there was an unmovable strength to it which told me how serious Brace was.

"You need to rest. I could count on one hand the amount of sleep you've had in the past few days, and you have to go to Earth. Grantham and Lalli can handle this. The fighting hasn't started yet." He waved his hand across to the regimented chaos which surrounded us. "Take your rest while you can."

I wrinkled my nose at him; our stare-off continued, neither of us bending, each wanting to control this situation. I knew Brace was right, but still … never hurt to push back. Give a man an inch and he would run a mile.

He grinned, reading my thoughts. "Please, baby." He softened his words and I knew he'd spoken out loud so that everyone would know he had caved first. He was giving me the power.

I closed my eyes briefly, before sucking in a ragged breath. "Okay, I'll rest for now." I strode across to hug my mother hard. "Please let me know the moment you find anything. If I'm asleep, come into my dreams."

She gave me an extra squeeze before pulling away. She ran a hand down my mass of curls. "Get some rest, sweetheart. I need to know that you and Sammy are okay. That lets me focus on finding Jos."

I grinned. "Don't you worry; I have my guard dog." Cerberus shifted on my shoulder. "And my guard mate to keep me safe."

As soon as I stepped away from Lallielle, Brace swept

me into his arms, his shirt soft beneath me. Cerberus gave a barking growl before readjusting himself in the crook of my neck.

"I can walk," I protested, but I wasn't struggling very hard. It was too damn nice being in his arms.

"Indulge me," he drawled. "I like to carry you."

Colton stepped up next to us, Lucy's hand firmly clutched in his much larger one. "Are you going to Abernath?"

Brace nodded. "I'm taking Abby to our home."

I still got trills of tingles up and down my body, my actual blood heating at those words. Brace's arms tightened as he felt my joy.

"Lucy needs sleep too. We might as well come with you and rest at our home."

Lucy blinked a few times and then her beautiful blue eyes welled up. Colton's expression was almost comical as he struggled to figure out what was wrong with his mate. If he stopped panicking for a moment I'm sure he'd read it in her mind.

"What's wrong, pretty girl? What happened? Did you have a vision?"

Eventually Lucy pulled her hands free and fluttered up. When she and Colton were face to face, she kissed him. It shocked the words right out of his mouth. They both seemed lost in the moment, and the rest of us exchanged smiling glances. Except for Fury, who was still glaring at Crete, and Dune, who was watching his mate with an amused expression.

Finally they pulled apart.

"I've never had a home." Lucy's voice was soft, but we all had excellent hearing. "Abby and you are my home, but to have a place that's ours ..."

She trailed off as tears trickled down her porcelain skin. A tender half-smile crossed Colton's lips.

He gathered his pixie into his arms. "I'll give you anything you want, pretty girl. Everything is yours."

Some of her tears dried up, and a scary grin crossed her features. "So you're saying I have free rein to decorate?"

I snorted. Colton was in for it. But I had to give it to him. He never showed an ounce of apprehension.

"If you want me to, I'll rebuild the entire damn thing for you."

Lucy kissed him again.

I sighed. "This could go on for hours."

My best friend managed to flip me off as well as continue kissing the love of her life.

EVERYONE DISPERSED. Fury and Dune took off to find the other half-Walkers – I promised I'd check in with everyone before taking off to Earth. Grantham and Lallielle went to the Doreen princeps, and the four of us – my very bestest friends – were heading to Abernath.

I was still in Brace's arms. It always amazed me that he showed no strain despite the fact he'd been holding my weight for at least twenty minutes. We all entered the doorway, Lucy's wings shimmering as she fluttered through.

As we exited on to the other side, the gravity hit me immediately. The strain was all encompassing, but thankfully my body seemed to adjust far quicker than the last time I had been there. It sort of felt as if my body contained a memory cell of that world.

Colton had coated Lucy in a thin layer of energy, even though they hoped that with her pixie and faerie genetics she would be able to cope now. But no one wanted to risk it.

I closed my eyes for the journey across the green cardboard copy mountains, under the stream and into the town of Abernath.

The noise was immediate and jarring on the other side. There seemed to be celebrations going on in the streets.

I was awake enough now to glance around. "Put me down. I want to see." I struggled a little in Brace's arms.

With a kiss on my nose, he dropped me to my feet. His long-sleeved shirt fell down, and I quickly scooped it up, one of my hands keeping a hold on Cerberus so he wouldn't fall from my shoulder. The tiny hellhound had amazing balance.

Lucy danced a little as we continued to wander through. "What's all this for?"

Colton laughed. "We've had celebrations galore ever since Caty and Lasandra returned. And, well, the return of our princeps' melded mate tipped them right over the edge."

I continued to look left and right. "Aren't they worried with most of their men and warriors on First World to fight battles?"

"No, Que always had the men off on missions. The Abernaths are used to it," Brace said, and I could feel his overriding need to change things on this world.

Many stopped their revelry to bow and greet us. We

had more than one offer to join them, but sleep was what we needed most. I was dead on my feet.

"Where's your home, Colt?" I found the energy to shift my chin up and to the right to meet his gaze. I wondered when they'd be leaving us. I didn't want Lucy far away.

"Right next door," he said, flashing me all those flawless white teeth.

Lucy and I exchanged delighted grins. That was perfect.

The pair had to leave us at the start of Brace's spectacular home. Their residence was a slightly smaller but still opulent double-story home to the left of Brace's. We made plans to have breakfast in the town in the morning. For a brief moment as we chatted in front of our houses, our lives felt so normal, as if this was how we would live if the destruction of this star-system weren't imminent.

Brace stepped into my side. "Come on, Red, I'm failing as a mate at the moment. I'm not looking after you."

I knew he wanted to sweep me into his arms again, so to make it easier on him I snuggled closer. Gave him a sense of supporting me. Plus there was nowhere in any of the worlds I'd rather be. Cerberus took that moment to jump off my shoulder. He lumbered off to frolic in the garden, having shifted back to horse-size.

"Do you think Josian is okay?" I asked Brace. My father had not been far from my thoughts. I was stressed and missing him like crazy.

He dropped a kiss onto the top of my head, his scent and warmth surrounding me. "Josian is one of the strongest Walkers I know. If he didn't let his laluna beat him through all of these years, I doubt he has now."

Slivers of hope threaded the dark thoughts in my mind. As we made it onto the front porch, I lingered for a few moments, just enjoying the familiar scent of the flowers.

Brace must have had similar thoughts. "I really loved that date we had on First World. Even though I didn't remember our melding, it was still one of the best nights of my very long life."

I sighed. "It was one of the best nights I've had too, despite how heartbreaking it was to know you couldn't remember us."

Brace's eyes darkened, unspoken thoughts crossing the depths. "I wanted to kiss you all night. It took every ounce of my strength to hold back."

Desire tingled its way from the tip of my head down to my toes, and suddenly I wasn't that tired. "I hope that strength of will isn't working at the moment, because you have exactly eight seconds to kiss me or shit will be getting real."

Brace and I hadn't been properly together since the melding bond had been broken, and right then the need was slamming into me with the force of a freight train. He must have read that desire blazing through my eyes, or my thoughts were giving it away, because he groaned and placed both hands under my arms.

Bringing us up to the same height, he slammed his lips into mine. It was firm, uncontrolled, and full of passion. My back hit the front door and for a few endless moments I was floating in ecstasy. My Walker could kiss like no one else, full lips moving, tongues dancing, tastes and scents flooding every sense.

Brace shifted his hands. One went under my butt to support my weight and the other tangled into my masses of curls.

Somehow he managed to open the door behind us. Considering both hands were busy, he had to have used energy.

I wrenched my lips from his, my breath huffing in and out. "Bedroom now."

"Your wish, my command." His serious chocolate eyes stared into mine. They were soft and shimmery in the dim light.

"Ahem."

The clearing of a throat had my boiling blood go immediately to freezing. I bit my lip before burying my head into Brace's chest.

"It's your mother, isn't it?" In my impassioned state I'd forgotten about Lasandra and Caty.

I'd had no time to ask Brace if his mother and sister were living with him. I knew that this had been Lasandra's house, so there was every chance she still lived here.

Brace chuckled. "I'll protect you." He dropped me to my feet.

I was forced to turn and meet the icy eyes of my mate's beautiful mother. She had her slender arms crossed over her chest as she stared me down. Of course, her gaze softened on her son.

"I'm sorry to intrude on your privacy, Brace, but I need to speak with you ... alone."

Tension filtered through Brace's body and mind. He was upset that his mother was treating me so coldly, but I understood. He was her only son. She loved him more than life, and right then she didn't know or trust me. I got it.

"Anything you need to say to me, Mom, can be said in front of Abby. She's my melded mate. Even if I could keep anything from her, I don't want to. We're equal partners."

Lasandra's words cracked back at him like a whip. "She should have thought of that before breaking your heart and a sacred bond. If trust is so important between you two, why did she break yours so thoroughly?"

Ouch. I was way too tired to deal with this tonight. Angry mothers-in-law were really far down my list of priorities.

I reached up and gently rubbed my hand across Brace's lower back. "It's okay, I'm pretty exhausted. I'll just let you two chat."

His lips possessed mine again. It was not a show of dominance or an 'eff you' to his mother. I could feel that he simply needed to kiss me.

"Same room?" I asked.

He nodded and with one last soft kiss on the lips I turned to leave. "Goodnight, it was nice seeing you again." I was polite to Lasandra. I knew and accepted that I deserved some of her ire.

"Good night." Her reply was stiff, but still she replied.

Cerberus followed me into Brace's room. He explored for a minute before finally curling up in the corner. He was asleep in an instant. My faithful puppy.

I stripped off my clothes and, too tired for a shower, just washed my face and brushed my teeth in the bathroom. I slipped on one of Brace's shirts. It fell to mid-thigh and was soft and cozy.

Unconsciously I tuned into my mate for a brief moment. Brace had most of his thoughts open to me, but I didn't pry any further. If it was important, he'd tell me later.

Crawling across the soft sheets, I closed my eyes and tried not to think about the fact that Josian was missing. Not to mention that the next day we were going to Earth, and war was about to erupt on First World.

Instead I called on Brace to help and, with a whisper of his energy and warmth surrounding me, I drifted off to my first peaceful sleep since the bond had been broken. The thought which calmed me the most was knowing that very soon Brace would be in this bed with me. I was no longer alone.

This realization gave me the sweetest dreams ever, something to get me through the coming dark days, because I had no doubt things were going to get worse before they got better.

15

BRACE

Lasandra relaxed the second Abigail disappeared from sight. She stepped forward and wrapped her arms around Brace, drawing her precious son closer.

Brace pulled back.

"She's not going anywhere." His low tone was harsher than he'd normally use with Lasandra.

He loved his mother but would not tolerate her mistreatment of Abigail. Despite the fact his mate had been calm and polite, he'd seen the hurt in her jewel eyes. No one hurt Red on his watch.

"I don't want to talk about your mate." Lasandra's full lips curled as she said the last word. "I need your help. I've been trying to figure out what happened to Que. I know the evil bastard didn't die. I can still feel him."

Brace straightened. He'd always had doubts that the Seventine could have actually destroyed his father, but as the months had moved past and Que failed to return, he'd started to accept this as truth. Now his mother had just reinstated all his original doubts with a single sentence. His parents had been mated, but it had never been a true Walker match. They'd not had the proper bond, although connections had existed between them.

"So what do you think happened to Que? Is he out there just biding his time until the convergence?"

Lasandra pushed back her blond hair. "There's this chamber in his monstrosity of a house. He spoke of it, but never took me there. I know we'll find our answers there, answers to so many things."

Brace felt the hot ebb of anger flickering at the ends of his veins. "The experiment labs?"

For many years Que had talked about this room and the different creations he'd been trying to achieve. The evils he'd been prepared to unleash if anyone disobeyed him. But Brace had also never seen it. He'd had his men searching the glass monstrosity, but so far they'd turned up nothing.

Lasandra paled out. Even her lips barely held color. "Yes, and I think I've figured out how to get in there."

Brace examined her. She looked determined, and he would take the time to see if her knowledge had uncovered what his men could not.

"Give me an hour. I want to check on Abbs and clean up a bit." He needed to shower off the grime from the ash-filled dark mountain.

And, more importantly, he needed a few uninterrupted moments with his girl.

His mother nodded, going on her toes to kiss his cheek. "I'll meet you in front of the horror house in an hour."

She left using the side door. Brace had offered her this

place when she'd returned, but Lasandra had declined, deciding she wanted a new start. Which had been a good thing, since this house was the very place he wanted to make a home with Abigail. She'd told him how much she loved it, and above all else Brace needed her to be happy.

That was also part of the reason he'd *strongly* suggested Colton move into the dwelling beside theirs. Abigail and Lucy would be happiest living close to each other.

He exhaled forcefully as he used his energy to secure the perimeter of the house. Everything was going to shit right then. The Seventine had just one more to free, Josian was missing, and his poor beautiful mate had the weight of every world on her shoulders. Brace was determined to take some of that weight. Hell, he'd take it all if she'd let him, but her independence and sense of responsibility was strong.

He strode through the house, his long-legged stride eating up the distance between them and, as always, his heart rate increased at the thought of touching her again. Nothing else in his long life moved his emotions like Abigail. They had spent far too many nights apart, and he was over it; from now on, there was no more space between them. Brace was pretty sure he'd kill the next entity to keep them apart.

The room was dark when he entered, just the slightest spill of light from the bathroom. Without thought, he crossed the room, moving until he stood right at the edge of the bed. Abigail's frame looked small; she lay unmoving, her exhaustion knocking her out cold.

Brace couldn't stop himself from dropping to his knees and examining every detail of her beautiful face.

His mate was without any doubt absolutely heart-stopping stunning. He wasn't the only one to think so, but he also saw so much deeper than her perfect exterior. The fire and determination with which she threw herself into everything, the protectiveness and honor with which she made each choice. Even the difficult ones.

He had to touch her.

Sometimes he felt as if he'd go insane if he couldn't feel her soft skin, taste her full sensual lips. It was torture of the highest order. He'd been tortured by Que, but distancing himself from Red was pain beyond any he'd known.

He lightly stroked her cheek, and even in the deep of sleep she mumbled and shifted toward him. When Abigail had confessed about their broken melding bond, Brace had felt an actual gash carve through his heart. It was a wound he wasn't sure would ever be fully erased, one of those injuries which healed but always left some scar tissue behind.

Abigail shifted closer again, her features tightening as if, even in sleep, she was afraid or worried. Brace fought the urge to gather her into his arms. She needed rest, and he would not wake her because of his selfish need. Her mass of curls cut a fiery path across the light sheets, and as her shifting caused the blanket to lower Brace realized that she was wearing one of his shirts.

He groaned. Did women realize what it did to men when they wore their clothes? It was like she was wearing his name on her chest. The sight brought out his caveman – as Abigail would say. He knew then he was going to lose the battle. He had to hold her; he needed to feel her close; he had to wipe clear those fine lines of tension that were feathering her brow. He wasn't meeting his mother for an hour and he wanted that time with this woman who had not only stolen his heart but also his soul.

He could not exist without her, and he wouldn't want to.

Brace shucked off all of his clothes except for the tight boxer briefs and, doing his best not to disturb her, he eased in and gathered her close. She stirred but didn't wake. He considered that a success. She felt so delicate in his arms. He was constantly surprised at the strength she wielded because to him she was as fragile as a beautiful flower. She moved closer, her body craving the healing of their bond.

"Brace."

Abigail said his name so softly, as if she didn't want to disturb the moment.

Brace buried his face into her neck, her silky and fragrant curls caressing him.

"I'm sorry, baby; I didn't mean to wake you."

She laughed. The sound was like a shot of adrenalin to his body, and the same overwhelming desire he always felt around her exploded to painful levels. He forced himself to focus. Now was not the time. He was a man who prided himself on his control, even if one redhead seemed to be crumbling the foundation.

Abigail flipped over so they were face to face, and Brace was again grateful for his exceptional eyesight. He could see every facet of her stunning, emerald eyes. They were so wide and clear, and he could read the emotions pouring from her. He knew he was turning into a weak-ass Walker, but there was something about staring into those jewel-like depths, something which knocked him right on his ass.

"I've missed you so much." Her voice broke a little. "Every night since I severed our bond I've dreamed of being with you like this, of lying in your arms, and touching your skin."

To reiterate her point, she lifted both hands and pressed them against Brace's bare chest. Another sob choked from her. "Some nights I thought the pain would kill me ... sometimes, I wanted it to."

Brace had no idea how to control the flood of emotions he was experiencing right then. Her pain was killing him. He wanted to punch someone or throw a few energy balls, but mostly he would have done anything to erase the agony from her face. She was sobbing inside; he could feel her anguish.

He gently fisted two handfuls of her hair. They needed a moment to heal, a moment to bond. With that thought in mind, he slammed his lips against hers, pressing into her softness, but forcing himself to hold back his full strength.

Then as the intoxicating taste of her filled his senses and she returned the kiss with abandon, he had to fight himself not to pull her harder into him.

It always felt, no matter how close they were, it was not close enough. Her moan cut straight through to him. His body was hard and ready, every muscle rigid, and his control all but gone. The usual reaction he had to his mate.

"I need you, Brace." Her tone was begging and breath came in gasps as she lifted her lips from his.

Brace tried to force his body to calm a little. He did

not want to hurt her in his need. "Red, please. No more begging. I swear to the mother of all ..." He paused. "Do you know how much I love you? I love you more than I ever thought was possible; you destroy and rebuild me every day."

Her eyes softened, shimmering at him. His heart clenched at the sight.

"I love you too, Brace, so much. But right now if you don't kiss me again, I'm going to be pissed off."

He grinned. Her fire was as big a turn-on as her begging.

"Your wish, my command."

He touched his lips to hers again, softer this time, gently moving as their tongues tangled together in a dance as old as time itself. As the ever-present passion between them grew, the urgency increased. Brace freed one of his hands from her hair and fisted the shirt she wore.

He spoke between kisses. "You should always wear my clothes, like every day. But right now, this has to go."

She arched so he could strip her bare, his eyes feasting on the long expanses of skin on display. Abigail had a body which kept him up at night; perfect features and legs which went on for miles. It was standard for Walkers to be beautiful, but Brace couldn't actually imagine there were any more perfect than his Red.

Brace was already shirtless, but Abigail wasted no time ripping the boxers from him. She leaned back on her elbows, running her eyes over his body.

"You keep looking at me like that and this will be over before it's even started." His voice was low and husky, his need riding every word.

She licked her lips, clearly trying to kill him. Her gaze focused on his wide shoulders. "Did your muscles get bigger? I swear every time I get you naked, there are more muscles."

He grinned; it made him happy that she liked his body. He'd always worked hard in training, his muscles honed over hundreds of years. And the extra size she was seeing was the power boost from being Princeps. His strength was so much greater than before. Brace knew this strength was essential to him. His power was his weapon to keep her safe, protect her from any that would mean her harm.

Words were forgotten then as he reached for her again. There were no more pauses as they took the time to touch and taste, kissing along long limbs, relearning all the facets of each other. Their bodies had been apart for too many nights, and now, as the blood raced through them, it was as if some of the fissures within healed. As they moved closer and more in sync, there were less secrets, less hurt, and less pain. They were healing each other through the simple act of loving.

Afterwards they lay together in a tangle of overheated limbs. Brace held her tightly, unwilling to allow any space between them.

"I have to go meet Mom." He finally broke the silence. He was half tempted to cancel, needing to stay with his girl for a little longer. "She said there was something that Que was hiding in his house, a room which might hold some answers."

Abigail shifted her head to meet his gaze.

They lay less than an inch apart.

"She hates me, doesn't she?"

Brace lifted his right hand and traced a path down her cheek, before gently cupping her chin in his large hand. "No, right now she's fighting against the change, against everything she's lost. You know, I never even knew she was missing. I thought she was searching for Caty. I had no idea that Que had stolen her away and dropped her into the same world."

Guilt ripped through him. He'd thought his mother had abandoned him. He hadn't been mad with her, knowing she was searching for Caty, figuring she'd somehow cut her energy off. He should have looked for her too, had enough faith that his mother would have told him if she was planning on disappearing. Damn Que, filling his head with lies.

Abigail clued into his thoughts again. "Lasandra thinks I'm going to steal you away from her?" She was astute, as always.

Brace feathered a kiss across her lips. "Mom's always been protective of her children. When Walkers mate, it's everything ... our whole world. She knows now that she's no longer the most important woman in my life. She doesn't like the competition."

Abigail shifted as if she were uncomfortable. "I would never take you away from her." Her gentle heart shone through.

"It's a done deal, Red, I'm yours. From the moment you touched my soul, the moment we dreamed of each other, I was a goner. There's no hope for anything else, and I've never been happier. Mom's just going to have to learn how to fit into these new dynamics."

As he finished speaking, he pulled himself from the bed, and gathered his mate into his arms. He strode with determination into the next room and, using his energy, turned on the many shower heads that littered the ceiling of the large square stall. Powerful jets of water shot around. He made sure it was the perfect temperature, before easing them inside. Abigail had her legs wrapped tightly around his body, pressing her curves into him.

As the water beat onto their skin, massaging and caressing every sensitive nerve ending, she dropped her head back and let the water wash over her. Brace couldn't help but follow that movement, placing his lips against her throat. Kissing his way up to her mouth. Passion flared again, but they didn't have time for anything more than these few hot, drugging kisses.

Eventually he had to place her down so they could clean up.

"Do you want to come with me to Que's?" he asked.

Abigail had a toothbrush hanging from the corner of her mouth, she still preferred this method of teeth cleaning. She spoke around it. "Yes, I don't want you checking out anything dangerous without me." It was goddamned adorable that she thought she could protect him. "And Lasandra needs to get used to seeing me around."

His mate was beautiful and brave. "Okay, baby. Well, we have ten minutes, so unfortunately time is up in here."

Abigail dropped her lower lip in an exaggerated pout. "This is the best shower in all the worlds. I think I could live in here and be a happy, wrinkly-skinned person."

Brace threw back his head and laughed. "Walkers' skin doesn't wrinkle in the water."

She shoved him. "You know what I mean."

Dronish

THEY SPENT LONGER than planned in the shower. Dressing was also hindered by the fact they kept undressing again, but eventually they left their home and made their way hand-in-hand across Abernath. The parties had died off a little as the later hour approached, many retiring for the night. Brace knew they'd be back the next day. He could feel the ebbing flow of his people, nothing specific, just energy, but it was comforting all the same.

Lasandra was waiting in front of the building, alone, arms crossed over her body as she stared up into the darkened sky. The four suns which lit up the sky of Abernath had sunk to the other side of their world. They'd be back in a few hours. But for now there were only slivers of light from the stars.

His mother finally noticed them. Her face fell a little when she saw Abigail at his side, but she covered it up quickly enough.

"Follow me." Her words were short as she turned and slipped through the open door.

Brace hid his distaste as they entered the cold, glass-fronted building. He hated this dwelling. It was the place he had been brought to for punishments on those all too frequent occasions he'd dared to question Que. The former princeps had had this laser which actually marked the skin of Walkers. Brace still had slight divots littering his body. They were hard to see but they were there. It was also the place he'd lost his sister and mother, the space which had consumed the soul of his father.

They ventured further inside along the sparse walkways. Que was not big on personal possessions. The only room which had anything in it was his office, and that was a scene of macabre displays that made any normal individual want to run for the hills. Unfortunately, that seemed to be where Lasandra was leading them.

"This place is giving me the creepiest of creeps," Abigail muttered as she stared around, always very aware of her surroundings.

Brace pulled her closer. "Hold on to that thought. Pretty soon you're going wish we were back in this walkway."

"Awesome."

A set of stairs led up to the second level, most of which made up the office of the former princeps.

Lights flickered on as they entered. A series of gasps sounded from Abigail. Brace knew it was probably only his mother's presence which stopped the curses following, and he couldn't blame her.

"I should have had this place destroyed long ago." His anger cut through the air like the blades of swords. It renewed his pure hatred of his father every time he saw the trophies scattered around.

"Please ... please, for the love of my own sanity, tell me that these aren't body parts mounted on the walls ... and in jars." Abigail's nose screwed up as she tried not to stare too hard in any direction.

Brace rubbed her back in slow, reassuring movements. "This was where he brought Abernaths for punishment." He pointed toward a hand that was mounted above the huge black desk at the back of the space. "That's mine ... it's lucky we regenerate or plenty of our warriors would be lopsided."

The breath whooshed out of Brace as Abigail threw her arms around him. He could feel her barely concealed rage as she squeezed him tightly. A full range of emotions flooded him.

Besides Lasandra, no one had ever worried about him. He was the strong one – responsibility and risk were thrown at him without thought.

But this slip of a girl put his happiness and safety above that of all others. He'd never had any doubt, of course, but sometimes it was crystal clear ... he was the luckiest damn man in existence. With all the horrible shit he'd been involved in through Que over the years, he wasn't sure he deserved the gift that was Red, but even so, he was keeping her.

Lasandra was shooting Abigail narrow-eyed glares. Brace locked his gaze on his mother, warning her he would not tolerate any more of her bullshit attitude toward his mate. She dismissed him with a wave of her hand, but he'd seen the sadness draw across her features before she turned away.

He tightened his grip around Abigail, but his eyes were glued to his mother as she crossed the room. Lasandra paused at the back wall, and with barely a hesitation she reached out and gripped the hand that was attached to the wall. Brace's hand that he'd lost to Que in a fight just under three hundred years ago.

"What the hell is your mother doing? Has she lost her ever-loving mind?"

Brace hadn't realized that Abigail had her head turned to the side and was also watching the regal blond. A blond who appeared to be shaking hands with his long-ago removed and petrified arm.

Brace laced his fingers through Abigail's and together they crossed the space. He wanted to get close enough to see if his mother had lost her 'ever-loving mind', as Red had declared.

As they took the first few steps across, their footsteps echoing on the white and shiny tiled floor, the space directly behind the hand shifted and a doorway appeared.

Brace's stride faltered minutely, but he knew that this had to be the entrance to the experiment room. He wondered how Lasandra had known of it.

"Did your dead hand just open up a doorway to Que's secret torture lair?" Abigail's voice was a mixture of freaked out and impressed.

"Something like that," he replied.

They quickened their step. Brace did not want Lasandra to venture down there without him. The doorway was large enough to easily fit his height and width, so clearly it had been designed for Que. The stairs were steep, made of metal grates with large gaps separating each one. The path was too narrow for two, so Brace pushed Abigail directly behind him; he was going down first. He could see his mother a few steps ahead in the dim light. He felt a hand reach out and grasp the back of his shirt, which he was happy about. Red was exactly where he wanted her. Safe.

The descent seemed to take a really long time, and there was a weird energy in the air that he was unfamiliar with. And knowing everything Que was capable of, that was an ominous sign. Brace feared nothing for himself, but his mother and mate were here too, and he felt the slightest trickle of nerves – the unknown lay ahead and he wasn't sure if he could keep them safe. He was confident, not stupid, and Que was a monster.

Dronish

There was nothing to see for the first half of their descent, but twenty steps down a light started to filter up from below. Brace knew Abigail couldn't see much – his frame would be blocking most of her view – which was a good thing. Because when the first signs of the secret room came into his line of vision, it almost knocked him off his feet, and he had seen some pretty messed-up shit in his life.

"Is everything okay?" Abigail whispered to him. "You've gone all stiff and growly." She was pushing against him.

He knew she was trying to see over his shoulder.

"Prepare yourself, Red. You're not going to like what you see down here."

He heard her sharp intake of breath, and felt the way her hands, which were clutching his shirt, shook. They didn't speak anymore as they continued their descent. Brace could see Lasandra had stopped dead at the base of the stairs, staring, unmoving. He couldn't blame her.

Finally the stairs ended, and Brace had to step to the side so Abigail could move into the light of the large energy cage.

"Oh, my effing god. What the effing eff is happening here?" She gasped her words, and then strode forward until she was right on the edge of the dome.

Que had the same sort of energy dome set up here as had been on Nephilius, and contained within the walls appeared to be all kinds of things. But it was two tanks on the far back wall which had drawn the most attention and caused the most distress.

Suspended in one was Josian, the liquid encasing him whole. His eyes were closed as he drifted up and down in the solution. Brace couldn't tell if he was dead or not. He had no idea what Que had been experimenting with down here. Abigail turned back to him, tears tracking along her cheeks.

Brace crossed the space between them and gathered her into his arms.

"What does this mean?" she choked out.

He shook his head. "I don't know, Red, but we'll free him; we'll break the energy dome." He paused ... she deserved the rest of the truth. "If we break the dome we might free Josian, but I'm just not sure what else we might be releasing."

Especially given the fact that in the tank next to Abigail's father was his own.

Que's dark hair and craggy features were unmistakable. Well, most of his features were clear, but he was also changed – missing his right arm and leg. Although there were small growths protruding from the empty sockets, as if these limbs were being reformed. Only they didn't really look Walker any longer, as if the DNA of something else had been mixed in there.

Something really scary.

Abigail clutched Brace closer. "What the hell is going on here? What is Que creating?"

Brace shook his head, wishing he had an answer, but in reality no one knew but the man himself, and he was looking less than alive.

Just as he had that thought, Que's eyes flew open.

ABOUT THE AUTHOR

Jaymin Eve is the Wall Street Journal and USA Today Bestselling author of paranormal romance, urban fantasy, and sci-fi novels filled with epic love stories, great adventure, and plenty of laughs.

She'd love to hear from you, so find her at

https://www.facebook.com/JayminEve.Author

mailing list www.jaymineve.com

Or email jaymineve@gmail.com

CPSIA information can be obtained
at www.ICGtesting.com
Printed in the USA
FSHW020621150120
66114FS

9 781508 799405